MW01178854

By R. G. Thomas

THE TOWN OF SUPERSTITION
The Midnight Gardener
The Well of Tears
The Battle of Iron Gulch
The Midnight Gardener & The Well of Tears (Print Only Anthology)

Published by Harmony Ink Press
www.harmonyinkpress.com

THE
MIDNIGHT & THE
GARDENER WELL
OF TEARS

R. G. THOMAS

R.G. Thomas
Dearborn, MI
2017

Harmony Ink

Published by
HARMONY INK PRESS

5032 Capital Circle SW, Suite 2, PMB# 279, Tallahassee, FL 32305-7886 USA
publisher@harmonyinkpress.com • harmonyinkpress.com

This is a work of fiction. Names, characters, places, and incidents either are the product of author imagination or are used fictitiously, and any resemblance to actual persons, living or dead, business establishments, events, or locales is entirely coincidental.

The Midnight Gardener & The Well of Tears
© 2017 R. G. Thomas.

Cover Art
© 2017 Anna Sikorska.
Cover content is for illustrative purposes only and any person depicted on the cover is a model.

ISBN: 978-1-63533-417-3
Library of Congress Control Number: 2016917539
Published January 2017
v. 1.0

Printed in the United States of America
∞
This paper meets the requirements of
ANSI/NISO Z39.48-1992 (Permanence of Paper).

Table of Contents

The Midnight Gardener

For Holli, who so eagerly follows Thaddeus on his quest.

Acknowledgments

MANY THANKS to Lee Brazil and Havan Fellows for their continued support and cheerleading as my writing and this series in particular have taken shape. You both rock! Huge thanks to Fred, who makes every day feel like a first date. I love you more than words can say.

Chapter ONE

THADDEUS CANE stood in the exact center of his new bedroom and looked toward the west. His room was in the back corner of the house, and through the window on that west-facing wall, he could see down into the neighboring yard. A tall wooden privacy fence surrounded the house, but from this angle, Thaddeus could see the lush, green expanse of lawn, flowerbeds exploding with color like a fireworks display fallen to earth, and a long stretch of dark, loamy earth along the rear of the property where vegetables grew. In a far corner of the yard sat a massive, gnarled stump, surrounded by groupings of plants with long, dark leaves and bleached nearly white from being exposed to the elements.

Through the other window, which looked out over their backyard, he could see the brown, scraggly lawn that led to a thick wooded area. The trees stood close together, branches stretching up to the sky. The limbs of the trees were so entangled he had trouble telling which branch belonged to which tree. Thaddeus reasoned that it wouldn't take long for a person to get lost inside that wood, and he shivered at the thought.

Even though his room felt stuffy from being shut up for so long, Thaddeus didn't yet want to open the windows. He wanted to get to know the new house, smell it as it stood before fresh air rushed in and cleared out all of its history, all of its stories.

He closed his eyes and reached his arms up over his head, fingers spread wide. The ceiling was far out of his reach—he wasn't even six feet tall—but the stretch felt good in his muscles. A deep inhalation followed by a long, slow exhalation brought to him the scents in the room: old wood, moth balls, from the closet most likely, and something else, something old, much older than Thaddeus himself or even his father for that matter.

Not that his father was old. Well, he was forty-five now, which might as well have been 145 from Thaddeus's perspective.

As if summoned by Thaddeus's thoughts, his father cleared his throat from the doorway.

"Well?" his father asked.

6

Thaddeus opened his eyes. In the light that flooded in through the west-facing window, Nathan Cane's face looked drawn and gaunt. Just recently it seemed the crow's feet at the corners of his father's hazel eyes had deepened, and the small wrinkle just between his eyebrows, a tiny furrow of concentration or concern, had appeared. His thick brown hair, always slightly unkempt but somehow stylish, was threaded with gray. Thaddeus wasn't sure if it was the stress of them moving yet again or something else, but this relocation seemed to weigh more heavily on his father than all the others.

"It's nice," Thaddeus said.

"How's it smell?" Nathan asked.

Thaddeus grinned. "Good. Nothing bad."

"Not like the place in Eagle's Hollow?"

Thaddeus sneered and shook his head. "Not at all."

"Good." Nathan grinned back, but the furrow of concentration between his eyebrows didn't let up.

"Do you need help unpacking the kitchen?" Thaddeus asked.

Nathan shook his head. "Nah. I've got it down to a science by now. You get your room organized."

Thaddeus watched his father leave the doorway and listened to him walk down the steps to the first floor, where he started opening drawers and cabinets in the kitchen. With a final inhalation and exhalation, Thaddeus pushed up both windows to admit the fresh air, noticed there were no screens on the windows here, unlike other places they had lived, and got to work unpacking the few boxes of his personal belongings. It wasn't much, really, just some clothes, a collection of CDs, a few DVDs and video games, and a number of books, so many books. Having moved so often throughout his life, Thaddeus didn't own a lot of things. Physical belongings weighed a person down. The only really heavy items he owned were his books, and he wasn't about to go without them. He unpacked his well-read copies of Tolkien and Heinlein, Bradbury and Martin, and lined them up on his bookshelf.

The smell of the flowerbeds next door drifted in on the breeze, and every now and again he would pause to lean on the windowsill and stare down into the neighboring yard. The landscaping that surrounded the house he and his father had rented was quite inferior to their neighbor's. But as Thaddeus leaned a little ways out of the window and peered across and down the street, he noticed the neighbor's yard outshone a number of other residences on the block, so he didn't feel too bad about it.

Some people just had a way with gardening.

Later that night, following a dinner of pizza, Thaddeus and his father set up both beds. They worked well together, both very familiar with the jobs that needed to be completed after a change of residence. In his father's room, once they had managed to lift the box springs and mattress onto the frame, Thaddeus fell across the unmade bed and caught his breath.

"Guess we'll both sleep well tonight, huh?" his father asked.

He was bent over a box across the room, pulling out keepsakes and setting them atop the dresser. The photograph of Thaddeus's mother was set in its usual place in the left-hand corner of the dresser. It was black and white, and the camera had caught her midway through a laugh, her head thrown back so her thick, dark hair tumbled over her shoulders, and the spark of joy in her eyes was unmistakable. It was a great photo, a happy coincidence Nathan had snapped it when he had. Thaddeus had always thought his father placed the photograph in the upper left corner of his dresser because it mirrored where his heart lay inside his chest.

"I like that picture," Thaddeus said.

"You say that every time I unpack it," Nathan pointed out.

Thaddeus shrugged. "Doesn't make it any less true."

Nathan abandoned the box he was unpacking and lay on his back across the bed beside Thaddeus. Both of them stared up at the dusty ceiling fan above, hands clasped over their bellies.

"This move might be an easier adjustment for you," his father said.

"Because school's already out for the summer and I might be able to meet some kids ahead of time at the local hangouts?" Thaddeus asked.

Nathan chuckled. "You're always three thinks ahead of me, aren't you?"

Thaddeus turned his head on the mattress, feeling static build up in his hair with the movement, and they smiled at each other.

"Maybe two thinks," Thaddeus said. "I'm not that much smarter than you."

"Oh, thanks."

Nathan rolled over and grabbed him, and they tussled for a moment. Thaddeus protested and struggled to get away, shouting, "Dad!

I'm fifteen!" but couldn't help laughing as his father growled deep in his chest like a woodland creature.

Finally, Thaddeus's laughter and struggles rendered him breathless, and he managed to say between gasps for air, "Okay, I'm sorry! I'm sorry! I surrender! I'm just one think ahead of you. Just one!"

Nathan growled once more, the sound deep and resonant in his broad chest. Then he released Thaddeus, pushed up off the bed, and reached down to pull him to his feet.

"That'll teach you," Nathan said in a mock serious tone.

Thaddeus straightened out his T-shirt and glared at his father. "I'm fifteen, Dad. I'm too old to be wrestled with."

"Remind me of that when I do it again. Now, go get showered, brush your teeth, and then hit the sack," Nathan instructed. "It's been a long day."

Thaddeus snapped his feet together and saluted. "Heil, Father!"

Nathan glared, and Thaddeus hurried to the bathroom where he shut the door.

That night, Thaddeus couldn't sleep. He always found it difficult to sleep the first night in a new house, though he figured it shouldn't matter because they had moved so often: thirty-two times, by his count, and all since he was just a baby. All since his mother had died.

Thaddeus didn't really know what had happened; his father didn't like to talk about it. He used to ask questions about his mother—what she had been like, how she had died—but Nathan never fully answered him, and so Thaddeus just stopped asking. From what Nathan had said, she'd died in some kind of accident, but whether it was in a car or something in their home, he'd never found out. His father loved his mother and didn't have anything to do with her death, that much Thaddeus knew for certain, because each time they moved, Nathan still put her picture out on top of his dresser, and Thaddeus figured he wouldn't do that if he harbored any guilt.

He had left his windows open a bit to enjoy the night air, and the sound of someone humming drew him to the one that faced west. Thaddeus peered down into their neighbor's yard where the light of the moon bleached the color from the flowers and the grass. Someone was out in the yard, moving from flowerbed to flowerbed, humming an odd tune. Fireflies danced around the figure, and Thaddeus frowned as he watched them move along with the person. He'd never known fireflies to trail after someone like that. This deserved a closer look.

The grass was wet and cool under his bare feet, sending a shiver up Thaddeus's legs. He crept along the tall, wooden privacy fence, looking for a space between the boards or a knothole he might be able to peer through. But the fence was solidly built, and Thaddeus couldn't find even the smallest crack to try and get a glimpse of the mysterious neighbor.

On the other side of the fence, Thaddeus could hear the humming gardener moving closer to the fence. A few fireflies drifted over the top and circled Thaddeus's head, their lights flashing in rhythm. He moved a few steps back, and the fireflies spun around the place where he had been standing before rising up and slipping back over the fence.

Just as Thaddeus parted his lips to call a greeting over the fence, the skin at the back of his neck prickled, and he stopped. Someone was watching him.

He turned slowly toward the wooded area at the edge of their property. Just inside the closely spaced trees, Thaddeus saw something standing very still and staring at him. It was an animal of some kind, a big one, but he couldn't tell if it was a dog or a wolf, or maybe even a cougar, as the moonlight didn't reach far enough between the trees to illuminate it.

Chills rattled through him, stilling his voice and freezing him in place. He stared at the creature in the woods, trying to decipher form from shadow. It stared back, not moving or making a sound, and that was more frightening to Thaddeus than if the thing charged him.

The humming grew louder as the midnight gardener moved to a flowerbed just on the other side of the fence from Thaddeus. Thaddeus swallowed and tried to find his voice to shout a warning to his neighbor, but decided it would be unnecessary since his yard was completely closed in. Instead, he willed his legs to move and stepped backward toward the house. The shadowy creature remained standing in place, but it lowered its large head, and moonlight flashed within its eyes.

That sparked a reaction within Thaddeus, a thawing out of his fear, and he turned his back to run to the house, glancing over his shoulder every second step. Nothing pursued him, however, and he stepped through the side door and quickly closed and locked it behind him. Now that he was safe inside, shivers took him, and he stepped up and down in place to get them out of his system.

"Okay, so, no moonlit strolls," he said to himself with a firm nod. "Got it."

He crept upstairs, being quiet so as not to wake his father whose room was at the top of the steps. After pausing in the bathroom to wipe the grass and dew from his bare feet, he entered his bedroom and leaned out the window that overlooked the neighbor's yard. The mysterious gardener was gone, and the fireflies now meandered around both yards, sparking and fading like normal insects. Thaddeus leaned a bit farther out of the window to see the place in the woods where the animal had stood and watched him. He squinted but couldn't tell if the creature still lurked in the shadows.

With another shiver, he drew back inside and closed the window. After a second's hesitation, he latched it even though his bedroom was on the second floor. Despite the excitement of his midnight sojourn, or maybe because of it, a yawn crept up on him. He slipped beneath the sheets and curled up on his side. He yawned once more before drifting off to sleep, where he dreamed of walking through a dense wood while a large creature followed him, both of them trying to track down the person who was humming a tune among the trees.

Chapter TWO

DESPITE THE unique, and slightly creepy, name of his new town, Thaddeus soon realized there wasn't much to do in Superstition. Unless it involved browsing or possibly working at one of the dozen or so odd little souvenir shops scattered up and down Main Street, and he didn't want to do either. Instead, he spent the next three days walking around the town, nodding in response to his father's warnings to be cautious and not stay out too late each time he left the house.

"Home by dark," his father called, and Thaddeus waved a hand in acknowledgment as he pushed out the screen door.

Superstition was a small town, but not too small. They'd only lived there a few days, but to Thaddeus, it felt big enough for him to remain anonymous but small enough that he didn't feel overwhelmed. Tall, broad-limbed trees lined the streets, throwing shade on the sidewalks and the nicely maintained houses. Some homes had hedges, the leaves a mossy dark green, with densely packed branches trimmed into box shapes or, in a couple instances, animal shapes. Thaddeus nodded to people he passed, glad to see only a few stopped to stare.

It was always tough to be the new kid in town.

The town library was a marvel of dark fieldstone and turrets. Thaddeus stood and stared at it, feeling a kind of dumbstruck awe. This was no dull brick government-style building. This was a timeless place, with an air of mystery and ancient secrets. He was torn about entering the library. Part of him was eager to see what the interior looked like, run his fingers along the bindings of all those books standing in neat rows. But another part was a little nervous about a building such as this, with a strong personality and an alluring face. What if the secrets it harbored were of the dark and wicked kind?

In the end he decided to return to the library another day, maybe with his father in tow. The minute the thought went through his mind, Thaddeus frowned and shook his head. That would never do. He was fifteen now, not a child; he didn't need his father to protect him. He huffed out an exasperated breath through his nose and turned away from the gothic building to continue with his exploring.

As he roamed the sidewalks, getting familiar with the names of streets and the layout of Superstition, Thaddeus saw a few kids his own age but kept his distance. He wasn't ready to start answering questions about where they had moved from, why they had chosen Superstition, and what had happened to his mother. Those questions always made him feel as if he were being interrogated, especially when he didn't know the answers himself.

Finally weary from all his walking, Thaddeus headed for home. He had circled the town one and a half times and, if he had picked up the layout at all, his house should be directly across from his current position. His feet were tired and scuffed the sidewalk as he walked alongside the thick woods. He stopped when he caught sight of a narrow path that seemed to head off in a more direct line toward his house. He debated with himself a moment, arguing about the safety of sticking to a known route in a new town versus venturing off through the woods on an unknown path, especially after having seen that shadowy animal watching him from the edge of the trees a few nights ago. The sidewalk, however, would take him blocks out of his way as it skirted the dense woods. Thaddeus figured the woods must look from the air like a long finger jabbing into the heart of Superstition.

And his feet really were tired.

"Nothing ventured," Thaddeus said to himself and stepped onto the path.

The air was cool and close in the shade of the woods, and all the sounds of the town—the mowers running in yards, children playing on lawns, car radios blasting, and the occasional truck rumbling past—were dampened and soon lost altogether by the closely packed trees. Birds darted and fluttered overhead, and small things rustled about in the fallen leaves that lay like a thick carpet at the feet of the trees.

Thaddeus didn't feel threatened, but he wasn't inclined to tarry either. He walked briskly along the dirt path, careful not to trip on the occasional exposed root or fallen limb. He looked all around the woods but saw no menacing creatures. In time he came to a much narrower path that split off from the one he was following. Thaddeus peered down both, then stepped onto the new, more confined route as it appeared to head toward his home.

An hour later the light was fading, and Thaddeus's feet were numb. He should have listened to his father and not strayed too far from home until he knew the town better. And he definitely should not have wandered off into the woods alone either.

A small ball of anxiety tightened inside his chest, and the nerves across his scalp tingled. He couldn't panic, not yet. And if for some reason he couldn't find his way home tonight, he wouldn't die of exposure. He might be damp, cold, scared, and hungry come morning, but he would be alive. And his father would be out looking for him if he didn't get home soon, of that Thaddeus was certain.

The light fled the woods faster than Thaddeus anticipated, and before long it was full-on dark. All he had to navigate by was the occasional slice of moonlight and the tiny flashlight app in his smartphone, which had no signal this deep in the woods and was close to the end of its battery.

Thaddeus paused to lean against a tree and catch his breath, staring into the darkness around him with wide eyes and the taste of copper in the back of his throat. Something was different now, but he couldn't tell what it was. He stood very still, the tree bark rough beneath his fingers and grounding him in place as he slowly turned his head, trying to see into the woods around him. It was so dark and so quiet, he could hear himself breathe.

The realization hit like a lightning strike. It was quiet all around him; every other living thing had fallen silent. And he'd seen enough horror movies to know what that meant. When the crickets and frogs stopped making noise, something bad was nearby. Something evil.

A twig snapped.

Thaddeus's heart pounded. He knew whatever it was that stalked him could most likely hear it. It could probably smell the fear gushing off him like a fire hose too. He had to keep moving. Standing still would be like offering himself up as a meal.

His stride lengthened as he continued along the path. Off to his left, he heard the crinkle and crackle of something big stepping through the fallen leaves, and a jolt of fear burned through him. Whatever the thing was, it seemed to be keeping pace with him on a parallel course, not coming toward him, and Thaddeus kept his gaze straight ahead, trying to make out anything that might be lying across the path that could trip him up. If he had thought to fully charge his phone before leaving the house, he would have just turned on the flashlight app and been done with it, but he wanted to save the light for an emergency. Like when the beast finally attacked.

A new sound reached him, and Thaddeus stopped fast and cocked his head to listen. His legs trembled and his breath came in short, quiet pants. What was that sound? It sounded like…. He understood in a flash, and relief and excitement collided inside him, sending out a shivery chill of comfort.

It was someone humming; more specifically it was the sound of the midnight gardener who lived on the other side of the fence from his house.

A tiny yellow spark ignited a few feet in front of him, making Thaddeus jump. It faded away, then lit up again a few feet deeper into the woods, off the narrow path, and he realized it was a firefly. More of them appeared around him, sparking and dimming, all gliding in the same direction between the trees. They were headed toward the humming, and Thaddeus took off at a run, dodging between trees as he followed them. He tried to listen for any sound of pursuit, but he was making too much noise to hear anything else above it. Blood pounded in his ears, and his breath rasped in and out, burning his throat. Any moment he expected to feel sharp claws tear into his skin, rip muscle, and dig into bone as the thing in the woods pounced on his back and drove him face-first into the dirt.

But nothing touched him, and with a shaky cry of relief, Thaddeus burst out of the tree line and staggered across the shaggy lawn of his new house. He stopped halfway to the house to catch his breath. He didn't want his father to see him in this state, otherwise he'd never be allowed to go off on his own again. Leaning over with his hands on his thighs, he gulped in air and stared at the moonlit grass beneath his shoes. The humming went on as his mysterious neighbor worked in his yard, and the sound warmed and calmed him. He had made it. He was home.

Leaves crunched from within the woods behind him, and Thaddeus spun around, gaze darting between the dark spaces amid the trees. Nothing moved except for the small, flickering fireflies that drifted out of the woods and over the top of the privacy fence to join the humming gardener next door.

With slow steps Thaddeus moved closer to the fence, keeping his gaze on the woods and his hands in fists. When he finally stood beside the fence, Thaddeus cleared his throat and said, in as loud a voice as he dared, "Hello there, over the fence."

The humming stopped, and a palpable tension blemished the cool evening air. Thaddeus wished he could take the greeting back, but it was too late. All he could do was push on and try to get a response.

"I really like your garden. I can see it from my bedroom window here. There must be something to gardening at night, I guess."

Silence was his only response.

"I'm sorry if I startled you," Thaddeus continued, still watching the woods. "I had a bit of a scare myself just now. I came through the woods, and it took longer than I thought, so it got dark before I could get back here, back home, you know? I was followed by... something. I don't know what it was, but I get the feeling it's been around here before. Do you have any idea what it might be?"

More silence.

Thaddeus's stomach rumbled, reminding him he'd skipped lunch and had a very long day of walking. And running for his life through the woods. He let out his breath and turned to give a sharp, sarcastic salute to the fence.

"Okay, then, nice talking with you. Keep up the good work with the garden."

He turned his back to the woods and walked quickly to the side door of his house, where he let himself in. His father stood at the kitchen sink, just opening a jar of spaghetti sauce. When he saw Thaddeus, he raised his eyebrows and asked, "Long day exploring?"

"Something like that," Thaddeus replied. He kicked off his muddy shoes on the landing, bolted the back door, and walked up the steps into the kitchen, then past his father.

"Did you go into the woods?" his father asked.

"Not far," Thaddeus lied.

"Thaddeus." It was his father's stern "don't try to lie to me" tone.

Thaddeus sighed and turned to face him. "There was a path, and I thought it would be a shortcut home." He shrugged. "It wasn't."

"Did you get lost out there?"

"No. Just... turned around."

His father stared at him.

"I know, all right?" Thaddeus said with a heavy sigh. "I won't do it again." He turned and headed for the doorway to the living room.

"I got a job today," his father called after him.

16

Thaddeus stopped and turned back. "Oh yeah? Where at?"

"Superstition Sporting Goods," his father replied. "Might be some late nights. I guess they stay open a little later than some of the bigger stores to cater to the younger, weekend-getaway types. Will you be okay with that?"

Thaddeus nodded as he thought about the thing in the woods. "Yeah, I'm okay with that. I'm glad you found something so soon."

"Me too. I didn't want us to scrape by like we did that one time."

Thaddeus raised his eyebrows. "Just one time?"

His father blushed and waved a hand to shoo him off as he stirred the sauce. "Yeah, yeah. All right, smart guy, it was more than once. Never mind. Go get cleaned up for dinner."

Upstairs in his room, Thaddeus plugged in his phone to charge, then leaned out the open window. The yard next door was quiet and dark; even the fireflies had departed, and he couldn't help feeling bad about chasing away their neighbor. He had only been trying to be friendly. He guessed some people just didn't like to talk to strangers.

He squinted as he peered into the woods, but the night had taken over completely, and he saw nothing. Whatever had been keeping pace with him had vanished as well.

"Curiouser and curiouser," Thaddeus whispered before pulling back inside the window and sliding it shut.

Chapter THREE

THADDEUS LEANED on his windowsill and stared down into the neighboring yard. The garden was overgrown now. Well, overgrown compared to what it had looked like prior to him speaking to the night gardener. Since that night the week before, Thaddeus had waited at his window each evening, anxious to catch a glimpse of the happy, humming gardener, who only came out when the sun went down. But he never showed. After the first night of his absence, even the fireflies stayed away.

A cold, empty space seemed to open wider and wider inside Thaddeus when each sunset brought no further sign of his neighbor. His father was working long hours at Superstition Sporting Goods, so Thaddeus was on his own for much of the day. He had spent the better part of the past week walking around their own yard, looking over the grass and flowerbeds with a critical eye. Their yard could use some attention as well, and Thaddeus decided to ask his father to take him to the local nursery on his next morning off from work, whenever that might happen. If his father kept these hours up, Thaddeus might as well be living here on his own.

Now, as the sun eased down behind the distant mountains on this first day of July, Thaddeus sighed and rested his chin on his palm. If his neighbor did not make an appearance tonight, it would make eight straight nights. It felt to Thaddeus as if the vacant space inside him was opening wider and wider, oozing guilt into his system. If he hadn't tried to rush some kind of communication with the night gardener, then maybe he could have eased into a conversation one night this past week.

Instead, the garden was neglected, and something in the very air felt different. Thaddeus had caused a disruption in the order of things, and all he wanted was for everything to be as it had been before he'd come running out of the woods, away from whatever had been following him, and called over the wall.

Movement among the deepening shadows in the neighboring yard, furtive and quick, caught Thaddeus's attention. His heart pounded and his breath caught in his chest as a tingle of excitement skittered up his back. Could it be?

He strained to listen, hope flaring alight inside him like a lighthouse beam. He had almost completely given up hope, but now the sound of the gardener's humming was back. It was low and melodic, just like it had been before.

Relief filled him, cool and soothing, and he sagged against the window frame, a dreamy smile spreading across his face. When the fireflies danced in from the dark of the woods, Thaddeus gasped aloud. He clapped his hand over his mouth and stared down into the yard beyond the fence, afraid he had made too loud of a sound and now might scare off his neighbor once again.

There, caught in a silver slice of moonlight, stood a boy. Before that moment Thaddeus had never seen more than a quick-moving shadow, and now he could see him in more detail. The boy—more a teenager, really, like Thaddeus himself now that he saw him better—stood looking up at him, the moonlight giving soft definition to his features. He was handsome in a country boy kind of way, with high cheekbones, a dark beard around his jaw, a rather large nose, and a messy thatch of hair that fell across his broad forehead. But what really captured Thaddeus's attention were his eyes. The gardener's eyes shone bright as he stared up at Thaddeus, reflecting back the moonlight like twin mirrors.

They looked at each other for a moment, no longer than it took Thaddeus's heart to beat three times, and then his neighbor dropped his gaze and resumed humming as he went back to his work.

Excitement thrummed along Thaddeus's nerves. His head felt light enough to float off his neck, and it was almost impossible for him to take a breath deep enough to satisfy his lungs. The gardener's humming now seemed meant just for Thaddeus, and the sound caressed his skin like a soft touch from the boy himself.

Thaddeus felt overloaded with sensation and needed to move. With a shudder, he stepped away from the window and paced the length of his room several times, shaking his hands and arms as he tried to catch his breath. He jumped onto his bed and curled up in the fetal position, hugging his knees tight as he stared at the darkness beyond the open window. The lamp beside his bed was on, and he reached up to switch it off, leaving his room lit only by moonlight. His muscles trembled, and he couldn't stop smiling as a giddy sense of joy swirled within him and his heart raced. The neighbor wasn't some older man who lived alone. He was a boy Thaddeus's age, and he had stood there in his yard and stared up at Thaddeus and not run away. They had made contact.

For quite some time now, Thaddeus had known he was gay. He'd spent enough lunch hours eating alone and staring at the handsome bookish types and muscular jocks around him to know he was attracted to other boys. He had, however, never acted on his attractions. Not once. He'd never even kissed a girl, let alone another boy. He had never thought any of them would have been interested in kissing him back.

But maybe now that might all change. Now he lived next door to a mysterious, handsome boy who wasn't as afraid of Thaddeus as he had first feared. And there was a sense of magic around that house and yard, an enigmatic air that called to something inside him, piqued his curiosity and interest.

Thaddeus pushed up off his bed to pace his room again, all the while listening to his neighbor hum as he worked among the plants. This was ridiculous. Thaddeus didn't even know his name, hadn't even gotten a clear look at his face, and here he was already thinking he might want this mysterious gardener to be the first one to kiss him.

"Ridiculous," Thaddeus whispered.

The humming stopped, and Thaddeus paused in his pacing.

"Ridiculous." The word had been spoken quietly, but the calm night air carried it up to Thaddeus's window as if by special delivery.

A tremble started low in Thaddeus's belly, and he stood frozen in the middle of his room, his leg muscles locked in place. Had the guy next door just overheard him whisper and repeated it back to him? Could he hear everything Thaddeus did up here in his room?

He forced his feet to move and edged up to the window as the humming resumed. He peered down into the yard and watched the broad back of his neighbor as he moved from plant to plant. With slow, cautious movements, Thaddeus put his hands on the window and started to push it closed. The shape in the yard beyond the fence stood up and turned to look at him. Moonlight shimmered in the whiskers around his jaw, and when he smiled and gave a small wave, Thaddeus nearly shouted in surprise. Instead, he gave the boy a salute, then turned away from the window, his face burning as he blushed.

What the hell had he done? Given a salute? What was he thinking?

He collapsed on his bed and lay sprawled on his back staring up at the ceiling. *A salute? Really?*

Closing his eyes, Thaddeus agonized over the salute until the gardener's humming lulled him into a deep sleep.

Chapter FOUR

"YOU MUST be Master Thaddeus!"

The man's voice was loud, and it felt like an assault. Thaddeus couldn't help wincing as he turned to face the barrel-chested man striding toward him. A button-down plaid shirt stretched across the broad expanse of the man's chest, the buttons straining to hold on.

"I-I-I…," Thaddeus stuttered, his senses swamped by the man's presence. He was big—huge, really. Tall and broad and loud, and as he came to a stop right in front of Thaddeus there in the middle of Superstition Sporting Goods, the man loomed over him.

"Ah, cat got your tongue?" The man smiled, displaying big, white teeth. He leaned down close and lowered his voice to something Thaddeus considered normal conversation level, but for him was most likely a whisper. "Gotta watch 'em. They do that, you know."

Thaddeus blinked and nodded. A cat didn't have his tongue; it just felt too thick for his mouth and unable to form words. Who was this man? All he'd wanted when he stepped through the door of Superstition Sporting Goods was to see where his father worked and maybe have a few minutes to speak with him.

"Thaddeus?"

The sound of his father's voice rescued him. A wave of relief washed through Thaddeus, energizing his muscles enough to take a step back from this big, boisterous man. When he had some distance, Thaddeus noticed the name tag pinned to the big man's shirt pocket: Edgar.

As in Edgar Marcet, the owner of Superstition Sporting Goods. Great. He'd just acted like a complete dumbass in front of his father's boss.

Before Thaddeus could introduce himself properly, his father arrived beside him and laid a strong, comforting hand on his shoulder. "What are you doing here? Everything okay at home?"

"I'm fine, yeah," Thaddeus replied. "I was just walking through town and thought I'd stop in."

"Bored, eh?" Edgar asked with a smirk. He folded his arms, and the bulging muscles threatened to tear his shirtsleeves. "We could use a youngster in the back room. You interested? Unpacking boxes, counting inventory, running errands?"

"Uh, I think he was just getting a feel for the town," his father said, "but thanks for the offer, Edgar."

"Young kid like that probably needs some spending money," Edgar continued, keeping his gaze on Thaddeus. "Still taking an allowance from your dad here?"

"Um…." Thaddeus looked between the two men as anxiety twisted into a ball inside him. How was he supposed to answer that question?

"Since we just moved here a couple of weeks ago," Thaddeus's father continued in a firmer tone of voice, "I was going to let him enjoy a summer off before he had to start classes at a new school in the fall. Let him get to know the town a bit. But, again, thank you for the offer, Edgar."

That got through to the big man. He nodded and stuck out a giant hand that nearly crushed Thaddeus's when they shook. "Well, the offer stands. Think about it." He walked off, greeting a man and woman by name that stood browsing a wall display of tennis rackets.

"Wow," Thaddeus whispered to his father. "He's…."

"Outgoing?" Nathan offered.

"At least."

He grinned. "I know. He knows everyone in Superstition, and most from the surrounding towns. He does a lot of business, which is why he stays open so late."

"I didn't mean to get you in trouble or anything," Thaddeus said as he looked around the big, brightly lit store. "I just wanted to see where you worked."

"You didn't get me in trouble." Nathan squeezed his shoulder. "Want to hang out until my lunch break and eat with me?"

Thaddeus shrugged. "Sure. Okay. How long?"

"Thirty minutes." Nathan pointed out toward the street. "Why don't you take a walk and see what kinds of stores there are on Main Street here, then meet me in front of the shop at twelve thirty?"

"Yeah. Okay."

Thaddeus had walked through the town before, but today he stopped in some of the stores. In a town named Superstition, one had to expect at least a few souvenir and oddity shops, and Thaddeus wasn't disappointed. There was Superstition SuperStore, Superstitional Things, Things That Go Bump,

The Grackle's Roost, Finer Things, and Wards and Wonders. Some of the stores were devoid of customers, with an employee at the register engrossed in a magazine or book or smartphone. Thaddeus browsed up and down the aisles of each store, finding the standard spooky items like voodoo dolls, ceramic skulls, and small jars with labels like "Eye of Newt" or "Lizard's Tongue" written in a spidery script. Along with those items, he also found crystals and beads, Native American dream catchers, joke bottles of magical cure-alls, T-shirts, and, of course, a few plastic dinosaurs.

In the back of The Grackle's Roost, he came across a large paperback book titled *A Superstitious Town: The History of Superstition*. It cost more than he had on him, but he made a mental note to come back and get it once he had some more money.

Which made him think of Edgar Marcet's job offer. He could save some money up while he worked in the back room, where he wouldn't have to interact with customers. He wondered if he would mind working at the same place as his father, then decided it might be the only chance they would have to see each other with the schedule his dad was working.

Then he thought about the hours. Would he be able to be home shortly after nightfall so he could listen to his neighbor hum as he worked in the garden? Maybe some evening soon, he'd even get a chance to talk with him now that they'd looked at and acknowledged each other.

His phone buzzed in his pocket, and he found a text waiting from his father: *Where are you?* He sent a quick note back and hurried to the front of the shop, nodding to the woman with the dark hair and eyeliner behind the counter.

"Come on back now," she called after him. "We'll be waiting."

"Okay, yeah," Thaddeus said and fought back a shiver as he stepped out the door. Were there any normal people living in this town? As he walked along the sidewalk, he swore he could feel her watching his back.

At lunch with his father, Thaddeus asked what he thought about him working at Superstition Sporting Goods. Nathan considered it in silence for a moment, then shrugged. "If you want to. I just wanted to give you one more summer of freedom, but if you're interested, I can talk to Edgar. Take the week to think about it, though, okay?"

Thaddeus agreed and after lunch, headed back to the house. He played a video game for a while, read some chapters of a fantasy book by a new author he'd been trying to get through since May, and then fell asleep on the sofa for a couple of hours. His father was working late again, so his dinner consisted of a mixing bowl of cereal, which he ate while watching some old TV show episodes online. After that he wandered around the yard and ventured a few feet into the woods to stand and peer into the cool, damp shadows. Birds called and danced between the trees, and the sun managed to get slivers of light down to the soft, mossy floor. Thaddeus listened for any other sounds, but only the birds and a few squirrels were out. Nothing larger or more threatening.

When the sun finally set, Thaddeus used the bathroom, put on a dark hoodie and black track pants, and slipped a small flashlight in his pocket. He'd come up with the idea while out in the yard earlier. He was excited and nervous about his plan, but he had to see his neighbor closer than from his own windowsill. He just hoped he wouldn't scare him off for another week.

As the night stretched shadowy fingers out from the trees, slowly closing its grip over the yard, then the house, then the block, Thaddeus stepped into the woods. He didn't go far, just a couple of feet before he turned to walk along the line of the neighbor's tall, solid privacy fence. Halfway down the length of the fence, he came to a tree with a branch low enough for him to reach. He climbed carefully and quietly into the tree until he found a spot where he could see over the fence into the lush shadows of the yard beyond.

Movement in the yard made his heart pound. He stilled his muscles and his breathing. He heard the rustle of something, and then the familiar humming started up, and Thaddeus relaxed against the trunk of the tree. Fireflies meandered in from among the woods and lifted up and over the fence to float around the dark shape of the gardener. Thaddeus sighed and wished he were able to float over the fence and get a closer look at his mysterious neighbor. He had no idea what he would talk to him about, but a good start would probably be why he gardened at night and who shared the house where he lived.

A sound from beneath the tree startled him. Looking down, Thaddeus sucked in a breath and tightened his grip on the branch as he watched a large animal circle the tree. It was cloaked in shadows, but he could hear the snuffling sound it made as it sniffed around the trunk. Thaddeus's blood pounded in his ears, drowning out all other sound, including his neighbor's humming, as he watched the beast prowl around the tree, nose to the ground, sniffing and snorting. He still could not see the animal clearly, so he had no idea what it was or if it could climb up into the tree and attack him.

The bark was rough beneath his fingers as he tightened his grip even more, his gaze locked on the broad back of the creature beneath him. It stopped and lifted its head to stare at the fence, and then it looked up into the tree and right at Thaddeus. As he stared down into the glowing golden eyes of whatever the thing was, Thaddeus's body went cold. He pulled his feet up and slowly stood on the branch where he had been sitting, wanting to get as much distance between him and the creature staring up at him.

With a deep snarl, the beast jumped up against the tree, huge claws gouging the bark half a foot below Thaddeus as it snapped its jaws. Thaddeus felt the tree tremble beneath the animal's attack and heard himself moan with terror. He had to get higher, get clear of this thing for good. Moving carefully, he stepped around the trunk to branches on the other side and climbed higher. The monster lunged again, and the tree shook, more violently this time. Thaddeus lost his grip on the trunk, and his feet went out from under him.

As he fell, panic exploded inside his chest. His scalp tingled, and he let out a short, high scream before he hit the ground, landing on his side. His teeth clicked together, just missing his tongue, and his breath left him in a rush. He heard the leaves crunch beneath the beast's paws as the thing rushed him, and he grabbed the only thing he had brought with him: the flashlight. The batteries were fresh, and the bright white beam hit the creature full in the face, startling it enough that it staggered back from him a few steps. It moved quickly, and it all happened so fast; the only thing Thaddeus managed to see was a big, brown muzzle, glistening, sharp teeth, and the flash of its golden eyes.

Thaddeus crab-walked away from the beast, until his head bumped against the fence. Suddenly, someone from behind grabbed his hood and gave a hard tug. The zipper raked up against the underside of his chin, catching on the few whiskers he had managed to grow since spring and yanking them out. He gagged and coughed as he was dragged along the ground away from the beast. He reached up to grab the front of his hoodie in an effort to unzip it, but then he was released and fell against the ground where he coughed and sputtered until he sat up, eyes wide as he looked back and forth for the thing that had attacked him, or the person who had saved him.

The grass beneath his palms was cool and thick, as soft as a finely made carpet. Thaddeus's pulse slowed and his breath evened out as his location became clear. He was inside his neighbor's fenced-in yard. Rounded mounds of rich, fragrant earth supported even more fragrant flowers. Even in the muted light of the moon, Thaddeus could see a variety of shades of color and shapes.

A tiny yellow shape darted before his face, and he jumped, then looked around. Just a firefly, buzzing past to check him out. He tried to get to his feet, but his balance wasn't quite back yet, so he stayed on his butt.

Then it hit him. He was *inside* the fence. He was with his mysterious neighbor.

Thaddeus looked all around, and then stopped when he saw the shadowed form crouched a dozen feet away to his left.

"H-Hello," Thaddeus said.

The form rose to its feet and approached. Thaddeus's heart pounded, and his mouth went dry.

His neighbor stood over him, staring down at him, then suddenly dropped into a deep crouch so they were nearly eye to eye. Because the gardener's back was to the moon, his face was in shadow, but Thaddeus could see heavy whiskers along his strong jaw, his large nose, and deep-set eyes.

Then his savior smiled, showing wide, blunt teeth, and reached out a meaty hand to grasp Thaddeus's shoulder.

"Hello!" his neighbor said, his voice deep and rich, immediately soothing Thaddeus's nerves and anxiety. "That was close, eh?"

Chapter FIVE

THADDEUS SAT on the ground and stared up at his neighbor. It seemed to be all he could manage at the moment, after almost being mutilated by whatever animal had knocked him out of the tree. Here he was, finally inside his neighbor's beautifully maintained yard, looking right at the mysterious gardener he'd been pretty much obsessed with these past weeks, and Thaddeus had no idea what to say. And he didn't think he would have the ability to put words together in a coherent fashion anyway. His mind was spinning, filled with words disassociated from each other and snapshots of childhood memories as well as what he had just lived through.

"Are you hurt?" the gardener asked. His voice was smooth as a river stone, and the sound of it helped to still Thaddeus's racing mind.

"No," Thaddeus managed, though his voice was a whisper. "I'm not hurt. Thanks to you."

The gardener shrugged and glanced away, embarrassed, it seemed, by Thaddeus's appreciation. When he looked back at him, the neighbor stuck out his big hand, and Thaddeus took it. As the gardener pulled him easily to his feet, Thaddeus noted the smooth, dry feel of his palm and the heat of his strong fingers closed over the back of his hand.

"Thanks," Thaddeus said when he was upright once again, his hand still caught in the gardener's strong grip.

"You're welcome," his neighbor replied, then pumped his arm up and down in greeting. "I'm Teofil."

Thaddeus frowned and leaned in, repeating slowly, "Tay-oh-fill?"

Teofil nodded and spelled it for him. "It's a family name."

"It's nice," Thaddeus said. "I like it."

Teofil gave a single nod and, still pumping Thaddeus's arm, cocked his head. "Do you have a name?"

"Oh my gosh, sorry!" Thaddeus exclaimed. He laughed then stuck out his tongue and shook his head. "Still rattled by that... whatever that thing was out there, I guess. I'm Thaddeus Cane."

"Teofil and Thaddeus," Teofil said, then smiled. "I like how it flows together."

"Oh, well, yeah. So do I. They are a very good fit. Our names, I mean." Thaddeus felt himself blush and was very glad it was nighttime so Teofil wouldn't be able to see it. He looked down to where Teofil was still shaking his hand and said, "I think we've pretty much met now, don't you?"

Teofil laughed and released Thaddeus's hand. The night air was cool against his palm, and Thaddeus curled his fingers closed tight in an effort to retain as much of Teofil's warmth as possible. His heart beat fast, and his breathing was quick and light, making him giddy.

"Want to see my gardens?" Teofil asked with a boyish grin that nearly made Thaddeus swoon.

"Yes!" Thaddeus practically shouted, then put a finger over his lips and looked around. "Sorry. I'll try to be more quiet."

Teofil shrugged and walked past Thaddeus toward a mound of dark, rich earth from which a number of beautiful flowers sprouted. "It's okay. My grandfather doesn't hear very well anymore, so he'll sleep through anything."

Thaddeus hurried to keep up with Teofil's long strides. "Oh, you live with your grandfather?"

"I call him Leo."

"That's his name?"

"Leopold Solobiec." Teofil grinned at him over his shoulder. "It takes about a year before it rolls right off your tongue."

"So your last name is Solobiec?"

Teofil cocked his head and looked up at the starry sky. "Huh. You'd think so, wouldn't you?" He shrugged and smiled again. "Here, let me introduce you."

"Introduce me? To your grandfather?" Thaddeus asked, suddenly nervous.

Teofil threw back his head and laughed, then dropped to his knees and waved his hand above the flowers. "No, silly. To the garden." Fireflies circled his head, darting in close to his ears where they hovered a moment before swooping away. Teofil chuckled and patted the ground beside him. "Come on. Kneel down here beside me."

Thaddeus knelt beside Teofil. He listened as Teofil explained about the plants, but he didn't hear any of the words. All he knew was he knelt alongside someone truly unique, who not only had saved his life but had captured his interest like no other. It was as if he had been visiting a foreign country where he didn't speak the language, surrounded by people chattering away using incomprehensible words and expressions, and suddenly he had found his way back home and everything made perfect sense. It wasn't the garden plants or Teofil's explanations that touched something deep inside Thaddeus but the boy himself.

They moved around the yard, kneeling before the flowerbeds as the fireflies danced and spun around their heads. Teofil explained specifics about the soil and the amount of light each section received, the sound of his voice lulling Thaddeus into a dreamlike state.

As they walked to another section of the yard, Thaddeus stopped and looked toward the far corner at the massive tree stump. It stood about five feet tall, and its bark looked silver in the moonlight. A large, blackened scar ran in a ragged pattern along one side. Around its base grew spiky plants with what appeared to be bloodred blooms, all crowded in close together so their spiny branches intertwined.

"That must have been some tree," Thaddeus said.

Teofil followed his gaze and nodded. "I think so too. It's just been a stump as long as I can remember. Leo's pretty firm about that corner of the garden. Only those plants can grow there."

"Do you know what kind of plant that is?" Thaddeus asked. "I've never seen it before."

"Those are drachen narcosis." Teofil leaned in close, and the musky smell of his sweat mingled with the fecund scent of earth washed over Thaddeus. He took a deep breath, pulling the smell deep inside him, hoping to be able to retain it for when he was alone.

"Pretty smelly stuff," Teofil continued, his voice lowered. "But beautiful blooms. They need bonemeal to really thrive."

"Bonemeal," Thaddeus repeated in a whisper.

Teofil nodded, his face only inches from Thaddeus's. His wide, handsome face filled Thaddeus's vision, and he stared into Teofil's eyes that were the blue of stormy ocean waves. Needing to look away for fear of losing himself, Thaddeus dropped his gaze and took in how Teofil was dressed. He wore all earth tones: forest green pants, pale yellow shirt, and brown boots that laced up his lower legs. Brown suspenders stretched over his shoulders, and his thick, dark blond hair lay across his forehead. His beard was of the same color as his hair, full and thick. The fireflies spun around them, and from somewhere off in the distance, Thaddeus heard the high-pitched giggle of a young girl as well as church bells, and it all came together for him in a chilling rush of understanding.

The church bells were ringing, so it was at least 6:00 a.m., plus he could see the details of Teofil's face, which meant the sky was lightening. It was dawn, and he had been out all night. His father was going to be pissed.

"Oh crap!" Thaddeus nearly shouted. The moment that had seemed to stretch out to eternity between them snapped, and Teofil drew back.

"What's wrong?"

"The sun's coming up," Thaddeus said. He turned in a circle, unsure of where in the yard he stood. He saw the top of his house beyond the tall fence and ran toward it. "I need to get home!"

He reached the fence and jumped for the top, but it was too tall. Then he remembered the beast that had tried to eat him and took a step back, heart pounding, and bumped up against the solid form of Teofil. Thaddeus caught his breath as Teofil put his large hands on his shoulders and squeezed gently.

"You okay?" Teofil asked, his voice soft and gentle in Thaddeus's ear.

Thaddeus nodded, started to reply, but couldn't find his voice for a moment. He took a breath, cleared his throat, and tried again.

"Yeah, I'm okay. I just remembered that thing that tried to eat me earlier." He turned in place and looked into Teofil's eyes, only a few inches away. "Do you think it's still out there?"

Teofil smiled and brushed a strand of hair off Thaddeus's forehead. "I think it left hours ago."

Thaddeus smiled as he trembled. What was it about Teofil that affected him so much?

"Well, good. I'd hate to jump the fence and be chewed up on my own lawn."

Teofil rolled his eyes up to the stars slowly fading from view as if in thought, then said with a smile, "I would think being chewed up would be bad no matter where it happened."

Thaddeus laughed, then covered his mouth when he heard how loud it sounded.

Teofil laughed as well, much more quietly, and guided him toward the back of the fence where he opened a nearly invisible gate. "Here. Try the gate."

"Sure, do it the easy way," Thaddeus grumbled. He leaned out and looked both ways along the back of the fence. There was no sign of the beast, and he stepped out of the yard into the woods, then turned back to Teofil who remained inside the yard. He had hoped Teofil would walk him home, but the boy's feet seemed planted in the soft, thick lawn on his side of the fence.

"Have a good day, Thaddeus," Teofil said. "It was nice to finally get a chance to talk with you."

"Yeah, for me as well," Thaddeus said. He fidgeted in place a moment, then lifted a hand and smiled. "Okay, then. Guess I'll see you around."

"I hope so." Teofil looked up at the sky, then back at Thaddeus, and his expression had changed, shifting to something akin to concern. "You'd better get home. Sun's almost up."

"Oh. Yeah. I should go." Thaddeus nodded. He was about to ask if they could meet for lunch later when Teofil closed the fence on him.

A bird called from behind him, giving him a start. Thaddeus looked around, then back at the fence. It appeared completely intact, with no sign of the gate at all, even when he leaned in close and squinted. He noticed a small stone near his foot and placed it on the ground where he remembered the gate opening, then turned to hurry along the fence toward home.

Chapter SIX

THADDEUS SLOWLY opened the side door and crept into the house. Outside, loud birdsong greeted the rising sun as he turned and eased the door closed. He moved quietly up the landing steps into the kitchen, then came to a sudden stop at the sight of his father sitting at the kitchen table. Nathan's hands were balled into fists on the tabletop, and he glared at Thaddeus with his lips pressed into a thin line of anger.

"Dad," Thaddeus said, his voice a much higher register than normal. "I didn't expect to see you."

"Didn't expect to?" his father asked in a low, frighteningly calm tone. "Or didn't want to?"

"Um...." Thaddeus let the word fade out and shifted his weight from one foot to the other. "Both?"

"Where in the almighty hell have you been all night?" his father asked. Before Thaddeus could answer, his father pushed up from the chair and approached him, finger pointing in Thaddeus's face, anger blazing in his eyes. "Do you have any idea how worried I was about you? I came home from work at eleven last night and went upstairs to check on you, but you weren't in your room."

"Dad—"

"I tried your cell phone but got no answer. I drove up and down streets all over town looking for you. I had no idea where you were or who you were with or if you were in trouble." His voice broke on the last word, and he paused to take a breath. Dark circles bruised the skin beneath his eyes, and he looked so lost, so devastated, that an icy pit of guilt opened within Thaddeus.

"Dad, I'm sorry. I wasn't far, just next door. And I'm sorry, my phone was off. I was—" *Being sneaky* were the words he almost said, but he stopped himself in time. Instead, he explained, "It was late, and I didn't want my phone to ring and bother anyone."

Nathan frowned. He looked toward the window—toward the fence behind which Teofil toiled every night—and then back at Thaddeus. "You were.... You were next door?"

His father seemed deflated now, his anger spent with his outburst. As Nathan sank back down, Thaddeus sat across the table from him and nodded vigorously. He was too amped up on having spent the night talking with Teofil to be tired. Now that the storm of his father's anger seemed to have passed, he was eager to have someone to tell about his nighttime adventure. Minus the near-death experience with the beast that prowled the woods, of course.

"I was. There's a kid who lives there who gardens at night. Well, I think he's a kid. He seems to be my age. Anyway, I've seen him now and then from my window but haven't gotten a chance to talk with him yet. Until last night."

"You were next door the whole time?" Nathan asked.

Thaddeus nodded. "Right on the other side of the fence. They have these amazing gardens full of awesome, colorful flowers. And these fireflies come in each night and circle Teofil's head and—"

Nathan's gaze sharpened, and he snapped his head up, suddenly alert. "Teofil?"

"Yeah. That's the kid's name. Teofil. Isn't it cool?"

Nathan got up from the table and crossed to the sink. He leaned on the counter and stared out the window at the tall privacy fence behind which Teofil lived. Thaddeus watched his father stare out the window, noted the high set to his shoulders, the muscles that stood out in his arms, and how his fingers clutched the edge of the counter. As he observed all of this, a number of questions he should have asked Teofil swept through his mind. Why did Teofil only garden at night? What had happened to Teofil's parents? Why did the fireflies come in from the woods each night and follow him around the yard? Did he go to school here in Superstition? Was he going to be there in the fall?

"You're not to see that boy again," his father said.

At first Thaddeus thought it was a joke, and he let out a single, surprised laugh. His father was always pushing him to make friends, to get to know other people in whatever town they were currently living. But after a few times of making and then losing friends when they moved once again, Thaddeus had stopped trying to get to know anyone. It was easier to be the strange, quiet kid who sat in the back of the class than to make friends and establish a connection with one or more kids his own age, only to be uprooted once again and moved God knew where.

Then his father turned to face him, and Thaddeus saw his expression. It felt like hands made of ice had reached inside him to squeeze all his organs. He pushed to his feet and walked up to glare into his father's face. "You can't forbid me from seeing the kid who lives next door to us. It's impossible."

Nathan set his jaw and put his hands on Thaddeus's shoulders. "Son—"

Thaddeus shrugged out from under his father's touch and pointed a finger at him now. "You're the one who is always telling me to make friends. To hang out with kids my own age. Every single city and small hick town we've lived in, I've heard the same line. Now that I've made a friend I really like, someone who gets me and seems like he could be a really good, close friend, you tell me I can't see him anymore. Well, you go to hell, and take your psycho-head-game parenting techniques with you."

He strode past his father, pulling away from his reach and stomping up the stairs. After slamming his bedroom door, he braced a chair under the knob, then lay on his back across his bed. He stared up at his ceiling, ignoring his father calling to him through the door. When Nathan finally walked away some time later, Thaddeus closed his eyes and drifted off to sleep.

It was late afternoon when he awoke, and he really, really needed to pee. He pulled the chair away from the door and hurried across the hall to the bathroom. Afterward he made his way down the steps. The house was quiet, so he was certain his father had already left for work. A note was waiting for him, written in Nathan's familiar slanted script. It was short and precise, standard procedure for his father.

> *Thaddeus, I don't like arguing with you. You're all I*
> *have left in this world that means anything to me. Please*
> *try to understand.*
> *Love, Dad.*

Thaddeus sighed, and a tiny flicker of regret flared into life within him. Now he felt guilty. And, well, maybe he should. He hadn't been honest with his father about the large animal that had tried to claw him out of the tree.

Nor had he mentioned the spark of attraction he harbored for Teofil. He didn't know what it was about his neighbor, but something in Teofil seemed to be the perfect match for Thaddeus's lonely heart. He checked the time and decided it best to get his apology to his father out of the way now, rather than wait for him to come home. Following a bite to eat and a quick shower, Thaddeus rode his bike into town. The day was warm, but the wind felt good against his skin and hair. He chained his bike to a rack at the end of Main Street and walked along the sidewalk, humming to himself as he stopped in front of each shop and examined the goods on display in the windows. He knew he was postponing his apology, but it wasn't five o'clock yet, and that's when he knew his father took his dinner break. Thaddeus could talk with him then. Now, he wanted to explore a bit more.

At the end of the street, he once more found himself in front of the library. Unlike the first time he had come upon the dark fieldstone building with rounded turrets at each corner—when a feeling of foreboding had prevented him from entering—Thaddeus was intrigued by the place today. He stepped inside and breathed in the smell of old books and newsprint. A woman stood behind the main desk, and she glanced up at him, then did a double take and openly stared. Her red hair framed her face like flames, and she narrowed her emerald-green eyes slightly as she watched him walk past the desk. Thaddeus nodded to her, and the woman gave him a slow, single nod in reply.

That wasn't weird at all.

He spent some time wandering up and down the rows of books, trailing his fingers lightly over the spines and looking over the titles and authors. There were a number of recent bestsellers on the shelves, along with the old classics. He could get some serious reading done for school this summer if he could focus long enough. And if he didn't take the job at the sporting goods store. Money or education and free time. Wasn't that what it always came down to with these kinds of decisions?

Since no patrons stood at the desk, Thaddeus decided to ask about applying for a library card. Later, if he found a book he was interested in, he could just check it out and be on his way. He was slightly unnerved at the way the red-haired woman stared at him as he approached the desk, but he was determined to follow through with his plan.

"Hello," Thaddeus said, glad his voice didn't shake.

"Good afternoon, young man," the woman said, her voice soft and smooth, like velvet made audible. "How may I help you?"

"I was wondering what kind of information is required to get a library card?"

"You're new to town," she said.

"Yes. Just moved here a few weeks ago."

"Well, normally we like to have a young person's parent here with them to provide proof of address." She looked around to make sure no one was listening to them, and Thaddeus couldn't help looking around as well, though there was no one standing anywhere near them. The librarian then leaned closer over the desk and lowered her voice even more. "But you seem like a trustworthy sort, so I'll just trust you're giving me the correct address." She narrowed her eyes and moved in even closer. "You are trustworthy, aren't you?"

Thaddeus nodded. "Yes, of course."

"Of course you are." She turned to the computer beside her, poised her fingers over the keyboard, then said, "Name and street address please."

Thaddeus relayed the information, and she tapped the keys in time. Soon, he heard the quiet hum of a printer, and the librarian cut out a card, fitted it within a plastic sleeve, and ran it through another machine. Moments later, she handed over a laminated card and gave him a smile that did not show any teeth.

"Not many people move into Superstition anymore," she said, her voice dreamy and a little sad. "Mostly, people move out of Superstition."

"Why is that?" Thaddeus asked.

"Not much call for work here," she replied. "Unless you like low-paying retail jobs."

"No other industry around?"

That small smile appeared once again, and her green-eyed gaze met his. "Not anymore. Sometimes things just wither up and die."

Thaddeus fought back a shiver at the quiet listlessness in her tone. He cleared his throat and shifted his weight, suddenly nervous and wanting nothing more than to be out of this cool, shadowy building and back out in the sunshine. Holding up the library card, he nodded once more. "Thanks for the card."

"Come back and use it soon."

"I will. Good-bye." He turned and headed for the door.

"Until we meet again," she said to his back. "Be well and be wary."

Thaddeus stopped to look over his shoulder. "Wary?"

"All kinds of things out and about these days," she explained. "People being just one of them."

He opened his mouth to ask if she knew anything about the large beast in the woods, but just then the door opened and three teenagers walked in, their laughter lowering to a respectable volume at the sight of the librarian behind her desk. The trio, two boys and one girl, parted around Thaddeus, each of them giving him a long look as they walked past.

Thaddeus turned and left the library, his question about the beast in the woods unasked and still troubling.

He was just in time to catch his father, and when he stepped inside the store, Nathan walked quickly up to him.

"Is everything all right?" Nathan asked.

Thaddeus nodded. He looked away, then met his father's gaze and took a breath. "I wanted to come in and say I was sorry."

Relief softened Nathan's features, and his shoulders dropped an inch, maybe more. More pangs of guilt burned within Thaddeus's gut at the thought that he had caused his father so much stress and worry.

"I'm glad," Nathan said. He squeezed Thaddeus's shoulder and added, "I'm sorry too. I was just really worried about you. The worst thoughts kept running through my head."

"Well, I'm sorry," Thaddeus repeated. "Really."

"Thank you, son." Nathan took a deep breath and let it out. "You hungry?"

Thaddeus grinned. "What do you think?"

Nathan laughed and turned him toward the door. "Come on. How about pizza? My treat."

Thaddeus rolled his eyes but couldn't fight back the grin. "Oh, okay, you can buy this one."

"Again?" Nathan added.

Thaddeus's grin widened. "Again."

An hour and a half later, as the last streaks of sunlight faded from view, Thaddeus coasted his bike up the driveway and tucked it away in the shed behind the house. As he headed back to the house, he walked close to the fence that stood between his yard and Teofil's, running his fingers over the smooth surface of the boards.

Inside he brushed his teeth and got ready for bed, then turned off the lights in his bedroom and pushed his window all the way open. Stars blazed in the night sky. The cool evening air filled the room, caressing his face and rustling papers on his desk. Thaddeus sighed and leaned on the windowsill, staring down into the yard beyond the fence.

From the darkness, a low humming started, and Thaddeus sat up straight, squinting as he strained to see Teofil among the night shadows. Fireflies flickered and danced, and then he saw the large familiar shape of him. Teofil crossed from one flowerbed to another, humming as he knelt to prune off dead blossoms, aerate the earth, and pull an occasional weed. Thaddeus was tempted to call down to Teofil but held his tongue, his father's demand to stay away from their neighbor echoing in his memory. Plus, he enjoyed the sight of Teofil at work.

Teofil stood to move to another part of the yard and looked up at the window, right at Thaddeus. The soft silver light of the moon allowed Thaddeus to see the smile on his face. Teofil waved and said in a loud whisper, "Come down! Come visit!"

Thaddeus looked toward the woods. Nothing moved in the deep shadows between the trees. He hesitated, thinking about his father's demand; then he nodded. "I'll be right over."

Teofil pointed toward the rear of the yard. "I'll meet you at the gate."

Thaddeus pulled on his hoodie, grabbed a flashlight, and ran downstairs. He scribbled out a note for his father, then hurried out the door and across the grass toward the trees, his heart pounding and his breath hot in his throat. Tonight he would ask all the questions he had completely forgotten about the night before. Tonight, he would get some answers.

Chapter SEVEN

"YOU LOOK good," Teofil said as Thaddeus stepped past him and into the yard.

Thaddeus was glad it was nighttime as he felt himself blush, and he let his gaze travel around the yard, over the flowerbeds, anywhere but to Teofil's face. "Oh? Really?"

"Yes," Teofil said and leaned in close to whisper, "Really."

A loud, nervous laugh burst out of Thaddeus, and he slapped a hand over his mouth as he stared at Teofil with wide eyes. He lifted his hand long enough to whisper, "Sorry," before covering his mouth again.

Teofil smiled, lighting up areas of Thaddeus that no other boy had activated. "You're pretty cute, you know that?"

More heat flared across Thaddeus's face. The only thing he could think to do was give a shrug and turn away to let out a breath. He felt dizzy and giddy, his thoughts pinging around like pinballs. What was it about Teofil that brought out such a strong attraction?

"What did you do today?" Thaddeus asked as he approached a flowerbed and stood before it, staring down at the blooms painted with moonlight.

"The usual," Teofil replied. "How about you?"

"Well, I slept a lot," Thaddeus said and looked at him. "Guess that was to be expected since I was here with you all night."

"Guess so," Teofil agreed. He knelt down and pushed his fingers into the dirt.

"Why do you garden at night?" Thaddeus asked, kneeling beside him.

Teofil shrugged, his gaze on his fingers working in the dirt, the tip of his tongue stuck out of the corner of his mouth. "Always done it, that's all."

"Always?" Thaddeus asked. "Like, since you were born or something?"

Teofil smiled at him and winked. "Something like that, yeah." He took Thaddeus's hand, his fingers cool, damp, and gritty with dirt. "Feel this."

Thaddeus opened his mouth to protest, thinking Teofil might be moving faster than he was comfortable with, but let his protest go unvoiced when Teofil guided his hand down to the dirt. The earth was soft and light, cool against his skin as Teofil pushed his fingers deep.

"Feel around," Teofil said.

Thaddeus wiggled his fingers in the dirt, a little nervous about what he might come in contact with. "What am I supposed to be feeling?"

"The dirt. Tiny stones. The roots of the flowers." Teofil leaned in again and said in a low voice that sent shivers down Thaddeus's spine, "Life."

Thaddeus stared into Teofil's eyes, and the moment seemed to stretch out into minutes, hours, days, weeks, as Teofil held his hand within the dirt. A yellow glow flickered between them—quick like a will-o'-the-wisp—and then was gone again. Thaddeus blinked and leaned back, his fingers coming out of the dirt and Teofil's grasp. Sense returned to him, and as he brushed the dirt from his hand, he asked, "Are you, like, some kind of firefly shepherd or something? Why do these lightning bugs follow you around the yard?"

It was Teofil's turn to laugh. He threw back his head and laughed up at the moon and the stars. Thaddeus looked over his shoulder at the windows of the large house, but they all remained dark. No sudden illumination announced the awakening of Teofil's grandfather, and he relaxed a little and looked back at his friend.

"It's a valid question," Thaddeus said, feeling a little bit defensive. "They hover around you like sheep or something."

"Oh, you might want to watch what you call them," Teofil said, his voice lowering to a whisper but his eyes still twinkling with amusement. "They don't take kindly to being compared to livestock."

"What?" Thaddeus threw his hands up in the air and shook his head. "You're talking about them as if they were rational, thinking beings." A tiny, high-pitched trill made him look around. "Who was that?"

"It was the livestock that hover around my head," Teofil said. He nodded toward Thaddeus's shoulder. "Take a look."

Moving slowly, very, very slowly, his stomach tight from nervousness, Thaddeus turned his head and looked down at his shoulder. The yellow glow filled his vision, and he squinted against it. Then a form within the glow began to take shape. A tiny, glowing girl stood on his shoulder, completely nude, arms folded and an expression of annoyance on her tiny face, bright yellow hair spilling over her slender shoulders.

Four thin, translucent wings, very similar to those Thaddeus saw on dragonflies, flapped slowly on her back.

He held very still, his eyes wide and his breath caught in his chest. For a long while, no thought went through his brain at all. He sat as still as stone and stared at the tiny woman standing on his shoulder glaring up at him. He'd seen some weird stuff in the thirty-two times they had moved around the country, but this took the cake.

"What is it?" he finally asked in a dry whisper.

"A fairy!" Teofil replied. "You've never seen a fairy before?"

Thaddeus slowly shook his head, never taking his gaze off the fairy on his shoulder and not moving any other part of his body. "No. Never seen one before. Never knew they were real."

The fairy threw her hands up in the air in disgust and turned her back. She pushed off from his shoulder and flew away out into the night. Thaddeus's eyes were wide as his gaze followed her path. Tremors wracked his body, the sudden release of pent up adrenaline, no doubt, and he put a hand down on the grass to support himself.

"You okay, Thaddeus?" Teofil asked, leaning in close and placing a big, warm hand on Thaddeus's shoulder. "Hey, you okay?"

Thaddeus stared at him a long, stunned moment. "Fairies?"

Teofil smiled and tightened his grip a bit. "You've never seen one before? I thought you…." Teofil cocked his head. "You know what I am, right?"

Thaddeus swallowed hard and shook his head. "A teenager?"

That smile again. In that expression, Thaddeus saw nothing to be afraid of. No matter what Teofil told him he was—vampire, werewolf, anything—Thaddeus knew deep inside that he had nothing to fear from his new friend. The weight of Teofil's hand on his shoulder calmed and grounded him as his mind tried to spin right out of his skull and up into the air to dance with the fairies.

"You wondered why I garden at night," Teofil said. "Well, it's because I'm a gnome."

Thaddeus blinked. All he could think of was the ceramic gnomes people placed in their yards as decoration. But Teofil didn't fit that image at all. For one thing, he was young and handsome, as tall as Thaddeus himself and broad across the shoulders. And he definitely was not wearing a colorful jacket and pointy hat.

"A gnome?"

Teofil nodded. "A gnome." His eyebrows went up. "You scared of me now?"

"What? No! Of course not. I just… I just need to get used to it. Just saw my first fairy a minute ago, and now I find out my new friend is a gnome." Thaddeus took a deep breath, let it out, took another, and let that out as well. A few fairies floated between them, and now that Thaddeus knew what he was looking at, he could see them watching him, observing his reaction. One of them, he noticed with a bit of surprise, was a male, his lean, nude body glowing with a golden light.

"So you're a gnome," Thaddeus said, setting the word in his mind and trying to get his previous concept of what a gnome was to match up with Teofil.

"Garden gnome, of the Rhododendrons."

"Rhododendrons?" Thaddeus repeated.

"My tribe," Teofil said with a smile.

"Oh!" Thaddeus smiled back. "Your family?"

"Yes! My family!" Teofil squeezed his shoulder once more, then removed his hand and stared off toward the gate in the length of fence, sadness softening his expression. "Though I haven't seen them in a long time."

"I'm sorry," Thaddeus said, thinking of his mother and how her death seemed to weigh heavily on his father even after all these years. "I know how it feels to miss someone like that."

Teofil glanced at him from the corner of his eye. "You do?"

"Yeah. My mom…." Thaddeus shrugged and looked down, plucking blades of grass. "She died in an accident. Or something. My dad's been pretty vague about it all these years. I don't know exactly what happened. He doesn't like to talk about it. My father, I mean. I never knew her because she died when I was a baby. But I've seen pictures, and I know she held me in her arms at least a few times."

"That's hard," Teofil said. "Growing up without a mother, not knowing what happened to her. At least I know where mine are."

Thaddeus looked at him in surprise. "You do?"

"Sure. They're out in the woods," Teofil said with a wave of his hand toward the trees. "Forest gnomes and garden gnomes are pretty much the same tribe." He shrugged. "I was better with garden plants than forest plants, so I was chosen to come here."

Thaddeus frowned. "Chosen? For what?"

"Thaddeus!" His father's voice coming over the fence startled them both, and they stood up, hands at their sides and staring at the fence as if guilty of doing something more than talking.

"It's my dad," Thaddeus whispered.

"Do you think he heard us?" Teofil asked.

Thaddeus shook his head. "I left him a note telling him I'd be over here." He looked up at Teofil. "I got in trouble for staying out all night last time."

Teofil looked guilty. "Sorry."

"My fault, not yours," Thaddeus said. He stepped up to the fence and called over it in a loud whisper, "Dad! I'm here."

"Come home," his father demanded. "Right now."

"But, Dad—"

"No buts. Get home."

Thaddeus sighed. "Fine." He faced Teofil again and stood for a moment just looking at him. Fairies slowly circled his head, their golden glow lighting his face enough for Thaddeus to see that Teofil stared at him with more than just friendship, more than mere affection.

"Now, Thaddeus!" His father's command snapped the moment between them.

"Thanks for coming by and talking," Teofil said. "I really like you, Thaddeus."

They walked toward the gate side by side, shoulders bumping now and then as the fairies floated around them.

"I like you too, Teofil," Thaddeus said. "Maybe sometime we can see each other in daylight."

"Oh, I don't come out in daylight," Teofil said. "I garden at night."

"Does sunlight burn you or anything? Like vampires?"

Teofil chuckled. "No. Nothing like that. I just prefer to work in the dark." He thought a moment, then shrugged. "Maybe I could try it in the daytime, though. If I had someone with me."

Thaddeus smiled. "I'd like that."

"Me too."

They looked at each other in silence, and then Thaddeus's father called over the fence again.

"Dammit!" Thaddeus grumbled. "I gotta go. Let me know when you want to meet up again."

Teofil tipped his head toward the fairies who were now doing tricks in the air nearby. "I'll send one of them over to get you."

"Is that the gnome version of a text message?" Thaddeus asked.

Teofil frowned. "A what?"

"Never mind. I'll keep an eye out for a fairy-gram." He lifted a hand and backed toward the fence. "Good night."

"Good night, Thaddeus." Teofil leaned in, and for a second Thaddeus thought they might kiss. But, instead, Teofil reached past him to open the gate. "Sleep well."

"You too. Tomorrow, I mean. During the daylight." He turned to go, then turned back quick and waved to the fairies. "Good night, fairies. Nice to finally meet you all."

The fairies did loop-the-loops in response, their high-pitched, tinkling laughter sounding like far off glass wind chimes in a gentle breeze.

Thaddeus stood outside the gate and watched Teofil push it shut. He trailed his fingers over the boards as he walked along the fence and rounded the corner to see his father standing in their yard, his arms folded and his mouth set in a thin line.

"I thought I told you not to see him again?"

"I was just talking to him, Dad," Thaddeus said as he walked past. "What's the harm in that?"

"Just…. Keep away from him," his father replied, his tone laced with anger and a trace of sadness. "For me."

"Fine. I'll sit in the house by myself all day." Thaddeus stomped into the house and up the stairs to his bedroom, where he threw himself on his bed and lay in the dark listening to Teofil hum as he tended the gardens next door.

Chapter EIGHT

IT HAD been a week since Thaddeus had seen Teofil. During that time he watched the Fourth of July fireworks from his bedroom window. As the thundering blooms of the fireworks lit up the sky, Thaddeus sadly smiled at Teofil, who paused now and then in his gardening to look at the spectacle above and give him a wave. His father had changed his mind and urged—insisted, really—that Thaddeus take the stockroom job at Superstition Sporting Goods. Now, Thaddeus found himself working most evenings and late into the night. When he would finally arrive home, a couple of times at 3:00 a.m., Thaddeus would be too exhausted to even try to call to Teofil over the fence. He would, however, push the window open and give Teofil a wave, then listen to his humming and fall asleep in minutes, sprawled out on his bed.

One of those nights, he fell hard into a deep sleep. With his muscles aching from moving boxes and stocking shelves, Thaddeus tumbled into a dream. It was blurred around the edges, and fairies floated back and forth at his peripheral vision. Whenever he tried to look at them directly, however, they darted away. Somewhere beyond the blurred edges of his dreamscape, he could hear Teofil's reassuring humming.

But something was different about this place. Someone else was with him.

When he looked around again, Thaddeus found himself in a kitchen. Sunlight poured in through the windows, lending a glow to the woman sitting at the small table. She stared down into a cup of coffee with an expression so troubled, so lost, it made something inside Thaddeus ache.

This was Claire, his mother. He knew her from the photograph his father unpacked and placed on his dresser with each of their moves.

His mother looked up, surprised to see him; then her face relaxed into a smile, and she spoke to him, the sound of her voice sweet and lyrical, like a favorite song happened upon while changing radio stations. Though she had been gone before Thaddeus could remember how she sounded, he was sure this was, indeed, her voice.

"Thaddeus," she said. "You look well."

"You do too," he replied. This all felt normal, as if Thaddeus had been the one away—maybe at summer camp or vacationing with a pack of giggling cousins—and the normalcy of it, so different from the reality of his life, made the ache inside him even more pronounced.

"I've missed you," she said. "So much."

"I've missed you too," Thaddeus assured her, then waved his hand as though his father, Nathan, stood beside him. "We both have."

Claire smiled. "I know."

Thaddeus drew in a breath. His body trembled, his stomach knotting tight as he took a few steps closer to the table. As he approached his mother, she and the table grew in size. Now it appeared he was a small child looking up at her, the sunlight in the kitchen even brighter.

"I don't remember you," he admitted. There, he had said it. He had purged a bit of the swampy mess that sat low inside him, feeding regret and guilt into his system a little at a time over the years, like a septic infection. He didn't remember his mother—how bad of a son was he? "I don't remember a lot about that time."

Claire's brow furrowed, but in concern instead of anger. All this time, all these years without her, Thaddeus had tried to find a memory of her to use for comfort. But all he had were the photographs his father kept in an album and the one in a frame on his dresser. There were no tactile memories for Thaddeus to cling to, no emotions tied to her memory other than loss.

"Oh, Thaddeus," she said and then stopped herself to lean back in the chair, hands limp in her lap, her gaze moving off toward the sunlight. "Oh, my boy."

"A year after your death…," Thaddeus began, intending to tell her how many times they had moved from one city to another.

Claire quickly sat forward again to lean on the table, her expression sharp as she looked down at him. "I'm not dead, Thaddeus."

A chill ran through him. "You're not?" A hot flash of anger followed the chill, burning like wildfire. He balled up his fists and steeled his gaze, staring into hers as he said, "You left us, then. You left me."

She was out of the chair and on her knees before him in an instant, faster than he could track her movements. He took a step back, startled, but she grabbed his upper arms, her grip strong as she stared right back at him. "I didn't leave you. I would never leave you. I was taken."

"Thaddeus!"

The dream began to break up, the sunlight fading, taking his mother's image with it.

"No!" Thaddeus shouted, looking all around him. He could still feel her hands on his arms, but the blurring at the edges of his dream crept in closer, erasing everything. When he looked back at his mother, her face was starting to fade, and panic erupted within him.

"Mother! No, come back. Wait!" he pleaded.

"I love you, Thaddeus," Claire said, her voice now garbled and distant. "We're closer now. So close. So very, very close."

Tears burned in his eyes and along his cheeks. He tried to surge forward and follow her as she pulled away from him, but he was rooted in place and could not move. "Mother!"

"Hey, lazy bones, time to get up!" His father's voice from the hall pulled him out of the dream and back into reality.

Thaddeus awoke with a start. His heart pounded, and the now tattered remnants of his dream lay just beneath his skin, like an itch he couldn't quite reach. His room was aglow with sunlight, and even though his eyes burned with the need to sleep, he pushed up from his bed and shuffled to the bathroom across the hall. He had taken an early shift after the late one the night before, and while it hadn't seemed like such a big deal at the time, he was definitely regretting it now. As he peed and splashed water on his face, the details of the dream began to fade, but the unsettled feeling still lingered.

ALL DAY Thaddeus was distracted by the swiftly fading images of the dream. He was quiet, withdrawn as he unpacked boxes and stocked the shelves in the large back room of the store. Edgar asked him more than once if he felt all right, and Thaddeus assured him he was just tired from the late shift the night before.

When it was close to time for Thaddeus to punch out, Edgar approached. His expression was so anxious, Thaddeus was at first concerned something had happened to his father out on the salesroom floor.

"What's wrong, Edgar?" Thaddeus asked, that odd, displaced feeling he'd had all day growing and shifting within him.

"Well, Logan was supposed to come in tonight to relieve you," Edgar said, referring to the clean-cut, scholarly high school junior Thaddeus had exchanged maybe five words with the entire week he'd worked there.

"Uh-oh," Thaddeus said. "I sense a 'but' coming on."

Edgar gave a weak smile and shrugged. "But he's gotten himself arrested for driving under the influence and is in jail."

Thaddeus widened his eyes. "Logan? Logan Augustine? He was just bragging to me the other day that he had had the highest grade point in his class this year."

Edgar lifted a shoulder in a half shrug. "It happens to the best of us sometimes. Anyway, we're expecting a big delivery from Rock Crick, and I know you worked late last night, but I was wondering if you'd be willing to stick around to help unpack it?"

Thaddeus sighed and looked out over all the shelves stocked with inventory. Where did Edgar think he would sell all this stuff? He looked at Edgar again and nodded. "Sure. I can do that."

Edgar's face brightened. "You are a lifesaver, Thaddeus. Thank you! I'll make sure you get time and a half for this."

Thaddeus went back to his work, feeling tired but a bit better that he would get more money for his efforts at least.

Sometime later, his father having left hours before, Thaddeus finished unpacking the last of the Rock Crick items and broke the box down, tossing it on the stack of flattened cardboard that needed to be taken out to the recycling dumpster.

"You all set back here, Thaddeus?" Edgar asked as he strode past, heading for the shelves stocked with shoes.

"Just finished up," Thaddeus replied. "I was going to punch out and take the boxes out with me on my way home."

"Your dad picking you up?" Edgar asked, but in a distracted way as he searched for a specific style and size of shoe.

"No, it's too late to call him. I'll just walk. It's not that far." He grabbed some string and got to work tying it around the flattened boxes.

"Be careful," Edgar said as he hurried back to the sales floor with boxes of shoes in his hands. "And go straight home, you hear?"

"Yes, sir," Thaddeus replied.

He finished tying up the boxes, punched out at the time clock, and then dragged the boxes with him out the back door. The cool night air was fresh with the smell of lake water and blooming plants. The mingled scents made Thaddeus think of Teofil, and a lonely ache pulsed within him. He missed talking with Teofil, and he still had so many questions for him! If any other person on the planet had confessed to being a gnome, Thaddeus would have thought him raving mad. But the sight of the fairies and the feeling of enchantment in the yard where Teofil toiled each night helped sell Thaddeus on the admission. But his father had specifically forbidden him from seeing Teofil again.

Still, what his father didn't know wouldn't anger him.

Thaddeus had too many questions to simply avoid Teofil. And he missed the rapport they had developed and the feeling that someone finally might understand him.

After tossing the boxes in the dumpster, Thaddeus wiped his hands on his jeans and started off for home. A half-moon rode the night sky, surrounded by stars, and somewhere deep in the woods to his left an owl hooted. He would need to walk ten blocks west and then three blocks north to get home. Though tired, Thaddeus didn't mind the opportunity to walk the quiet, shadow-drenched sidewalks of Superstition. It gave him some time to clear his head and try to remember more specifics from his dream about his mother.

She had said something significant before his father had awakened him, something he should be able to remember.

A twig snapped somewhere behind the line of trees to his left, stopping Thaddeus in his tracks. He stared into the blackness between the trees, heart pounding, mouth dry. Now that he was focusing, Thaddeus noticed that the woods had gone completely silent. No insects buzzed, no owls hooted, no rustle of small critters moving through the undergrowth—nothing but a watchful stillness.

Memories of the thing in the woods filled him with cold dread, and he realized his decision to walk home had been foolish. He had thought the fact that he was out in the open and there were streetlights at every corner would make a difference. But now he saw he could be wrong.

Thaddeus ran. He didn't wait to see what would come at him from the trees, he simply ran. He reached the end of the block and continued running, his breathing ragged, the night air cool against his face. After another block he risked a glance over his shoulder and nearly screamed.

The beast loped after him, head hung low, moonlight glinting off sharp teeth. It was close, much too close, and the sight of it lit a spark of panic in his chest. He put on a desperate burst of speed, afraid to look back again. Whatever this thing was, it was fast. And strong.

It hit him from the side and sent him tumbling across a lawn until he bumped up against something solid that knocked the wind out of him. He lay stunned for a moment, lungs burning and side aching where he had struck whatever had stopped him. When he looked up, he saw that he had landed against a stone garden gnome lawn ornament.

Before he could react to the absurd perfection of the gnome, the beast slapped a big paw on his thigh and sank in its claws. It backed up, pulling him away from the porch and toward a shadowed hedge.

Thaddeus screamed. He reached down to grab the beast's paw, feeling the muscles clench beneath the fur as it pulled him along. Its claws dug deeper into his leg, and Thaddeus screamed again.

A moment later the beast howled in surprise and pain, then released him. Thaddeus pressed his hands to his thigh, moaning as the warm, wet feel of blood squeezed through his fingers, and he rolled back and forth, eyes closed, pain burning through him like lightning. Someone knelt beside him, telling him he was safe, he would be okay, but Thaddeus kept his eyes squeezed shut as he continued to roll back and forth.

Over the new arrival's voice and the sounds of his own moans, somewhere off in the distance, Thaddeus heard an owl hoot, and another hooted back.

Chapter NINE

STRANGE SOUNDS floated around him. Whispered voices, sometimes laced with a frantic energy, undercut by a soft beeping. As Thaddeus circled the edge of consciousness, blurry memories came and went. He remembered dragging the boxes to the recycle dumpster before starting for home. The woods he walked alongside seemed peaceful, but then had gone silent. He recalled the panic that had exploded within him as he sensed the danger lurking in the woods so close, and he'd run. The thing chased him down, and it had clawed his leg.

With that memory Thaddeus jerked awake, then cried out as pain burned through him. He opened his eyes and stared through his tears up at a tile ceiling. A light just behind his head buzzed quietly.

"It's okay," someone said in a soft, soothing tone. It was a familiar voice, and the resultant rush of relief was like a cooling wave that tamed the heat of pain.

"Dad," Thaddeus said, his voice a dry croak.

Nathan leaned in over him. His eyes were bloodshot, and the skin around them was dark with shock and concern, but he tried to smile as if nothing was wrong. "I'm here, buddy. I'm right here. You're safe. You're all right. You're in the hospital."

"What happened?" Thaddeus asked.

"Well, that's what we'd like to know," Nathan replied.

"We?"

"The police are outside the room."

Nathan squeezed his hand before leaning in to softly kiss his forehead. A hot ball of emotion choked Thaddeus. How long had it been since his father had kissed him? It had been nice, comforting, but also a little disconcerting. Were things really that bad?

"Can I sit up?" Thaddeus asked.

"Sure, sure, sure," Nathan said and moved out of sight to grab the bed remote. "Here we go. Let me know when you want me to stop."

The bed rumbled as the top half rose, and when Thaddeus felt comfortable, he nodded to his father. "Thanks."

Nathan gave him an exhausted smile before setting the remote aside. He turned back, patted Thaddeus's shoulder, and asked, "Can you remember what happened?"

Thaddeus related the events he could remember. Edgar had asked him to work late for Logan, who had gotten arrested for drunk driving. He'd taken the boxes out, then started walking home. Something had been in the woods, the big beast he had seen behind their house.

"What kind of animal was it?" Nathan asked.

"Big," Thaddeus replied. "I've seen it a couple of times now. The first night I met Teofil, it knocked me out of a tree."

"What?" Nathan exclaimed, then looked around and lowered his voice. He looked shocked and angry, and Thaddeus dropped his gaze. "You never told me about that."

"I know, I'm sorry."

"Well what kind of animal is it?"

Thaddeus shrugged, unable to meet Nathan's gaze. He'd really been disappointing his father this summer, and he felt very guilty about it. "I'm not sure. It's nothing I've seen before."

"The doctor said it looked like the claws were big, like a bear."

"It's big like a bear, but it's not really a bear," Thaddeus replied.

"Are you sure?" Nathan asked.

Thaddeus nodded, remembering the hulking, shadowy form that knocked him out of the tree. "I'm sure. It's big, and it's mean, but I can't tell if it's a wolf or a bear or what." He swallowed hard and looked down at the lumps of his legs covered by sheets. "What did it do to me? How bad is it?"

"It was determined, but you'll be okay," Nathan assured him. "A couple of bruised ribs—"

"It knocked me down," Thaddeus explained, "and I hit a lawn ornament, I think."

"—and stitches in your leg to close the wounds. Fifty-eight in all."

Thaddeus's stomach did a slow roll, and he felt the blood drain from his face. "Fifty-eight stitches?"

Nathan nodded. "More than half internal. Shouldn't be any permanent damage, no muscle or ligaments were torn. Doctor is pretty confident you can go home today."

Thaddeus sighed. "Good."

"Thaddeus," Nathan said and leaned in closer to take his hand. "Look at me."

With great effort, Thaddeus met his father's stern gaze. "I know what you're going to say."

"Do you?"

"Yes. You're going to tell me I need to be honest with you about things, just like you're honest with me." Thaddeus raised his eyebrows. "Because you are being honest with me, Dad, aren't you?" His mother's words from his dream whispered through the back of his mind: *I'm not dead.*

Nathan sat back and looked away, and Thaddeus knew there was something, quite a lot of something, he thought, that his father was keeping from him. When Nathan met his gaze again, he looked even more weary.

"There are different reasons for keeping things from someone," Nathan said. "Sometimes it's done to keep someone you love safe. Other times, it's to be deceitful. I don't want to have to worry that you're being deceitful with me. Not now, not after all that we've been through."

Tears stung Thaddeus's eyes as he shook his head. "I didn't mean to be deceitful. I'm just really lonely, Dad. And Teofil is… he's different than anyone I've met before."

"That's all well and good, but for us to keep you safe, I need you to be honest with me about things that happen, okay?"

"Okay, yeah. I get it." But Thaddeus noticed his father hadn't really answered the question of whether or not he himself was being honest.

Nathan gave him a quick, tired smile and squeezed his hand. "Good. Now, the police have been waiting to talk with you. Are you up for that now?"

"Yeah. Let's get it over with."

"Okay. I'll be right here with you the whole time." Nathan stood and headed for the door.

"Hey, Dad?" Thaddeus asked.

Nathan turned back, his hand on the door's handle. "Yeah?"

"Something happened to interrupt the thing's attack," Thaddeus said. "Any idea what that was?"

"No. The homeowner found you on his lawn, shouting for help. He called the police. They found your library card in your wallet so they came to the house." He cocked his head. "When did you get a library card?"

"A week or so ago," he replied. "I almost didn't but darn glad I decided to get one now." He frowned and thought hard about the night before. He could remember the beast dragging him toward the heavily shadowed hedge, but then it cried out in surprise and pain and released him. What had happened to send the beast running off?

"Ready for the police?" Nathan asked.

Thaddeus looked up, took a breath, and nodded. "I'm ready."

THAT EVENING, after a hearty dinner, Nathan helped Thaddeus up to his room. He fluffed up Thaddeus's pillows and arranged on the nightstand a glass of water, a glass of soda, a bag of his favorite brand of chips, and the remote for the small television he had brought in from his own bedroom. Nathan opened both windows to take advantage of the cool evening breeze, told him repeatedly to stay in bed, and then left the room.

Thaddeus had taken a pain pill prescribed at the hospital, and as he watched sitcom reruns, he drifted in and out of sleep. Each time he fell asleep, however, he imagined he could feel the beast's claws dig into his leg and drag him toward the shadows beneath the hedge. He would jerk awake, sometimes with a hiss of pain when the stitches pulled from his movements.

It was one of these times that he noticed it was full dark. Only the TV lit his room, and some crazy infomercial was on, the host's voice digging at his nerves. Thaddeus switched off the TV and sighed with relief at the resulting silence. He checked the clock and discovered it was after midnight. The rest of the house was silent, so his father must have gone to bed already. Thaddeus thought about Teofil and wondered if he knew what had happened.

As if summoned by Thaddeus's thoughts, Teofil's familiar, comforting hum started up in the yard next door. Thaddeus's heart pounded, and a strong ache burned within him. He would love nothing better than to be able to go downstairs, cross his backyard to the woods, and follow the fence until he came to the gate that led into Teofil's yard. It would be so good to be able to go down and see Teofil, hear his voice, feel the warmth of his body alongside him as they knelt before the glorious flowerbeds Teofil tended.

But even as strong as that desire burned, Thaddeus knew he wasn't up to it. Not tonight, anyway. Probably not for a while.

A small, bright glow floated in through the window. It was a fairy, and Thaddeus pushed up onto his elbows to watch the tiny girl glide across the room. She clutched a large, perfect daisy, the weight of it causing her to dip now and then as she flew toward him.

"Hello," Thaddeus whispered when the fairy reached the side of his bed. "It's good to see you. Is that for me?"

The fairy smiled and nodded, then dropped the daisy onto his outstretched palm.

"Is it from Teofil?" Thaddeus asked as he smelled the flower.

The fairy nodded again, then blew him a kiss and turned to speed out the window and spiral down out of sight.

Thaddeus put the daisy in his drinking glass, making sure the stem reached what remained of his water. Teofil had sent him a flower. Somehow, Teofil had known about the attack.

A yawn interrupted his smile and eased him back into sleep.

THE NEXT day Nathan returned to work. He helped Thaddeus down the stairs and set him up on the sofa with things in reach, made him promise to stay inside the house, then hurried out the door. Thaddeus drifted in and out of sleep, and before he knew it, his father was back home and making dinner.

That evening the fairy brought him another flower. It was a deep red rosebud, and it was gorgeous. Thaddeus breathed in its scent before adding it to the water glass alongside the daisy. He got out of bed and limped after the fairy as she flew to the window. After grabbing his desk chair, he sat carefully and looked down into the neighboring yard. Teofil stood in the center of the yard, staring up at him. Moonlight shimmered in his eyes, and when Thaddeus waved to him, Teofil waved back. Then, humming, Teofil bent to his work. Thaddeus watched him for a time but grew sleepy and limped back to his bed where he fell asleep to the sound of Teofil's hum.

A FEW days later, the water glass beside Thaddeus's bed contained a variety of blooms, each delivered after sunset by a fairy before Teofil got to work. Nathan looked at the flowers but never asked where Thaddeus had gotten them. His leg felt better, he was able to get up and about easier, and Thaddeus could wait no longer. Nathan had a late shift at the store, so once the sun went down, Thaddeus walked out the back door and made his way across the lawn. At the edge of the trees, he stood and stared into the darkness for a moment, his leg quietly throbbing as he gathered his courage, then finally stepped off the grass into the woods and made his way as quickly and carefully as he could along the back of the fence. He was alert for any sounds of attack from the woods around him, but all he could hear were the normal sounds of critters rustling, owls hooting, and insects buzzing.

The gate opened the moment he reached it, as if Teofil had been watching his progress through the fence.

"I'd hoped you'd come see me tonight," Teofil said.

"I wanted to earlier, but…." Thaddeus waved toward his injured leg.

"I heard about the attack," Teofil said. "Come inside the yard."

Thaddeus stepped through the gate. He stopped and closed his eyes, breathing in a deep lungful of the fragrant evening air. His questions were building one after the other in his mind like LEGOs, but for now he just wanted to enjoy the peace of Teofil's world. When he opened his eyes, he saw fairies dipping and spinning around his head in greeting, and he laughed at their enthusiasm.

"See? We all missed you." Teofil leaned in closer and lowered his voice. "But I missed you most of all."

A blush burned in Thaddeus's cheeks, and he looked away, his gaze catching on the large shape of the tree trunk across the yard. The moonlight blanched it even more so that it appeared a ghostly thing, something that belonged on the other side of the veil of this world. He cleared his throat and took a breath to steady his nerves.

"I missed you all, as well," Thaddeus replied and was able once more to meet Teofil's gaze. "You especially."

The fairies giggled and flew in circles around their heads, talking all at once but in too high a register for Thaddeus to be able to understand.

He smiled and asked, "What are they saying?"

Teofil grinned, looked up at the fairies spinning around them, then back at Thaddeus. "They're telling me to kiss you."

Another blush, hotter this time. Thaddeus's throat was dry, burning, actually, like a brush fire, and he suddenly wished he'd brought along a bottle of water.

"Oh" was all he could manage to say.

Teofil leaned slowly toward him. Thaddeus's heart pounded faster with Teofil's increasing proximity. He took a breath and closed his eyes. The warm, soft touch of Teofil's lips sent his heart racing even faster, so that blood pounded in his ears and the wounds in his leg pulsed in time. The voices of the fairies circling them blended together into one gentle and sweet song that floated away on the night breeze. Heat prickled across Thaddeus's skin in waves, and his scalp tingled.

It was a gentle kiss, tentative and sweet, and before Thaddeus knew it, Teofil pulled back. He couldn't help the resulting smile as he met Teofil's gaze once again. It had been his first kiss, and it had been perfect.

"You taste like magic," Teofil said.

Thaddeus knew, at that moment, that he had fallen in love with Teofil. Whether he was a gnome or was insane and thought he was a gnome, Thaddeus didn't care. He had finally met someone who made him feel special, someone who made him feel welcomed and loved and funny. He had met someone who made him laugh and want to ask questions and listen to for hours. This was the man—the gnome—he had been destined to meet.

The back door of Teofil's house banged open, and an old man stomped out onto the porch. He wore a bright yellow tracksuit that practically glowed in the moonlight, and his long, gray beard hung almost down to his waist, nearly obscuring the entire length of the jacket's zipper. This, Thaddeus assumed, was Teofil's grandfather, Leopold. And he looked angry.

"Trespasser!" Leopold shouted and shook his fist in their direction. "I'll call the police! I'll have you arrested!"

Teofil's grandfather descended the wooden steps to the lush lawn and stormed toward them. Thaddeus's heart pounded for an entirely different reason than it had just minutes ago. His fear built as the old man approached, and he had just turned to hurry toward the gate and escape Teofil's grandfather's fury when someone pounded on it from the other side.

"Thaddeus! Open this gate right now!"

Thaddeus's fear doubled, tripled, and finally all but consumed him. His father was on the other side of the gate, pounding to get in, angry at Thaddeus for disobeying him once again. He was caught, and now Thaddeus was going to have to face not only his father's wrath, but that of Teofil's grandfather as well.

And all because he had shared his very first kiss with another boy.

Chapter TEN

"I DEMAND that you open this gate!"

Thaddeus's father pounded harder, almost drowning out the angry words Teofil's grandfather was shouting as he approached.

Panic bloomed inside Thaddeus, shutting down his ability to think. Why were Teofil's grandfather and his own father so angry about this? His father had never once said a disparaging word about anyone, no matter their race, gender, or sexual orientation. While Thaddeus had never truly come out to his father, Nathan had let him know he would have no problem should Thaddeus choose a gay relationship. So what was it about Teofil that made him react so strongly?

"You there! Out!" Teofil's grandfather shouted and pointed toward the gate. "Stay away from him!"

"No!"

The denial was more of a roar, and suddenly Teofil stood in front of Thaddeus, shielding him from his grandfather. Thaddeus let his gaze slide over Teofil's broad shoulders, tracing the lines of taut muscles in his outstretched arms visible beneath the thin T-shirt. The fairies had scattered, frightened away by the commotion, no doubt, but as he peered over Teofil's shoulder, the moon gave enough light for Thaddeus to see the shocked look on the old man's face.

"You defy me?" Leopold asked, his voice quiet and stunned.

Nathan pounded on the fence again and made more demands. Fear rolled in Thaddeus's gut, slick and cold, and his wounds throbbed as his father carried on. He was worried about facing his father in his present state, yes, but a larger fear had coalesced that the commotion Nathan was causing would attract the beast in the woods.

"He's making too much noise," Thaddeus whispered and gathered the tail of Teofil's T-shirt in his hand, resting his fist against the small of his back. "He'll bring it right to us."

Teofil looked over his shoulder at him, frowning. "What will he bring?"

"That thing that's attacked me twice," Thaddeus said. "The monster in the woods."

"Well, there's no getting past any of this now, is there?" Teofil's grandfather said. He turned toward the gate, paused to let out a deep breath, as if he'd been holding it in for years and years, and then he stepped up and pulled on the handle.

Nathan marched through the gate and right up to where Thaddeus and Teofil stood. A combination of hurt and anger clouded his expression, and guilt dug its claws into Thaddeus's belly. Teofil stepped between Thaddeus and his father, and the look of surprise on Nathan's face would have been funny if Thaddeus hadn't been the focus of Nathan's anger.

"You're a brave one, I'll give you that," Nathan said. "Step aside."

"It's taken you this long to find us, and I don't even warrant a greeting?" Teofil's grandfather said.

Thaddeus watched from behind Teofil as Nathan's expression shifted. He went from outright anger to barely suppressed rage. His father's lips tightened into a thin line, and the furrows in his brow deepened. Nathan held Thaddeus's gaze a moment before he turned to face Teofil's grandfather.

"Where is she?" Nathan's voice was cold, edged with the threat of violence.

Thaddeus wanted to scream at the top of his lungs for everyone to stop, to just hold still a moment, but he couldn't speak. There were too many layers to what was happening right before him, too much he didn't understand. He strained to hear every word said, understand the nuance of this revelation that his father and Teofil's grandfather seemed to know one another, to have some kind of history.

"She is safe," Teofil's grandfather responded. "No thanks to you."

Nathan clenched his fists at his sides and took a step closer to the old man. When he spoke again, his voice was quiet. "That's not fair, Leopold."

It was Leopold's turn to take a step, and he closed the distance between himself and Thaddeus's father with no hint of nervousness. "It is fair, Nathan. It is fair because you should have known better. You should have seen the signs." He stepped closer again as Thaddeus's heart hammered.

"You should have listened to me," Leopold said, his voice losing the edge of anger and sounding more sad and tired. "All those years ago, Nathan. You should have listened to me."

Thaddeus didn't realize his father was crying until Nathan bowed his head and put a hand over his face. His shoulders shook with the power of the emotion he released. When a hoarse sob broke from his lips and Nathan sank to his knees, Thaddeus's body broke the paralysis that fear had brought on, and he limped hurriedly out from behind Teofil. He lowered himself carefully beside his father, wincing a bit at the tug of the stitches, and put an arm around his shoulders, pulling him close.

"Dad, I'm here," Thaddeus whispered. "What is it? Tell me. What's wrong?"

He had no idea what to do or say. He'd never before seen his father cry, let alone sob like this. He'd seen him with a sad expression, especially when looking at pictures of Thaddeus's mother, but not once had Thaddeus seen him cry. Until Teofil's strange grandfather had spoken just a handful of sentences to him.

"Nathan—" Leopold started.

"No!" Thaddeus struggled to his feet and pointed a finger in the old man's face. He could feel the heat of his anger crawling across his skin, slipping into his pores and knotting up his insides. "You leave him alone. I don't know who you are or how you know my father, but you step back and give us space."

"Father?" Leopold looked from Thaddeus to Nathan and back again. "So you're Thaddeus, then, are you?"

Thaddeus straightened his spine and pushed out his chest. "I am Thaddeus Cane. What of it?"

The old man gave him a single nod, moonlight twinkling in his brown eyes. "You have grown into a fine young man, that's all. I am Leopold Solobiec. I am an old, shall we say, associate, of your family."

"What do you mean by that?" Thaddeus asked. "How do you know my father?"

"As I said, I used to be an associate of your parents," Leopold replied.

"I don't know what that means," Thaddeus said.

"Thaddeus," Nathan said as he got to his feet beside him. He put an arm around Thaddeus's shoulder and pulled him close against his side. "That's enough. Let's go home."

"No!" Thaddeus shrugged out from beneath his father's arm and took a step away. "I want to understand what this is all about. From what it sounds like, you've been searching for this man all these years, is that right?"

Nathan looked at Leopold then back at Thaddeus, his expression depleted of anger so that now he just looked exhausted. "That's right. We have, actually."

"All the moves, all the upheaval and new schools and new towns and friends left behind." Thaddeus felt the sting of tears and bit his lip to try and hold them at bay. He succeeded, for now, but the threat of them still lingered. "All those years we kept moving, you said it was to find a better place. You never told me you were searching for someone." He drew in a breath. "Does this have to do with Mom?"

"It's complicated," Nathan replied. "There's much you don't know." He put his hands on his hips and looked up at the stars, quiet for a moment as he gathered his thoughts. Finally, he met Thaddeus's gaze again. "We moved around so much for different reasons. One of them was that I was searching for Leo, and, yes, he knew your mom. I didn't know for sure that he was here, but Superstition felt different from the moment we moved in. I based our move here on an instinct, on rumors I'd heard from others I met along the way. When I heard about this town, I had to come see. I couldn't give up looking for Leo, for finding out about your mom. I had to know for certain whether or not she was dead."

"She's…." Emotion blocked the words in Thaddeus's throat, and he had to swallow hard before he could finish. "She's alive?"

"Well, she's not dead," Leopold interjected. "I can tell you that right now."

Thaddeus and his father turned their heads quickly to stare at the old man.

"What does that mean?" they both said at once.

"She's alive," Leopold assured them. "But she's different than you remember, Nathan. She's been changed."

"Changed how?" Thaddeus asked. Thoughts spun inside his mind as though within a tornado, slamming into one another, breaking into fragments that made no sense. "Where is she? How is she?"

"She's safe," Leopold said. "From others as well as herself."

Beyond the fence, deep within the dark shadows of the woods, something let loose with a howl so loud and chilling it made Thaddeus shiver. Teofil stepped up behind him and put a hand on his shoulder. The warmth of Teofil's touch steadied Thaddeus, and he reached up to put his hand over Teofil's, unconcerned whether or not his father or Leopold saw.

Leopold had turned to the gate and now looked at them both. His eyes were wide and his face tight with tension. "It's back. I've never seen it around here until just recently."

"Looking for Thaddeus, no doubt," Teofil said.

"And Claire," Nathan added.

"Mom?" Thaddeus looked at his father. "Why? What is that thing? What's going on, Dad?"

A barrage of knocking on the gate startled them all, and then a voice shouted from the other side of the fence, "Teofil, open up. It's us."

"Dad!" Teofil exclaimed happily. He ran to the gate, pulled it open, and a number of short, broad-shouldered beings lumbered into the yard. They carried a variety of weapons, swords and crossbows mostly, and were a mix of men and women. The men sported hearty beards, and all of them wore caps in various styles. Fairies swarmed in above the gnomes, swooping and looping, their golden light providing quick flashes of the gnomes' features: large noses, strong jaws, deep-set eyes.

The first gnome through the gate, a man shorter than Teofil with a dark beard and a large, rounded nose, grabbed Teofil and hugged him tight. Thaddeus reasoned that this was Teofil's father, and a swell of joy and amazement at seeing more of these magical beings almost brought him to tears, but he fought them back.

The scene must have affected Nathan as well because he moved to stand beside Thaddeus and put his arm around his shoulders once more.

"I'm sorry," Nathan said as each of the gnomes marching through the gate gave a hearty greeting to Teofil. "I had to keep things from you to keep you safe."

Thaddeus met his father's gaze. "I want to understand what's going on. I really do. But I can't when all I've been given are bits and pieces of the story."

Nathan sighed. "You're right. It's not fair to you. None of this has been fair, throughout your entire life. I've dragged you around on this quest of mine without any explanation. But many times we moved we did it because I felt we were in danger." He briefly tightened his grip on Thaddeus's shoulder. "You will get some answers tonight, I promise."

Teofil approached with his father by his side. There was a difference in height between them, as quite often happens between generations, but the two feet Teofil towered over his father made Thaddeus grin.

"Dad, I'd like you to officially meet Thaddeus Cane," Teofil said, beaming at Thaddeus. "Thaddeus, this is my father, Rudyard, son of Erich and Fleur, and leader of the clan Rhododendron."

Thaddeus hesitated, unsure how to greet a gnome, and a clan leader no less. Before he could decide between bowing and extending his hand to shake, however, Rudyard stepped up and pulled him down for a strong, hearty hug. Calm and steadiness swept through Thaddeus, and he breathed in the scent of fertile soil and flower blossoms.

"It is good to see you up and about once again, young Thaddeus," Rudyard said as he stepped back. "That beast just about had you as a midnight snack."

Thaddeus blinked in surprise. He looked from Rudyard to Teofil to his father and back. "It was you? You chased the beast off?"

Rudyard grinned and tipped him a wink. "You can thank me later." In one deft move, he unslung the crossbow from around his shoulders and held it up. "Gave him a shot from this, right in his hindquarters." He let out a loud, strong laugh. "He won't be sitting down for a week, that's for certain."

Nathan stiffened beside him, but before Thaddeus could turn and ask him about his reaction, Rudyard looked at Nathan and said, "Good to see you again, Nathan. It's been a long time."

"That it has, Rudyard," Nathan replied and leaned down to give the gnome a quick hug. "My thanks to you for saving Thaddeus."

Rudyard glanced at Thaddeus, then looked back at Nathan. "He could have protected himself, you know, if you had trained him."

Tension draped over the scene, and Thaddeus exchanged a nervous glance with Teofil.

"So he could suffer the same fate as Claire?" Nathan asked.

"This must be Thaddeus!" A female gnome with a large bosom and rounded hips stepped up and grabbed him in a strong hug. She released him and waved her hands as she continued to talk. "I'm so glad to finally meet you. I'm Miriam, daughter of Jozafat and Isobelle of the Peony clan, and I'm Teofil's mother. We've heard about you, of course, from the fairies and what little we speak to Teofil. Not that he ignores us, mind you, he's just busy with his work here. Oh, look at him. He's gotten so tall." She winked at Thaddeus. "He gets that from my side."

The howl came once again. It sounded closer this time, and everyone in the yard turned toward the gate. One of the girl gnomes giggled nervously, and Miriam shushed her with a stern, "Flora, be still!"

Leopold heaved a heavy sigh. "It will be cramped, but we should all get inside the house, at least until sunrise."

Several of the gnomes groaned, and a few of them, male and female combined, raised their weapons amid shouts of "We want to fight!" and "We've beaten it before!"

"Now, young ones," Rudyard shouted over the hullabaloo. "The battle is not to be fought tonight. We will choose the time to fight, and it will be soon. But for now, let's all thank Master Solobiec for his hospitality and go inside."

"Boots off at the door!" shouted Miriam; then she turned to smile sweetly at Thaddeus and, taking Rudyard's arm, headed for the house.

Thaddeus looked at his father. "I intend to follow them inside."

Nathan nodded. "We both shall. It's time you knew the truth."

"All of it?" Thaddeus asked. "Not just the parts you want me to know?"

"All of it." Nathan tipped his head toward the house. "Let's go."

Thaddeus walked toward the house where Teofil stood holding open the back door for the long line of gnomes busy toeing off their dirty boots before stepping inside. The fairies darted back and forth around the heads of the gnomes and followed them inside as well. Thaddeus's brain tipped as a new reality started to take shape. Beneath the fabric of the "normal" world, where he had never felt like he'd fit in anyway, existed this magical world of fairies and gnomes and giant beasts. Was this true all around the world or just here in Superstition?

"You know, Thaddeus," Nathan said as they crossed the lawn, "I do like Teofil. I think he's got a good heart. I don't care that he's a boy or a gnome or anything. The reason I didn't want you over here was so you wouldn't learn about your past without me here to help you understand it, that's all."

Thaddeus stopped at the foot of the porch steps and smiled at his father, the quivering nerves in his belly easing somewhat. "Thanks, Dad, for saying that."

"You're a good boy," Nathan said, "and you're going to grow into a great man."

Nathan hugged him tight, then released him and climbed the steps. Thaddeus followed his father and smiled at Teofil, who still held the door open. Nathan stepped through the door, and before Thaddeus entered Leopold's house, Teofil leaned down to give him a soft, swift kiss on the lips.

"Ready?" Teofil asked.

Thaddeus nodded. "I'm ready."

Teofil took his hand and gave it a squeeze. "Me too. Let's find out the truth together."

Thaddeus glanced once more over his shoulder at the spectacular flowerbeds suffused with moonlight, the tall, tightly spaced trees in the woods beyond the fence, and the peak of his house in the lot next door. He had a feeling it would all look different—*he* would be different—when he left this house in a few hours. When the dust finally settled from all of this, he was going to be someone new. But that was all right; he was ready for that. He turned and followed Teofil inside.

Chapter ELEVEN

THADDEUS COULDN'T stop smiling. The house he stepped into was cluttered with knickknacks and furniture of all sorts. A table hewn from what appeared to be a number of logs with chairs that matched was pushed into the corner of the kitchen. Pots and pans hung from a variety of hooks, along with dried herbs and other plants that generated a fragrant blend of aromas. Countertops were crowded with a number of teakettles in all sorts of strange shapes, sizes, and colors.

Even though he tried to pause and soak in the atmosphere of the kitchen, Thaddeus was borne along with the entire group as they shuffled through a doorway and into a large sitting room. Mismatched chairs and footstools were strewn about, crammed into corners and jostled up against each other. Small ceramic jars with cork stoppers lined shelves all along every wall. There were electric lamps, but scarves draped the shades, and a number of flickering candles chased the shadows from the corners. Large oil paintings hung on the walls, the colors dark and the subjects stoic men, women, and, Thaddeus assumed, gnomes. Most of the depicted battle scenes brought to mind stories by Tolkien, and he had to remind himself to stay in the moment, to be present in what was about to happen. This was the oddest and most important gathering he'd ever been involved in.

Once this meeting was over, he sensed he might lose this initial thrill he felt at being in the company of so many mythical beings: a family of gnomes, a number of fairies, and Teofil's odd grandfather, who could not be a simple human based on what Thaddeus had seen so far. When the sun rose in the morning, Thaddeus knew his view of the world would be changed, and he wanted to hold on to this feeling of awe and wide-eyed wonder as long as possible. With the beast roaming the woods and the sense of urgency he sensed from those here now, this might be his first step into true adulthood, and he wasn't entirely sure he was ready for it.

"All right, all right, settle down everyone," Leopold said. He stood before a large fireplace with a wide mantle atop it. A massive hourglass stood on the mantle behind him, the sand trapped within deep red, and Thaddeus noticed that the bottom contained more than the top.

Time for something appeared to be running out.

The group positioned themselves on chairs, love seats, footstools, and in open spots around the floor. Thaddeus sat beside his father on a love seat, adjusting his leg to a comfortable position. He smiled when Teofil gently nudged his legs apart so he could sit on the floor between his feet and lean back against the love seat. Thaddeus's heart pounded, and his injured leg throbbed quietly, his muscles thrumming like taut wire due to Teofil's proximity. Thaddeus avoided looking at his father, focusing his attention instead on Leopold, who stood across the room.

"Friends, there's been a change in the wind." Leopold looked directly at Thaddeus, then gestured to him. "Those who had been cast aside and believed dead by some have returned. Our enemy has sensed the return of these much-sought-after friends of ours, and so a time of reckoning has awakened from its long slumber. The hunters, it would appear, have flushed out those they've been searching for all these years."

Thaddeus couldn't breathe. He felt dizzy and was very glad he was sitting down because if he had been standing, he was pretty sure he would have fallen over. He took a shallow breath, then another, and tried to get his thoughts to stop spinning, but questions flooded his brain, and he felt as if he were drowning.

He looked at his father and wasn't surprised to find him looking back.

"Hunted?" Thaddeus asked.

Nathan nodded slowly. "One of the reasons we moved around so much."

"Hunted by whom?"

"Why don't you let me explain?" Leopold said. "I was present for the majority of it, after all."

Nathan glared at Leopold. "Including your final act of cowardice."

A great roar of disapproval rose from the gnomes, and the fairies zipped around in the air over everyone's heads, voices high and angry. The sudden noise startled Thaddeus, and he jumped in his spot on the love seat. Teofil remained silent, however, and wrapped his arms around Thaddeus's calves, careful to avoid his injury. His touch grounded and calmed Thaddeus.

"Enough!" Leopold shouted, and the room quieted. The fairies settled back in place, interspersed between the tiny clay jars along the shelves, some sitting atop the stoppers, and Thaddeus thought he could feel them glaring at him and his father across the room.

"Nathan is allowed his opinion of what transpired," Leopold said. "He was there that day, as well, and has had to live with the results all these years like the rest of us. He witnessed the final spell before he was forced to flee. All he could do was save the baby."

His father tensed beside him, and Thaddeus looked at him. "Me?"

Nathan nodded but kept his gaze locked on Leopold, his lips pressed tight together until he said in a low, almost threatening tone, "Easy, Leopold."

The old man nodded to Nathan. "We shall only discuss what is needed, for now."

"What does that mean?" Thaddeus asked aloud.

"I'll tell you what it means," said Teofil's father, Rudyard. He pushed up from his seat beside his wife, Miriam, and stomped over to stand in front of Leopold, his head coming up to Leopold's waist. He turned his back to Leopold and crossed his arms over his broad chest as he fixed all of them with a steely look. "It means this beast knows Thaddeus and Nathan are here, and it would love nothing more than to finish its mission once and for all. But it's a wily beast, and it takes a different shape when the sun is up, allowing it to move among the humans unnoticed."

"Like a shape-shifter?" Thaddeus asked, and Teofil turned his head to look up at him. "They exist too?"

"You okay?" Teofil asked.

"Yeah, it's just... it's a lot to take in." Thaddeus looked up at Leopold. "What is it? I mean, I know it's a shifter of some kind. I've read about them in books but never believed they were real. But what is it? A wolf or a bear or what?"

"It's what we call the Bearagon, a mixture of bear, wolf, and dragon," Leopold explained.

"Dragons exist too?" Thaddeus whispered.

"It's brutal is what it is," Nathan said. He put an arm around Thaddeus's shoulder and gave him a one-armed hug. "And it could have killed you."

"I was surprised to see it out in the open like that," Rudyard said with a shake of his head. "Got me thinking it was time to come in and see how Teofil was doing."

"Awful as that thing is, I am glad to see you, Dad," Teofil said, and Rudyard smiled at him before returning to his seat next to Miriam.

"You've made us very proud, son," Miriam added. "You've been away so long, and it was difficult to let you go. But you've done so well."

"I tried to please you," Teofil said. "I just never really knew what was expected of me."

"That, I'm afraid, was my doing," Leopold admitted.

Thaddeus raised his hand, and when everyone in the room looked at him, he said, "I'm confused. What exactly are you, Leopold? How did Teofil end up here with you? And what was his purpose here?"

Leopold nodded and smiled. "We've jumped ahead. You need to know the full story, and so I shall tell it. After I've finished, we'll need to discuss what to do about the Bearagon."

Leopold lifted the hourglass from the mantle and held it before him. A reverent hush fell over the room as all of them watched the red sand slowly falling into the bottom of the glass.

"I, like your parents, am a magical being. A wizard, to cut right to it. This hourglass has been tracking the time since danger and death came to our small village," Leopold said. "Fifteen years, to be exact. You were six months old, Thaddeus, and many of us enjoyed spending time with your family. We all lived in a mountain village many days' journey from Superstition. It was a remote place unseen by the outside world. Wizards, witches, gnomes, dwarves, fairies, and other magical creatures lived in peace. Your mother, Claire, was a witch, gentle, kind, and gifted with powerful magic. She loved you more than anything, everyone could see it."

A lump of searing hot emotion sat in the bottom of Thaddeus's throat, and he blinked back tears as he listened to Leopold's deep voice. The sense of loss he'd lived with all his life welled up strong within him, flooding his chest with a chilling cold.

"Your parents were very involved members of the community and had been rumored to be the next in line to ascend to the highest positions in our realm, known as Heralds. All of us would have been pleased to see that happen. All of us, that is, except for a few who were envious of your family. They talked among themselves about how to overthrow the existing Heralds and those standing by, ready to ascend. Their envy grew into jealousy, dark and brooding. Jealousy soon became anger, which eventually led to hate. Their personalities changed because of their emotions, and it stained, as well, their very souls. They morphed into evil beings, drawn to creatures of the night and the dark places of the world, and they lashed out at those in the light. One of them, a witch known as Isadora, became fixated on your family, especially on Claire and yourself. She was unable to have children of her own, and seeing your family so happy, so loving, stoked her envy into something dark and twisted. Isadora gathered together those who shared her vision and started an uprising.

"The attacks caught all of us by surprise, though looking back we should have expected them." Leopold sighed and his shoulders drooped. He returned the hourglass to the mantle and, when he turned to face them again, Thaddeus was struck by the sadness in his expression.

"A great number were lost in the ensuing battle," Leopold continued, "including the sitting Heralds, a very kind and gracious witch and wizard. Our village was destroyed, and many of us fled into the wilds. Your mother and father fought bravely, saving many, but mainly fighting to protect you. They did the best they could that day, but we were not prepared, and the number of Isadora's followers was greater than we could have anticipated."

Thaddeus's heart pounded, and he clenched his fists in his lap. Teofil's arms tightened around his legs, so Thaddeus knew the story was affecting him the same.

"Your parents became separated in the conflict," Leopold continued. "Your mother hid you in the woods before rejoining the fight. She engaged Isadora in a battle of spells, and they fought all through the town, bringing down homes and felling trees as each tried desperately to kill the other. Your mother, Claire, had been backed up to the edge of a cliff. Isadora cast a spell and she tried to dodge it. She lost her balance and toppled off the cliff. Isadora thought she had killed your mother, and she marched through our devastated village in triumph, but, in truth, her spell had been deflected at the last moment by a dear friend of your parents, someone they trusted with all of their heart. Because of the deflection, instead of killing Claire, the spell changed her. It was I who found Claire at the bottom of the cliff, and understanding the danger she would be in if it were to be revealed she had survived, I carried her off and hid her from everyone else."

Leopold paused to take a deep breath and wipe a tear from his eye.

"You did what you thought was best at the time," Miriam said in a soft, comforting voice. "It was a terrible time for all of us, and I don't know what anyone else would have done had we been in your position."

"I appreciate the sentiment, Miriam," Leopold said with a nod. "I know that some in the room feel I went too far, but I had my reasons, and I still do. Claire had changed drastically. She had become a danger not only to herself, but to those around her." Leopold fixed Thaddeus with a sad look. "Even to those she loved with all her heart."

"Where is she?" Thaddeus asked, his voice a dry whisper.

"Hidden and safe," Leopold assured him.

"Hidden from those who love her and could have helped her," Nathan said, his tone edged with anger.

"It had been a powerful spell cast by Isadora," Leopold replied. "Do not think I didn't try to break it before finally admitting defeat and hiding her away."

Thaddeus frowned. "She's been locked up all these years?" He looked from Leopold to his father and back again. "Does she know we're looking for her?"

Leopold sighed. "She is safe and comfortable, and that's all I will say about it. In her condition, if Isadora were to manage to get some influence over Claire, if perhaps she held her son hostage, she could extend her power from the few magical creatures who remain under her rule out to the human world. Then much more than a simple mountain village would be lost."

"How has she changed so much?" Thaddeus asked. "How could she have been changed so much if she was a good person by nature?"

"She might have physically changed," Nathan said, "but inside, deep inside, she is still your mother."

"She's not dead," Thaddeus said. "That's the important part." He nodded, more to himself than those in the room, and thought a moment. He recalled something said earlier and asked, "How does Teofil fit into all of this?"

Leopold looked to Rudyard and Miriam. "Would you like to explain?"

Rudyard nodded. "Leopold needed a garden gnome to help protect his house and grounds from Isadora's prying magic. We gnomes have a gift for cultivating and nurturing plants that provide a shield from magic. Teofil was young when Leopold asked for our help, but we could tell he had a special gift with the kinds of plants Leopold required in his yard. So we sent Teofil to live here with him, told him to tell any who asked that Leopold was his grandfather. There were a few close calls in the early days, as the humans who lived nearby were curious about him and the yard. So, to keep them both safe, we encouraged Teofil to garden at night, away from prying eyes, and…." Rudyard's face turned red, and he looked down into his lap, unable to finish.

"We cast a spell on the fence to keep him inside," Miriam finished for him. Tears filled her eyes, and she reached over to pat her husband on the thigh.

"It nearly broke my heart to pen him in that way, but if we were to keep everything we had fought for safe, it was the only way we could think to do it." Rudyard pulled a kerchief out of his pocket and blew his nose with a loud honk. As he stuffed the kerchief back in his pocket, he looked at Teofil with such love and affection it stole Thaddeus's breath. "Will you forgive us, son?"

Teofil got up and crossed the room. He wedged himself between Rudyard and Miriam and put his strong arms around them, hugging them both tight.

"I forgive you," Teofil said. "It's the only life I've known. And being here, with Leopold, allowed me to meet Thaddeus. I do have to admit, however, that I am curious to see more of the world."

"That will come in time," Leopold said. "I can assure you of that. But for now, I still require your expertise with the plants."

"I understand," Teofil said and smiled over at Thaddeus. "But you can still come over to visit."

Thaddeus smiled back. "I'd like that." He thought of something and looked at Nathan. "Is that why you didn't want me over here spending time with Teofil?"

Nathan nodded. "I could feel the magic around this place, and it concerned me. I didn't know if it was someone from our side or a member of Isadora's group. We all scattered, and they've become quite adept at hunting us down."

"Can't you all recognize each other?" Thaddeus asked.

"Some of us have changed our appearance," Leopold replied. "Most of Isadora's tribe have done so. It can be exhausting to keep a spell running that long, but many of them have altered their appearance enough to catch us by surprise. Sadly, quite a few of us have been lost because of this. If only we'd stayed together, we could have reorganized and launched a counter attack."

"We can't go back and change the past," Miriam said. "We did what we could."

Nathan startled them all by pushing to his feet and pointing at Leopold. "Some of us could have done more!"

"Dad!" Thaddeus exclaimed and stood beside him.

"Stay out of this, Thaddeus," Nathan said, his voice low. "I've spent years on the run, alone and afraid for both of our lives. I've been hunted while I've been hunting him. I saw him pick up your mother from the base of the cliff, watched him carry her off into the trees and disappear for good. I knew where Claire had left you and couldn't leave without you, so I was unable to pursue him. It's taken me this long to find him, and I intend to have my say!"

Chapter TWELVE

THADDEUS LOOKED from his father standing beside him, to Leopold who stood in front of the fireplace, his brow furrowed and his brown eyes narrowed, then to Teofil, who had gotten to his feet and hovered just behind him. The tension in the air made the family of gnomes shift and fidget and the fairies take wing to float quietly up by the ceiling.

"Dad, don't do this," Thaddeus pleaded. "Not now, just when we've all found one another again. It's been so many years. Please, it's our only chance to find Mom."

"I'm not sure Nathan is ready yet to see your mother, Thaddeus," Leopold said, his voice a deep rumble.

"You don't decide when I'm ready to see Claire!" Nathan shouted.

Thaddeus put a hand on his father's arm, felt the tight muscles, and said in a low voice, "Dad, please. Let's sit down and talk some more. I've never known this part of my past. Let me ask questions, let me understand this new world."

Nathan glared at Leopold a moment longer, then turned to look at Thaddeus. As he looked into his father's eyes, Thaddeus saw the anger fade to a reluctant acceptance. When his father sighed and nodded, Thaddeus was finally able to take a deep breath and relax a bit. They sat down on the small love seat once again, and Teofil resumed his position on the floor between Thaddeus's legs.

"Very well negotiated, Thaddeus," Leopold said, giving him a crooked smile. "You are very much your mother's son."

"She was a good negotiator?" Thaddeus asked.

"Oh, everyone loved Claire," Miriam spoke up, smiling bright at her memories. "It was like a fresh mountain breeze whenever she entered the room. She was lighthearted and kind and compassionate." Miriam stopped and looked around, suddenly embarrassed. "Oh, I beg your pardon. Listen to me just yammering on and on."

"It's all right, ma'am," Thaddeus said and gave her an assuring smile. "It's nice to hear such good things about my mother."

"She was the best of us," Nathan said in a low voice. He stared at a spot on the faded living room rug, his gaze clouded with distant memories. "That's why Isadora went after her and…." He paused and blinked, lifting his gaze to meet Rudyard's. He glanced at Leopold, then cleared his throat and finished. "Well, that's why she was high on their list of targets."

"So, do you all believe Isadora is here in Superstition?" Thaddeus asked.

Leopold nodded slowly and stroked his beard. "It's entirely possible. She has most likely changed her appearance drastically."

Thaddeus thought a moment, then asked, "This might be a silly question, but could she be the creature that attacked me?" He looked between Leopold and Rudyard. "What did you call it?"

"The Bearagon," Rudyard replied. He shook his head slowly and clucked his tongue. "Big, nasty beast." He looked at Leopold. "What think you, Leopold? Could Isadora be the beast in question?"

Leopold shook his head. "I don't believe so. During the battle so long ago, I witnessed Isadora and the beast fighting side by side."

"There's only one Bearagon?" Thaddeus asked.

"So far as we know," Leopold replied.

"No wonder it's so mean," Thaddeus said in a low voice. "It must be very lonely." His statement made him think about Teofil's situation, growing up within the confines of Leopold's fenced-in yard, only seeing his family on occasion and never able to make any friends. Without a second thought, Thaddeus put a hand out and stroked the side of Teofil's head, feeling the soft, thick strands of hair between his fingers.

Across the room Miriam ducked her head and dabbed at her eyes with a kerchief, perhaps thinking along the same lines as Thaddeus.

"What we need to do now is work as a team and uncover the true identities of Isadora and the Bearagon," Leopold said. "Until we can flush them out from behind their disguises, we're all in danger."

Nathan grunted and stood abruptly. "I've had enough. It's almost dawn, and I need to be at work soon." He looked down at Thaddeus. "We both need to go home and get some rest. I'll meet you on the back porch." He strode across the room and through the doorway into the kitchen.

Thaddeus stared around the room at the others who stared right back. It wasn't an outburst, but he felt embarrassed for his father's reactions.

"I'm sorry for all of that," Thaddeus whispered. "He's been so angry."

"He's harbored deep feelings of abandonment and loss all these years," Leopold said. "He just needs some time to adjust to all this. And to introduce you to the world into which you were born."

"I've always felt like such an outcast," Thaddeus said. "Every place we moved to, I never seemed to fit in, and I never understood why."

Teofil tightened his arms around Thaddeus's legs and looked up at him. "You're not an outcast any longer. You have me."

"All of us," Rudyard stated.

"Aye!" another young gnome shouted. "And me."

"Me too!" one of the girl gnomes added.

A chorus of *yeahs* and *ayes* followed, and Thaddeus couldn't stop smiling by the time it was done. Two of the fairies even flew over to place kisses on either of his cheeks, kisses that felt like the lightest brush of a feather.

"Thanks, everyone," Thaddeus said, blushing and smiling and close to tears. He looked up at Leopold. "I should go meet my dad."

Leopold nodded. "That you should, young man. And as you go about your day-to-day activities, keep an eye out for those in town who act differently toward you."

Thaddeus gave a derisive snort. "That's pretty much everyone, but I'll be way more alert now."

"Very good," Leopold said. "Be safe, young Thaddeus. And it's been quite a pleasure making your acquaintance."

Thaddeus left the room amid a chorus of good-byes, Teofil trailing behind him. They stepped out on the porch into the cool air of predawn. Nathan was walking slowly around the garden, looking at the flowerbeds, reaching down now and then to stroke a plant leaf or gently cradle a blossom.

"You're worried about him," Teofil said.

Thaddeus nodded, his gaze still on his father. "I am. He's angry and hurt, and I'm afraid it might affect his focus, distract him from the bigger issue, which is discovering the identity of Isadora and this Bearagon."

"We all have a path to walk," Teofil said, his low, soothing voice bringing Thaddeus's gaze back to meet his. "Some walk in sunlight, some in shadow, others along a sun-dappled path."

"I like that," Thaddeus said with a smile. "Is it a proverb or something?"

"I don't know what that is," Teofil confessed with a gentle shrug, "but I've heard that said once or twice by my mother."

Thaddeus grinned. "I like your parents."

Teofil grinned back. "They like you too."

Thaddeus glanced out to the yard where his father stood staring at the sun-bleached tree trunk set in the back corner. In the last of the moonlight, the trunk glowed ghostly white, the pale leaves of the plants surrounding it shimmering as well. What had Teofil told him those plants were called?

He turned back to ask Teofil about the plants, but was surprised by the press of Teofil's lips. The whiskers of Teofil's beard were soft, his lips full, and it all made Thaddeus's head spin. Then the tip of Teofil's tongue stroked the length of Thaddeus's upper lip, sending a shiver through him and stopping all basic thought.

"Thaddeus," Nathan called gently from the yard. "Time to go."

Thaddeus stepped back, unable to breathe as he stared at Teofil. He'd never been kissed before he met Teofil so he had nothing to compare the sensations to, but, wow, he didn't think everyone kissed like that. Did they?

"Did you feel it too?" Teofil whispered.

Thaddeus tried to speak but couldn't find his voice, so he simply nodded instead.

Teofil smiled. "Good night, Thaddeus Cane."

After clearing his throat, Thaddeus was able to respond, "Good night, Teofil Rhododendron."

Thaddeus crossed the lawn to join his father, who now stood at the gate. The grass was wet with dew, and it soaked his shoes and the bottom of his jeans. As the feeling of Teofil's kiss continued to whirl around his mind like a tornado, Thaddeus didn't even feel the wound in his leg from the Bearagon.

"You be careful with him," Nathan mumbled as he pulled open the gate and leaned out to look both ways along the fence. When he was satisfied they were alone, he motioned for Thaddeus to follow.

With a last look back at Teofil, who still stood on the porch, Thaddeus slipped through the gate behind his father and pulled it shut. He rested a palm against the wood a moment, trying to detect the shielding magic spun by Teofil's parents, but all he could feel was the smooth wood. Dropping his hand, he hurried after his father and, as they turned the corner of the fence and entered their own backyard, asked, "What do you mean I need to be careful with Teofil?"

"You each come from very sheltered backgrounds and an attraction, especially a first attraction under such unique circumstances, can quickly lead to heartbreak." Nathan opened the side door and waved for Thaddeus to enter the house ahead of him. They kicked off shoes dampened by dew and moved up the two steps into the kitchen.

"I like him," Thaddeus explained. "And I'm not thinking beyond that right now. I just like how I feel when I'm around him." Now that the excitement of the meeting and the massive download of his unknown history was behind them, a heavy sense of exhaustion settled over him, and he yawned loudly.

"Why don't you get some sleep?" Nathan suggested.

"When do you go into work?" Thaddeus asked.

"I need to open the store today," Nathan replied as he began setting up the coffeepot.

Thaddeus yawned again. "I will go up and sleep for a while. But I'd like to come into work later. I don't think I'm on the schedule until noon anyway."

THADDEUS LOCKED his bike to a rack outside the entrance to Superstition Sporting Goods at 11:55 a.m. and stepped into the store. He had had to pedal slowly on his way to work due to his injured leg, but he'd made it. On his way to the back room to punch in, he waved to his father, who was helping a man in the fishing equipment section. After punching in, Thaddeus poked his head into Edgar's office to find the big man seated at his desk.

"Hi, Edgar," Thaddeus said. "I'm back today, just wanted to let you know."

Edgar smiled brightly. "Thaddeus! How are you? Is your leg better?"

Thaddeus nodded. "It is. It's getting better every day."

Edgar got up and rounded the desk to lean back against it, folding his big arms over his broad chest. "Sounded like a scary situation. Any idea what it was that attacked you? Wolf? Bear?"

Thaddeus shrugged as the word "Bearagon" drifted through his mind. "Not really sure. It was big and angry, and I got really lucky because something scared it off." He sent a quiet thought of thanks out to Rudyard for shooting an arrow into the beast's backside.

Edgar shook his head. "Terrible. We've never had a problem with something like this before." He leaned in closer and sniffed the air. "Maybe it liked the way you smelled?" He sniffed again, drawing in deep breaths through his nose. "I don't smell anything unusual."

A nervous feeling fluttered through Thaddeus's stomach, and he took a couple of backward steps out of the office. "Yeah, I'm not sure what it liked about me either. Maybe it *is* my smell, who knows?" He lifted his hand in farewell, but before he could turn to walk away, he bumped into someone behind him.

"Watch it, newbie," a guff voice grumbled.

"Sorry," Thaddeus said and stepped aside.

Logan, Thaddeus's coworker who he had needed to work for the night he was attacked, walked past, heading into Edgar's office. He had wavy hair that fell just past his shoulders, a two-day scruff of beard, and small eyes so dark they were almost black.

Thaddeus started to turn away but stopped when he noticed Logan was limping and holding a hand pressed against his left buttcheek.

Realization and fear spun together within him, sending his blood rushing through his system. He took a step backward, then another, his gaze locked on Logan's hand where it rested over his buttock, right where Rudyard said he had shot the Bearagon with his crossbow.

He needed to tell his father, and, most of all, he needed to tell Teofil and Leopold.

"Thaddeus?" Edgar asked, looking around Logan at him. "You all right? You're white as a sheet."

Thaddeus snapped his gaze up to Edgar's face, still stunned by the thought that Logan was the Bearagon shifter. He nodded and blurted out, "Fine. I'm fine. No problems. I'm good. Thanks." He pointed his thumb over his shoulder. "I'll get to work now. Working."

Edgar nodded. "Okay, you do that. And take it easy today. I don't want you to injure yourself any further."

Thaddeus fled to the door that opened onto the sales floor and stepped out of the back room, pausing to let out a breath of relief. His hand trembled as he clung to the doorknob, and he thought back over the few days he'd worked alongside Logan. The other boy had always acted like a snob, like he was better than Thaddeus, but he'd never given the impression he wanted to harm him.

Just as he released the doorknob and took a step onto the floor, a woman approached him. She looked familiar and striking, her pale face surrounded by a mane of fiery red hair, and her dark green eyes were wide as she asked, "Thaddeus Cane?"

"Yes?" Thaddeus replied, his voice low and hesitant.

"I'm Vivienne Redding, the head librarian," she explained.

"Oh, yeah," Thaddeus said with a nod. He glanced out over the sales floor, trying to find his father. "I'm not a sales floor person, but I can track down someone to help you find what you're looking for."

"Actually, I was looking for you," Vivienne said. "I wanted to check on your condition. The police came into the library to ask some questions after your attack. Your library card was found in your wallet, which is how they contacted your father, and they saw it had been issued recently." She took a step closer and lowered her voice. "Are you all right? Were you badly injured?"

A mental alarm started going off inside Thaddeus's head like a klaxon, and he took a step back. Vivienne could be Isadora in disguise. "I'm all right. Thanks for asking. I'm sorry the police felt the need to come talk with you and get you involved." He watched her reaction carefully as he added, "You had nothing to do with it, after all. It was an animal attack."

"Well, of course I didn't," Vivienne said. She seemed flustered for a moment, trying to find the words to explain herself. Finally, she gave him a single nod and said, "I see that I may have upset you, and I'm sorry. I just… I needed to check and make sure you were all right. Be careful, Thaddeus. There are some strange characters here in Superstition these days."

"I would have to agree with you," Thaddeus replied.

"Good-bye, then," Vivienne said and turned to walk through the store to the front door. As she went Thaddeus noticed that every customer and employee in the store, men and women, watched her walk away, and he wondered if that might be a clue that Vivienne was Isadora, or if she was just that beautiful.

Thaddeus found his father as he finished helping a customer choose a life jacket. "I need to talk with you, Dad. I think I know who the Bearagon is."

Nathan looked at him with an intense expression. "Who?"

Thaddeus looked around, then gestured for his father to follow. "Not here. We have to get away from the back room door. Come over to the camping equipment."

As Thaddeus led his father through the store, he couldn't stop thinking about Logan Augustine limping past him, holding his sore buttcheek. Trying to picture Logan changing into the beast known as the Bearagon, however, was proving more difficult. But maybe, once he told his father his suspicions, Nathan would be able to explain the possibility of it. And then they could discuss the possibility of Vivienne Redding actually being Isadora.

Chapter THIRTEEN

"LOGAN?" THADDEUS'S father repeated. "The Bearagon?"

"Yes, Logan," Thaddeus replied.

"Skinny Logan Augustine who works in the back room with you?" Nathan asked.

"Yes!" Thaddeus whispered, almost a hiss. "He was limping when he walked past me, and he held a hand to his butt, right where Rudyard said he'd shot the Bearagon with his crossbow."

Nathan glanced toward the door to the back room and then back at him. "I don't know, Thaddeus."

"Do you know how the Bearagon—" Thaddeus couldn't think how to describe the creature's transformation. "—works? I mean, when it's in human form, does it need to remain large?"

Nathan shook his head. "I don't think so. I've only heard stories of it, never seen one until the battle that day, when it—" He stopped and had to look away, his gaze haunted by the memories. "I just don't know."

Thaddeus put a hand on his father's arm. He realized this was all happening very fast, not just for him but for his father as well. All these years he had raised Thaddeus as a single parent, worked to ensure he had a normal life, kept from him, and everyone they knew, that magical beings were hunting them while they, in turn, were trying to find Leopold and Thaddeus's mother. It had been a lonely life for his father. Understanding that much now, he thought back—to all the times he had acted up, thrown temper tantrums at the mention of yet another move, the times he had pouted and been belligerent, accused his father of not loving him, not caring about him, when, in fact, his father had been trying to save their lives.

These memories churned within him, a whirlpool of emotions that spun together and condensed into a frigid ball of guilt that dug deep claws of regret into his lower belly. How could he have been so selfish? Though a layer of anger simmered just below the guilt—why hadn't his father explained all of this to him years ago? But Thaddeus understood the reasoning behind Nathan's decision to keep him in the dark. He'd wanted Thaddeus to have as normal a childhood as possible under their very unique circumstances.

"Hey, Dad," Thaddeus said.

Nathan looked back at him, his gaze focused once more, and Thaddeus wondered how often he'd had to rein in his emotions over the years.

"I'm glad this is all out in the open now," Thaddeus said. "You don't have to hide anything from me any longer. We can talk about everything openly and honestly. You must have gone through hell all those years I was growing up."

Instead of responding, Nathan grabbed Thaddeus in a tight hug. As his father's arms wrapped around him, Thaddeus pressed his face into Nathan's shoulder, breathed in the smell of his deodorant mingled with their detergent, and felt the familiar wave of comfort he'd always experienced over the years. It had been a long time since they'd hugged, and Thaddeus realized he'd missed it.

When Nathan pulled back and smiled at him, Thaddeus saw tears gather in his father's eyes and had to blink away tears of his own. They laughed quietly at each other as they wiped them away and looked around to make sure no one was watching them.

"Now what?" Thaddeus asked.

"Well," Nathan replied, "we try to find a way to get Logan alone and see what happens. The sooner we know if he is the Bearagon, the sooner we can deal with him."

A sick feeling churned within Thaddeus's gut, and he swallowed hard. "You mean kill him?"

"If we have to," Nathan replied. "But only in self-defense. Only if he attacks. Understood? We don't kill for the sake of killing."

Thaddeus nodded and took a breath. He felt light-headed, and his skin felt clammy. He hadn't really thought about killing anyone. He'd just been focused on figuring out the Bearagon's true identity. Killing the Bearagon, killing the person who became the Bearagon, was a different matter altogether. Logan Augustine was just a kid, a teenager like Thaddeus himself. Leopold had said their enemies had disguised themselves, so had the Bearagon chosen to look like a teenager to throw people off and, maybe, generate a little pity? Was it that manipulative?

The door to the back room opened, and Logan walked out. His wavy, shoulder length hair bounced as he walked, and Thaddeus nudged his father at the sight of Logan limping slightly.

"I'll keep an eye on him," Nathan said, his gaze locking on Logan as he strode across the sales floor toward the front door. "Looks like he might be going to lunch. You go in the back room and get to work. Come get me if anything happens. Got it?"

"Got it," Thaddeus replied. He started to go, then stopped. "Oh! The librarian came up to me when I came out here on the sales floor a few minutes ago."

Nathan frowned at him. "Librarian?"

"Yeah, the one who signed me up for my library card," Thaddeus explained. "She said the police came to talk to her since they found the card in my wallet and were able to contact you. She wanted to know if I was doing all right." He shrugged. "It made me wonder if maybe she could be Isadora?"

"I'm not sure," Nathan said and let out a breath. As he exhaled, he seemed to sag a bit, his shoulders slumping and his expression more grim, almost defeated. Thaddeus could see more clearly how exhausted his father was from the previous night, and he worried for him.

"I'm sorry, Dad. Maybe I shouldn't have said anything about her. I know this has been tough for you."

Nathan cupped the back of Thaddeus's head, his thumb rubbing the spot where his spine met his skull, and smiled. "I'm fine, Thaddeus. You be careful around Logan when he returns from lunch, all right? I'll watch him from out here and check on you often."

Thaddeus smiled back at his father. "Okay, Dad. I love you."

Nathan looked surprised for a moment, but then replied, "I love you too, Thaddeus. More than you could possibly understand."

"Thaddeus?" someone called, and he looked around to see Edgar leaning out of the door to the back room.

"I'm here, Edgar," Thaddeus said as he stepped away from his father toward their boss.

"Ah, there you are," Edgar said. He noticed Nathan standing behind him and took a step out of the door. "Is everything all right?"

"Everything's fine, Edgar," Nathan replied before Thaddeus could speak. "We were just discussing some plans for later tonight when we're both off work. Thaddeus was about to return to the back room and get to work."

"Very good," Edgar said. "We just received a large shipment that needs to be sorted out."

"I'll get right to work on it," Thaddeus assured him. When he approached the door, Edgar moved aside to allow him to pass. As Thaddeus stepped past, he heard Edgar breathe in deep, as if trying to catch a scent off him.

A chill went through Thaddeus as he hurried across the back room with its shelves piled high with inventory and shadow-drenched corners. A number of boxes had been stacked on the loading dock, the driver of the truck just pulling down the aluminum door before he would drive off. Thaddeus glanced toward the door of Edgar's office, where the man stood watching him closely, his face half obscured by shadow.

He turned to his work and got busy with a box cutter, opening boxes and pulling out inventory, all the while keeping half of his attention on the area around him in case of attack.

IT WAS late by the time Thaddeus finished with his work. He was sweaty, coated in dust that drifted up from the shelves in the back room. The wound in his leg was throbbing, and his shoulders and biceps ached. As he punched out, he noticed it was almost midnight and looked around the room. Edgar was in his office, working on his computer, engrossed in what appeared to be a sales spreadsheet. Logan had left at nine and had barely spoken ten words to Thaddeus the entire evening. Not that Thaddeus cared since Logan had most likely been trying to kill him the last few weeks.

Funny how that put so many things in perspective.

When his father left after his shift, he'd made Thaddeus promise to call him for a ride.

"But I have my bike here," Thaddeus explained.

"We'll throw it in the trunk," Nathan said. "I don't want you riding your bike through town that late at night. Understood?"

Thaddeus had agreed, so now he stepped out the front door of the store and sat on the wooden bench in front of the plate glass window with the store's name painted on it. He pulled his mobile phone from his pocket and called his father. Just as Nathan picked up, Thaddeus heard a sound from the corner of the store near the alley. He stiffened where he sat on the bench and kept silent as Nathan repeated his greeting, his voice now edged with concern.

"Thaddeus? What's wrong?" Nathan asked.

"I'm done with work," Thaddeus said in a quiet, distracted voice. "Can you come get me?"

"Are you all right?" Nathan asked.

"Yeah, I'm okay. I'm just…." Thaddeus paused to listen for a repeat of the sound, but the night was now silent. "I'm okay. Just come get me, please?"

"I'm on my way. Stay inside."

"Yeah, all right."

Thaddeus disconnected the call and got up. He backed toward the door, keeping his gaze on the shadowy mouth of the alley. Nothing moved, but he felt as if he was being watched, and the sensation made him shiver.

When he reached the door, Thaddeus put his hand on the curved handle. He turned, then stopped and shouted with surprise at the sight of Edgar standing on the other side of the glass, staring out at him. Edgar's expression was blank, devoid of any emotion, and before Thaddeus could regain his senses and pull the door open, Edgar locked it.

A growl from the alley grabbed Thaddeus's attention, and he stared at the shadows, his leg aching, his heart pounding, and his throat suddenly dry as bone. A shadow near the front of the alley detached itself from the rest of the darkness and Logan stepped into the glow of a streetlight.

"Thaddeus Cane," Logan said, his voice deepening. He slowly unbuttoned his shirt and shrugged out of it, exposing a broad chest covered with dark hair.

"Logan, what are you doing?" Thaddeus asked, trying to keep the tremor of fear from his voice but failing miserably. He realized he was still clutching the handle of the door and forced his fingers to open, then stepped back from the glass. From the corner of his eye, he could see Edgar standing and staring at him, watching him back away from Logan as he advanced.

"I'm taking care of some old business," Logan replied. He unbuttoned and unzipped his jeans, then pushed them down his legs and stepped out of them. He was nude now, his body shifting back and forth from shadow to light as he walked slowly toward Thaddeus.

"I-I don't know what you're up to, but I'm not into you," Thaddeus said, trying to keep his wits, trying to keep from screaming.

"Oh, this isn't about attraction," Logan said with a sneer. "This is about settling an old score."

He turned his head and twisted it at an odd angle, the resulting crackle of joint and bone gruesome. Thaddeus couldn't pull his gaze from the spectacle before him as Logan's body shifted. His chest broadened and his arms ballooned with muscles. His hands twisted and cracked and turned into clawed paws, and his head changed shape as hair sprouted all over his body.

In a matter of minutes, Logan Augustine was gone, replaced by the fearsome and dangerous Bearagon. Edgar stood behind the glass door and stared at the beast with a sly, seductive smile on his broad face.

The Bearagon roared at the night sky, the sound loud and terrifying. It startled Thaddeus back to his senses, and he turned to flee down the street. Panic scattered his thoughts, and he had no plan of escape, no route he had thought out ahead of time; he merely ran. He heard the beast behind him, its great paws pounding on the sidewalk, its breath rasping from its throat as it pursued him.

Thaddeus felt the Bearagon's breath on the back of his neck, knew he needed to change up his direction, so he dodged to the left between two parked cars, his leg throbbing in disapproval. The beast roared in anger as it skidded to a stop on the sidewalk and tromped across the hood of a car in pursuit, setting off the whooping car alarm. Thaddeus crossed the street and doubled back, hoping to meet up with his father, hoping to meet up with anyone who could help him. Why hadn't anyone come out to investigate the Bearagon's roaring? Or the car alarm? Was the whole town in on this plot to kill him and his father?

A figure stepped out of the shadows ahead of him. It was the slender, curvy shape of Vivienne Redding, the librarian, and Thaddeus came to a sudden stop. Was this it then? Was she truly Isadora and this had been worked out with Logan the Bearagon ahead of time to trap him?

"Come on!" Vivienne said and motioned for Thaddeus to approach her. "Hurry!"

With nothing but his life to lose, Thaddeus ran toward her, and Vivienne grabbed his hand, then turned to run with him, leading him between buildings as the Bearagon roared and pursued them. Vivienne led him across streets devoid of traffic and pedestrians, dodging around parked cars and in and out of alleys until he had no idea where they were. They'd put some distance between themselves and the Bearagon, when all at once Vivienne came to a corner and stopped. She pulled Thaddeus around behind her and turned to face the beast.

"What are you doing?" Thaddeus exclaimed, backing up a few steps. "It's still coming!"

"I know," Vivienne replied. "And I intend to stop it."

"With what?" Thaddeus asked.

Vivienne shouted some words that Thaddeus did not understand and thrust her hands toward the Bearagon. A flash of light erupted from her hands, bright and blinding, and the Bearagon reared up, roaring in pain, before it turned and ran off down the street, shaking its massive head.

Well, Thaddeus thought, *I didn't expect that.*

Vivienne turned to Thaddeus and blew a lock of red hair out of her face. "Well, then. That takes care of that."

"I guess so," Thaddeus said. "Thanks."

Vivienne nodded, then tipped her head. "Come. Let's go meet Nathan."

"Okay, yeah, sure, but… who are you?" Thaddeus asked. "I mean, I know you're the librarian, but who are you really?"

"Let's just say I'm an old friend of Nathan's and leave it at that, all right?" Vivienne said with a small smile. "Come on. The Bearagon could return, and he'll be angrier than ever."

Thaddeus nodded, then followed after her as she quickly crossed the street and ducked down an alley.

Chapter FOURTEEN

THADDEUS STOOD in Leopold's small half bath and studied his face in the mirror. He was the son of a witch and a wizard. Everything he thought he'd known about his life had been taken away and replaced by something extraordinary. He couldn't quite believe it yet. It still felt like a dream he was having after falling asleep while reading a really good book. There were witches and monsters after him, but he was protected by his wizard father, their wizard neighbor, a family of gnomes, and a host of fairies.

And Teofil.

The thought of Teofil made Thaddeus smile, and he kept smiling as he washed his hands and splashed water on his face. He dabbed away the water, then hesitated a moment before easing open the medicine cabinet. He felt guilty about it, but he really had to see if Leopold, though a great wizard, was just like every other man.

Deodorant, aspirin, toothpaste, Band-Aids, antibiotic ointment, and a prescription bottle. Thaddeus glanced toward the closed door, then looked back at the bottle, which was turned so the label faced the back of the cabinet. He had just considered turning it so he could read what had been prescribed when someone knocked softly on the door, making him jump.

"Thaddeus," Leopold said in a quiet voice. "Are you all right in there?"

Thaddeus felt the burn of a blush in his cheeks as he quickly closed the medicine cabinet door and practically shouted, "Yes!"

He cleared his throat, shook his head at his reflection, then took a breath and opened the door to find Leopold standing just outside it, grinning at him.

"Sorry," Thaddeus said, averting his gaze. "I may have been snooping."

"It's all right," Leopold assured him. "I understand." He leaned in closer and dropped his voice to a whisper. "The pills were for a minor infection I picked up last year. Nothing to brag about, and I should have discarded them months ago."

"Sorry again," Thaddeus said. "I just wanted to see if… I just didn't know if you needed normal things." He heard how his statement sounded, and his eyes went wide. "What I meant was, I didn't know if your kind needed to use normal stuff like we do." That sounded even worse, and he groaned with embarrassment.

But Leopold let out a big, booming laugh and squeezed Thaddeus's shoulder. "Oh, young Thaddeus. It has been a very long time since someone from the outside has come into our group. What a breath of fresh air you are. Come join us in the sitting room and tell us about your experience tonight."

Thaddeus followed Leopold into the sitting room where he had first learned about his past. This time, however, the group wasn't so large, just he and his father, Teofil and his father, Vivienne, and Leopold. The fairies had been asked to keep watch in the yard, and now and then Thaddeus could see one float past outside the window.

"Now, then," Leopold said as he sat in a high-backed chair covered with worn red velvet. "Tell us what happened."

Thaddeus relayed the details of his night to the point he'd met up with Vivienne, and then she took over the story.

"I zapped him," Vivienne said, referring to the Bearagon. "Then we met up with Nathan, and now we're here."

"So, the Bearagon has revealed himself," Leopold said as he stroked his beard. "And is entwined somehow with Edgar Marcet." He looked at Nathan. "I never liked that man. Much too forward when I met him on the street."

"You should have tried working for him," Nathan grumbled in reply. "I'm mad at myself that I didn't see it."

"So who is he?" Thaddeus asked, looking from one to the other. "Who are he and Logan? I mean, who were they back in the village? Before the attack?"

"Not sure yet," Vivienne said. "Their magic is powerful, and it disguises them well."

"Is it like a mask?" Thaddeus wondered.

"It's more like camouflage," Nathan replied. "Like a mask but not something that is removed, if that makes sense. It's just a spell that is constantly running, keeping their appearance different for those looking at them."

"And there's no way to see through it?" Thaddeus asked.

"If you know who to cast a spell at, there are some things that can be done," Leopold told him. "But they could be anyone. The spell can change not only appearance, but gender and, for the most powerful, even age. And now that we know the two of them are against us, we can certainly do that in the future to see their true faces."

Thaddeus nodded and looked at Vivienne. "So how did you know my parents back then?"

"Me?" Vivienne glanced at Nathan, then back to Thaddeus. "I was just a friend. Of them both."

"Vivienne helped me get you to safety after Claire...." Nathan stopped. "After I lost track of your mother, Vivienne helped me care for you for a few days before we decided it was too dangerous for us to travel together."

"Those were difficult days for all of us," Leopold said in a quiet voice.

Before anything more could be said, Teofil jumped up from where he'd been sitting next to Thaddeus on a love seat. His eyes were wide, and his voice was high-pitched in panic as he shouted, "Something's wrong!"

They all got to their feet, looking around the room and out the window.

"What is it?" Leopold asked. "What do you hear?"

"Not hear, feel," Teofil replied. "Something is trying to get inside the gate. They're using magic and have broken through the spell my parents cast around the fence. I can feel their magic trying to get past the garden spells."

A fairy popped up at the window, tiny fists pounding on the glass, high-pitched voice shrieking in alarm.

"Definitely something wrong," Nathan said, and they all ran after him as he headed for the back door.

By the time they got to the yard, Thaddeus could see the gate shaking as something rattled it from the other side. His heart pounded, and he stood on the wooden porch a moment, at a loss for what to do. A loud roar from the other side of the fence made him jump, and it spurred him into action. He followed Teofil to the middle of the yard and stopped, eyes wide as he watched the gate jerk and rattle.

"It's the Bearagon," Thaddeus said and turned to Vivienne. "Can you zap it again?"

"I can try," she replied, "but it's going to be expecting it this time. It might not work as well."

Leopold approached and dropped into a crouch beside Teofil, gripping his upper arms as he stared into his face.

"My boy," Leopold said. "You've kept this garden well maintained for many, many years. But I think our time here is drawing to an end."

Teofil nodded, his eyes wide in the moonlight. "It seems that way."

"We've made a good team, haven't we?" Leopold continued. "Working well together to keep ourselves safe. To keep our secrets safe."

"It's been an honor living here with you, Leo," Teofil replied.

Their conversation held such a tone of finality, Thaddeus's eyes welled up with tears. What was happening? Was it all coming to an end now, just when he'd found a family? It couldn't end this way, could it?

One of the hinges of the gate gave way with a loud shriek as the metal screws were torn from the wood.

"You must trust me now," Leopold said, his voice even more urgent. "Tear up the drachen narcosis."

"Leopold, no!" Rudyard shouted, turning to look at them over his shoulder. He had positioned himself between them and the gate, his crossbow loaded and ready.

"We have no choice, Rudyard," Leopold replied and pushed Teofil toward the back corner of the garden. "Thaddeus, help him! We'll hold the beast off."

Thaddeus followed Teofil to the corner where the tree stump stood, surrounded by dozens of bloodred drachen narcosis. They dropped to their knees and began tearing out the plants, throwing them off into the yard. The leaves, however, were lined with thorny spines that dug into Thaddeus's palms and fingers. Blood soon slicked his hands, making it harder to grasp the plants, and each fresh cut made him wince in pain.

"They have thorns!" Thaddeus shouted.

"I know!" Teofil shouted back. "Just try to get as many as you can."

More tearing sounds from the gate followed by a shout from Rudyard made both Thaddeus and Teofil pause to look over their shoulders. The gate tore away, and the Bearagon stalked into the yard, its big head lowered and swinging from side to side. Rudyard fired a shot, but the beast was expecting it and dodged out of the way, then lunged at him. With a swipe of its great paw, the Bearagon knocked Rudyard off his feet and sent him tumbling head over heels to land hard at the base of the fence that separated Leopold's yard from Thaddeus's.

"Father!" Teofil cried and took off at a run.

Thaddeus got up as well, but Leopold pointed to him and shouted, "No! Stay where you are and pull the rest of those plants! It's vitally important you do."

Thaddeus felt his heart leap in his throat as he watched Teofil dodge around the Bearagon to get to his father. Seeing that his love was safe, Thaddeus turned back to his task. His hands burned, and the wounds in his leg throbbed. Blood had soaked his jeans and the bottom of his shirt. It dribbled onto the ground and into the dark, rich earth as he pulled out the plants one after another. Behind him, he heard Leopold, Vivienne, and Nathan shouting as they fought to hold back the Bearagon. Light flashed as each cast spells, and Thaddeus desperately wanted to turn to see his father perform magic, but he kept his gaze on the ground before him, pulling up plants and throwing them aside.

When he was down to just six plants remaining, he felt the ground tremble beneath him and paused. He risked a glance over his shoulder and watched Vivienne blast the beast with a burst of light that sent it roaring onto its hind legs as she rolled out of the reach of its front paws. The ground beneath his knees shifted and seemed to roll, as if something beneath were moving, maybe turning over from one side to the other.

"Thaddeus, keep going," Leopold yelled. "Finish it. Hurry!"

Thaddeus yanked the last half dozen plants from the ground and then scrambled back, dragging his injured leg as he moved away from the weathered tree trunk that shone white in the moonlight. The ground was still for a moment as the battle behind him waged on. Then the tree trunk cracked up the center and exploded in a shower of wood chips. Thaddeus held up his hands to protect his face and felt the sting as bits of the trunk struck his injured palms.

The ground beneath him shifted and rose, lifting him up, and he rolled off the emerging hillock and into the yard. He got on his hands and knees, the dewy grass cool and slick against his injured palms, and watched as a large head, covered in scales, lifted up out of the dirt. The dead tree trunk splintered and fell to pieces around the spines along the back of the beast's massive skull, and the head rose higher and higher, impossibly high, balanced perfectly on a slender neck, which was also covered in scales. As Thaddeus stared, he watched the muscular neck move, the scales shifting to provide protection.

A great foot came up out of the ground, erupting from the rest of the flowerbed that had held the drachen narcosis, and it stomped on the lawn for leverage as the monster hefted its long, narrow body out of the dirt. The polished scales glittered in the moonlight, and Thaddeus was close enough to see his own image reflected back from some of them.

"Thaddeus!"

The shout from his father, the panic in Nathan's voice, snapped Thaddeus out of his amazed trance. He crawled away from the creature—dragon, he had to admit it to himself now, it was a dragon—but his blood-slicked hands went out from under him, and he crashed chin first to the ground. His teeth clicked hard together, and stars burst behind his eyelids. He rolled onto his back and blinked up at the night sky, frowning as he watched a number of shooting stars streak past. Was there supposed to be a meteor shower tonight?

Then he realized they were fairies and that they were rushing to defend him from the dragon. He sat up, swooning a bit with a head rush. When his head cleared, he stared in shock, unable to move as he watched the tiny fairies streak back and forth in front of the dragon, high-pitched voices taunting, tiny bursts of light from their spells making it flinch and roar.

The dragon pulled itself completely from the hole in the ground, dirt falling in clumps around its four large feet, and it turned, swinging its long, muscular tail. Thaddeus dropped flat on his back and felt the breeze as the dragon's tail passed over him. It roared and swung its tail back and forth, sweeping Thaddeus's father off his feet as he ran to help him up.

"Dad!" Thaddeus shouted and staggered to his feet, then stopped when he realized he had caught the dragon's attention and that it now crouched right behind him.

He turned, slowly, and stared into the beast's eyes. Surprisingly, they were nothing like he'd expected. Instead of being yellow or red, with a long, thin pupil like a snake's eyes, as he had seen in movies and TV shows, they were blue with a rounded pupil. Its nose was long, and the nostrils at the end flared as it took in his scent. Jagged teeth lined the long jaws, some the size of Thaddeus's entire arm. He swallowed hard and took a step back. The dragon rumbled a growl and leaned in closer.

"Hold still," Leopold whispered from behind him. "Let it get your scent."

"I don't want it to get my scent," Thaddeus replied in a desperate whisper but held still nevertheless. "I don't want it to be able to find me again."

"Trust me," Leopold said. "Just hold still."

"Thaddeus?" Nathan called, sounding confused from his tumble.

"Be still, Nathan," Leopold directed. "Let it take in his scent."

Thaddeus held still despite every instinct shouting for him to run, to get away. The dragon moved closer still and drew in a deep breath. Thaddeus closed his eyes and hoped it wasn't drawing in a breath before releasing a great blast of fire. Could this dragon even breathe fire? If he lived through this, he was going to need to sit down with Leopold and ask him some serious questions.

But for now, he needed to just stand still.

He opened his eyes and had to suppress a shout of fear at the proximity of the dragon's snout. Its blue eyes stared at him as it sniffed, and then it moved closer still. Its nose was very near now, an inch away, maybe less. Thaddeus could smell the damp earth the dragon had been slumbering in, and he had only a moment to consider that maybe he was being considered as a meal before two things happened in rapid succession.

The Bearagon roared from directly behind him, scaring Thaddeus into a crouch. He turned to see the big, hair-covered beast charging at him, knocking aside Vivienne and Leopold as it kept its angry gaze fixed on him. Thaddeus tried to scoot backward on his butt to escape the Bearagon, but his momentum stopped at the thickly muscled leg of the dragon as he bumped his back up against it.

The Bearagon jumped, its strong legs propelling it up high so it landed on the back of the dragon's neck, just behind its head. With a roar of pain and anger, the dragon shook its head and extended big, leathery wings. The wings flapped several times, the blowback pinning all of them to the ground and covering them in dirt as the dragon lifted up into the air with the Bearagon on its neck. The dragon shook its head back and forth, hovering over the yard as the Bearagon hung on with its strong jaws, teeth digging in between the scales.

Then a tiny light zipped through the night and right up to the Bearagon's face. Even from where he lay on the ground a dozen feet below, Thaddeus heard the sharp *snap* of the shock the fairy delivered to the Bearagon's nose. The monster released its grip on the dragon's neck to roar in pain and slid off the slick scales, claws scrabbling for purchase. Before it fell, the Bearagon swiped angrily at the tiny, glowing fairy that had been its undoing and sent it streaking down into the bushes by the house.

With a heavy thud, the Bearagon landed in the yard not far from Thaddeus. It slowly got to its feet, shaking its head before it caught sight of him. It lowered its head and tensed its muscles to pounce but never got the chance. The dragon reached down with one big claw and plucked it from the ground. As the Bearagon thrashed within its grip, the dragon looked down at Thaddeus once more, and then, flapping its large bat wings, it flew off over the woods, taking the Bearagon with it as it disappeared into the night.

Chapter FIFTEEN

THEY WERE, for the most part, all okay after the battle. Thaddeus helped his father up, and Nathan pulled him close for a tight hug.

"I thought I was going to lose you to that dragon," Nathan whispered.

Thaddeus couldn't help a nervous laugh and leaned back to look at his father. "Did you ever, in a million years, think you would say that to me?"

Nathan grinned and rested his palm against the side of Thaddeus's face a moment. "There are a lot of things I've said lately that I never thought I would. That, however, would probably be closer to the top of the list."

They went to Teofil and saw that Rudyard was not seriously hurt. He was stiff and sore with a cut on the side of his head and a swollen ankle, but it appeared his pride had been hurt far worse than his body. Vivienne was disheveled and sore but otherwise unhurt.

Miriam, Teofil's mother, appeared at the broken remains of the yard's gate, a number of Teofil's brothers and sisters gathered around her, and she gasped at the sight of the shattered gate. "By the stars and comets above, what happened?" She caught sight of Rudyard sitting next to Thaddeus, blood running down the side of his face, and she hurried over to him.

"We're okay," Rudyard assured her. "We're all okay. Don't worry your pretty head about it. Just a minor injury."

"Your ankle's the size of your head, you ridiculous gnome," Miriam scolded. "Don't you tell me you're okay." She looked around. "Who else is hurt? Let's check you all out."

"We seem to be all in one piece, Miriam," Leopold assured her. "Just some bumps and bruises."

Thaddeus smiled when Miriam's gaze found him and she looked him up and down. Then her gaze shifted to look past him at the large hole in the ground where the dragon had been slumbering, and her mouth dropped open.

"Was that where—?" Miriam started.

"It was," Leopold interrupted her. "And we have not yet discussed the matter further."

"Oh," Miriam said. She looked at Thaddeus again, but quickly this time, almost guiltily, then returned her attention to her husband.

Before Thaddeus could inquire about their exchange, Teofil asked, "Where's Lily?"

Thaddeus frowned. "Who?"

"Lily, the fairy who brought you the flowers when you were injured in your room," Teofil explained.

Thaddeus looked around. "Now that you mention it, where are all of the fairies?"

"Oh dear," Leopold said in a quiet voice. "I'm afraid we have lost someone."

Thaddeus looked in the direction Leopold indicated and felt a cold spot open inside him. "Oh no."

The fairies were gathered around some ferns at the side of the house, hovering above the tall fronds. At the base of the ferns, he could see two fairies lifting another, her body no longer glowing and her tiny arms and legs limp. All of the fairies were singing quietly as the two lifted their fallen loved one off the ground.

"Oh, Lily," Teofil said, his voice thick with tears. "She was always the first one to fly to someone's aid."

Thaddeus had no idea what to do. He wanted to comfort Teofil but didn't know if he could or should. Other than losing his mother, a woman he couldn't even remember, he'd never experienced the death of someone close to him, and he was at a loss on how to act or what to say. And there was a measure of guilt welling inside him over Lily's death. She'd been the one to zap the Bearagon as it had been biting into the dragon's neck, while Thaddeus himself had been sitting on the ground beneath them, unable to think of anything to do. He could have thrown a stone or a stick or something.

"Come on, lad," Rudyard said and put his arm around Teofil's waist, unable to reach his son's shoulders because he was so much taller. "Let's give her a proper burial."

They all stood in respectful silence as Teofil helped. The fairies folded Lily's arms, then her wings, over her chest. Small flower petals were placed over her closed eyes, and then she was laid out on a broad, soft hosta leaf Teofil cut from a nearby plant. The leaf was folded around her and tied in place with short lengths of ivy vines. The fairies stood around the tiny green coffin and sang a mournful song that brought tears to Thaddeus's eyes, though he could not understand the words. He held Teofil's hand in his own despite the cuts he'd received from the drachen narcosis, squeezing gently each time Teofil sniffled. When the song was finished, the fairies each took hold of the leaf and lifted it slowly off the ground, then flew out of the yard and into the woods.

"She'll be laid to rest with her kin in the fairy circle," Teofil explained. "And I shall miss her. Every day."

"Come now," Leopold said and waved toward the back door. "We have much to discuss."

They started toward the house, moving slowly, an exhausted and grieving group. Then one of Teofil's brothers stopped—Fetter, Thaddeus thought his name was. Fetter turned to face the woods, his eyes narrowed and his hand up, telling them all to wait. "Sh. Hear that?"

Thaddeus listened, straining to hear something, anything unusual. "I don't hear anything."

"Thought I heard a roar," Fetter said and looked at Rudyard. "Louder than the Bearagon."

"Aye," Rudyard said with a nod as he leaned on his wife for support. "That would be the dragon."

"Dragon?" Teofil's many brothers and sisters all exclaimed. A nervous and excited babble of questions followed to which Rudyard waved his hands for them to quiet down.

"Enough!" Rudyard shouted, finally getting them to be still. "Inside with the lot of you, and we'll all discuss it over tea and cakes." He looked at Leopold with narrowed eyes. "You do have tea and cakes enough to go around, I hope."

"Apparently I should," Leopold replied with a lifted eyebrow and turned to lead the way to his back door.

After having the wounds on his palms tended to, Thaddeus lingered in the kitchen with Miriam and Teofil while they put together tea and cakes, all of them quiet and subdued. Miriam apparently sensed they might want some time alone and ushered a few of the younger gnomes out of the kitchen with her as she carried a tray stacked high with cakes. Thaddeus checked the time on the pot of tea he was steeping—something with dried flower blossoms, grasses, and leaves—then caught Teofil's gaze and asked, "Are you doing okay?"

Teofil smiled sadly and nodded. "I am. I just can't believe Lily is gone. I know you didn't get to know her very well, but while I've been living here, she was my closest friend."

"I'm so sorry, Teofil," Thaddeus said and pulled him close for a hug. "She was very brave."

"I'm going to get that Bearagon," Teofil said, his face pressed against Thaddeus's shoulder, "if it's the last thing I do."

Thaddeus pulled back and cradled Teofil's broad, tear-streaked face between his palms. "We'll find the dragon and the Bearagon. I promise." He leaned in to kiss him softly on the lips.

"Thaddeus?" Leopold called from the sitting room. "Teofil?"

"Coming," Thaddeus replied. He checked the time and pulled the tea strainer from the pot. Then he and Teofil carried trays of cups and teapots into the room.

Once cups of tea had been distributed and Thaddeus had grabbed himself a small cake, he sat between his father and Teofil on the longer sofa and looked expectantly at Leopold.

"The dragon is free," Leopold said, his voice deep and rumbling as he sat in the high-backed chair once again. "The secret we have been keeping secure all these years is loose, and we must find it before it is seen by the human population, or found by Isadora."

"Where did the dragon come from?" Thaddeus asked.

Leopold hesitated. He sat forward in the chair and looked at his hands a moment, then met Thaddeus's gaze. The wizard looked between Thaddeus and Nathan, and just as Thaddeus's stomach had tightened nervously, Leopold said, "The dragon, Thaddeus and Nathan, is Claire."

"What?" Thaddeus and Nathan shouted together. Tea slopped out of Thaddeus's cup and onto his jeans, but he didn't care.

"Explain yourself, Leopold," Nathan demanded. "Quickly."

"I told you, Nathan, that the spell that struck Claire had changed her." Leopold gestured toward the window, which looked out on the now ruined backyard. "It transformed her into a dragon."

"The eyes," Thaddeus whispered, remembering the blue irises and rounded pupils that had regarded him so closely. "They weren't eyes like

I would have expected from a dragon. Like you see in movies. And the way she had smelled me."

"She recognized your scent," Leopold said.

Nathan pushed up from the sofa and paced, hands clasped tight behind him. "You're telling me, all this time I've been looking for you and expecting to find Claire being cared for, being healed, you've had her trapped underground as a dragon?"

Leopold got to his feet and raised his voice. "I was unable to change her back. Do you not think I tried? For weeks, months, I tried every spell I could think of to reverse Isadora's magic, but nothing worked. Claire was becoming more agitated, more prone to violence, and she was growing. Finally, I had no choice but to get her to hibernate. And to ensure she did not awaken until we knew how to reverse the spell, I asked Rudyard and Miriam to allow Teofil to tend the gardens and had them plant drachen narcosis above her to keep her sleeping."

"Drachen narcosis?" Nathan repeated and looked at Teofil. "Dragon sleep?" He pointed at Teofil, and his expression was so startlingly angry, Thaddeus took hold of Teofil's hand. "So you knew about this?"

"No, Teofil did not know, you hothead," Rudyard said, his voice gruff. He sat on a love seat with his swollen ankle propped up on an ottoman, one of his young daughters asleep in his lap and Miriam sitting beside him with two small gnomes drowsing in her arms. "He just knew Leopold needed someone to live here to tend the gardens and that it was very important."

Nathan paced some more, and Thaddeus watched him as questions and information spun inside his own head. There were so many questions, too many, but he blurted out the first that came to mind.

"Did she know me, do you think? Is that why she didn't attack me? Did she know I was her son?"

"It's difficult to say," Leopold replied, his expression softening as he returned to his chair. "She appeared to, Thaddeus, but she's been a dragon for many, many years and asleep for most of that time. Who's to say what she remembers of her life before?"

"A mother's love is strong, Thaddeus," Miriam assured him from across the room as she tightened her arms around the two young gnomes to either side of her. "Keep that knowledge in your heart."

"We have to find her," Thaddeus said. "We have to. We can't leave her out there. What if someone in town sees her? They'll call the army in, and they'll bring tanks or jets or something."

"We'll find her, Thaddeus," Nathan said, his voice quiet and reassuring as he took his seat beside him again. "I promise. We'll find her."

"We must find her before Isadora," Leopold told them. "Isadora may be able to control her since it was her spell that has changed her. If that happens, there's no telling what she could make Claire do, not only to us, but to all the cities of the world."

"We don't even know who Isadora really is," Vivienne said and put her head in her hands. "We've got so much to do, and so little time in which to do it."

"Have faith, Vivienne," Leopold said. "There are many of us here. We'll form two teams, one to search for Claire, the other to ferret out Isadora."

"Where do we even begin to look for her?" Vivienne wondered, and Thaddeus could hear the exhaustion and frustration in her voice. "We've been trying to find her for years."

Leopold nodded and smiled. "Yes, but now we know the identity of her cohort, the Bearagon, so we might be able to narrow our search a little more."

"I want to look for the dragon.... For my mom," Thaddeus said.

"You should definitely be in that search party," Leopold said. "The way she reacted to you gives me hope that your presence will be able to keep her calm."

"I'm going with him," Nathan said.

"Me too," Teofil put in.

"Count me in," Rudyard said, then winced as he shifted his ankle.

"Nonsense," Miriam told him. "You stay here and coordinate things." She nodded as she patted the backs of her children. "I'll go with them."

Thaddeus smiled as he pictured Miriam leading them through the woods and fighting the Bearagon. He imagined she was much tougher than she appeared.

"Very good," Leopold said. "Vivienne and Rudyard and I will work on finding out Isadora's new identity. Does anyone have any questions?"

Thaddeus looked at the faces in the room, then asked, "When do we start?"

"Why, no better time than the present, young Thaddeus," Leopold replied. "Let us divvy up supplies and weapons."

"Weapons?" Thaddeus said with a note of alarm. "I'm not going to hunt my mother down and kill her."

"No, but she took the Bearagon with her," Leopold said. "And who knows what other wicked beasts lurk in the deep heart of the woods."

Thaddeus swallowed hard and nodded. This wasn't going to be just a pleasant walk in the woods. One or more of them could be killed. He took a breath, let it out, then got up off the couch and followed Nathan and Teofil out of the room, nervous and anxious to get started and find his mother, dragon or not.

Chapter SIXTEEN

THADDEUS STOOD in his room beside his bed and looked down at the backpack his father had handed him a few minutes before.

"Bring only what's necessary," Nathan had said before hurrying off to pack his own things.

He had packed for their moves before but never for an extended trip. In the woods. On foot. To find a dragon, which was, in reality, his missing mother.

Thaddeus let out a breath and sat on the bed next to the empty backpack. He put his head in his hands and stared at the floor between his feet, trying to contain his madly spinning thoughts and find some kind of reality in which to root them.

Overall, even with the danger of these last few days, and the death of Lily, Thaddeus could not remember a time when he had been happier. He had read many books in all the years they had moved from place to place, finding friends and stability within the pages. In one book—he couldn't remember now which one—a character had stated that he had found a group of friends that felt like family, that he had finally found his tribe. That was how Thaddeus felt now. He had never fit in before, in any group in the schools he'd bounced between. But here in Superstition, he had discovered the people who made him feel good and normal and safe; he had found his tribe.

"Looks like you're swimming in deep thoughts there."

Thaddeus snapped his head up to find his father leaning in the doorway. A backpack stuffed tight with belongings sat at Nathan's feet like an overfed woodland creature.

"Oh, yeah," Thaddeus said, suddenly flustered and feeling bad because he should have been packing and not sitting there thinking. He got up and turned his back on his father, grabbing clothes off the piles on the bed and stuffing them into the backpack. "Sorry. I got behind. I'll be ready soon."

"Hey, hey, hey," Nathan said in a gentle voice. "Easy there, sport. Come on, sit down here with me."

Thaddeus felt his father's hands on his shoulders and stopped his frantic packing. Nathan moved him to the foot of the bed, and they sat side by side, both of them leaning forward with their hands dangling between their legs. A moment of heavy silence passed as outside the sun rose a little higher past dawn. The sound of voices drifted in the open window, the gnomes talking about how best to fix Leopold's fence.

"You've had to learn a lot of truth in a short amount of time," his father finally said. "A lot of truth. To borrow the phrase you kids use today, a whole shitload of truth."

Thaddeus had to laugh and slid a sideways glance at his father to find Nathan grinning at him.

"Dad, kids don't say that."

"Yeah, they do."

"No, they really don't."

"Well, they should, if they're normal kids." Nathan put a hand on his shoulder and gave it a gentle squeeze. "And that's my one true regret, Thaddeus. That you didn't get to grow up like a normal kid. We had to keep moving, either searching for your mom or running from someone I thought was acting suspicious. I really wish you had had the chance to grow up with friends around you, that you got the chance to laugh with them, and have sleepovers, and make up crazy stories about nothing at all, and learn a new swear word over the summer and then use it in the new school year and impress a whole new group of friends."

Thaddeus smiled at the imagery his father painted, and an ache that had always lingered inside him throbbed a bit harder, like a muscle spasm out of the blue. It was a lonely ache, a grieving for that imagined childhood he would never get to live.

"But, Dad, we never could have had that kind of life," Thaddeus said and was saddened by the slow fade of his father's wistful expression. Maybe Nathan had also longed for a childhood like the one he'd just described?

"You're right, I know," Nathan said with a nod.

"I'm not a normal kid in any sense of the word," Thaddeus continued. "I'm the son of a witch and a wizard. I'm like an American Harry Potter, just without the scar. And the wand." He looked at his father. "I don't have a wand, do I? When Vivienne was casting her spells, she didn't use a wand."

Nathan smiled. "No wands needed."

Thaddeus nodded and thought a moment. "How do I... do that? Perform magic, I mean." He laughed and threw his hands up. "I mean, I don't even know if I can do magic. Can I?"

"Oh, you can. You just need to learn to do it." Nathan shrugged and looked back down at his hands with a guilty expression on his face. "Maybe I should have told you the truth a long time ago, taught you all about your magical potential. We could have kept an eye out for clues together. But I didn't want you to have to worry, and I didn't want you to feel, I don't know...."

"Like a freak?" Thaddeus offered.

Nathan gave him a tight smile. "Like a freak. I wanted you to have as normal of a childhood as possible." He looked away, then back, one eye narrowed. "Did it work?"

They both laughed, and Thaddeus shook his head. "Not in the least."

Nathan held up a hand for a high five, which Thaddeus completed gently in deference to his injured hand. "Dad of the Year Award," Nathan said. "Right here."

Thaddeus put an arm around his father's shoulders and squeezed. "I think, given the circumstances, you've done a great job."

"Yeah?"

"Yeah."

They were quiet a moment, listening to the conversations of the gnomes in the yard next door. Through the discussions and gruff instructions provided by Rudyard—frustrated at being waylaid by his ankle and not able to do things himself, no doubt—Thaddeus heard Teofil's humming and had to smile.

"You've learned a lot of stuff recently," Nathan said, and his serious tone wiped the smile from Thaddeus's face and set off quiet alarms in the back of his mind. "I know I said that before, but you have. And not just normal, everyday truth stuff, either. But crazy, really out there kind of truth stuff."

"I've never seen anything like it on the daytime talk show shouting matches," Thaddeus offered and gave a quiet, nervous laugh. What was his father getting at?

"Yeah, nothing like that garbage. But there may be more things you learn in the days or weeks ahead. Things we don't have time to get into now, but I want you to trust me when I tell you that when the time is right, you will learn them, I promise."

"Dad, that's not really fair to say to me right now," Thaddeus said. "I think I deserve to know the truth. All of it."

"I know it's not fair, and I agree you deserve to know, but that's how it's got to be. For now." Nathan looked at him, an inner pain visible in his hazel eyes that made Thaddeus simultaneously sad and scared. "Just know that I love you, very much. Can you do that?"

"You're really scaring me right now, Dad," Thaddeus said.

"I know, and I'm sorry," Nathan said with a nod. "But right now's not the time."

Leopold shouted from downstairs, breaking the moment between them. "Nathan? Thaddeus?"

"I have to let him inside," Nathan said. "I've warded the house against entrants other than us."

Thaddeus widened his eyes. "You can do that?"

Nathan smiled. "I can do a lot of things, sport. You can too, in time."

"A shitload of things?" Thaddeus asked with a teasing grin.

Nathan laughed and pulled Thaddeus into a tight hug. "Yes, smartass, a shitload of things. Now pack a few changes of clothes and any important things you don't want to leave behind."

As his father got up and headed for the door, Thaddeus said, "You say that as if we're never coming back here."

Nathan looked at him over his shoulder. "We don't know what the future holds for us, Thaddeus." He gestured to the backpack. "Come on, we need to leave soon."

Thaddeus returned to his packing, a little more organized now but unsure what he really, truly had to take with him as they went on a quest to find his dragon mother. And the evil Bearagon; he couldn't forget about that beast.

"Ever since you moved in, I've wondered what your room looked like up here."

Thaddeus jumped and turned, then smiled at the sight of Teofil standing just outside the door to his bedroom. The gnome's broad shoulders would not fit through the doorway—he'd have to turn sideways to get through—and he was looking all around at the walls and the furniture with wide eyes.

"You can come in," Thaddeus said.

Teofil met his gaze and smiled, then did, indeed, turn his shoulders sideways and step into the room.

"Feel free to look around," Thaddeus said and turned back to his packing. "I have nothing to hide." He snorted a laugh. "Heck, we've moved so many times, I barely have anything of real value."

Thaddeus looked over his shoulder, watching as Teofil moved around the room, reaching out a blunt finger now and then to delicately touch something. Since Teofil was occupied looking around his room, Thaddeus took the opportunity to look him over. He noticed Teofil's beard had been neatly trimmed, most likely in anticipation of the long journey that lay ahead of them, and he wore his leather boots that tied up over his calves. His large blue eyes were wide as they took in all the things Thaddeus had collected over the years.

"You've got many small treasures here," Teofil said and held up a compass. "What's this?"

Thaddeus reached to take it from him, deliberately letting his fingers brush along Teofil's palm. "It's a compass. It's used to help you figure out which way you're going and probably something I should take with us."

"Are you nervous about our journey?" Teofil asked, coming up beside him.

Thaddeus looked at him and saw Teofil's eyes shift to the side and then widen as he smiled.

"This is where you sleep!" Teofil said, his voice lowered to a whisper.

Thaddeus laughed and turned to look at the rumpled covers of his bed. "Yes. This is where I sleep."

"It looks comfortable." Teofil put his big hands on the bed and pushed down a few times. The bed springs squeaked, making Thaddeus think of much more carnal reasons why they might be sounding off, and he blushed.

"I've often wondered how you look when you sleep," Teofil confessed, a blush reddening his cheeks, the sight of which sent a shiver through Thaddeus. "Many times I stood out in the garden and looked up here at your window as you slept. I wondered who you were, why I felt such a strong attraction to you, and what you might be dreaming about."

"I never knew that," Thaddeus said, his voice a whisper. "I'm just Thaddeus Cane."

Teofil stepped close and gently took his hands. Thaddeus looked into Teofil's eyes, amazed all over again at how his life had changed in the last weeks. He was nervous about the journey ahead but glad to be going with Teofil, Miriam, and his father. That, however, was in the future. For now, there was this moment between him and Teofil, and it stretched out longer and longer, the two of them looking at each other, Teofil's thumbs rubbing the back of Thaddeus's hands.

The kiss was soft and lingering, and this time Thaddeus had no idea who leaned in to initiate it. He felt the soft brush of Teofil's beard across his skin, then the touch of his tongue against his lips. He opened to Teofil and pushed his own tongue against his. It was his first openmouthed kiss and his heart raced as waves of tingles rushed up and down his body. They tipped their heads as the kiss deepened, and Teofil put his arms around Thaddeus, pulling him tight against him. Thaddeus felt his own physical reaction to the kiss and his attraction to Teofil reflected by the gnome and moaned quietly.

Moments later they parted, both of them panting slightly, staring at each other dumbstruck.

"I've never—" Thaddeus managed.

"Me neither," Teofil replied.

They laughed together, and then Teofil leaned in to give him a soft, gentle kiss, with no tongue and no lingering.

"We need to go soon," Teofil said. "The sun is well up by now."

"Right. We have to go. Let me finish up here."

In a matter of minutes, Thaddeus had finished packing some clothes, his toothbrush, a few favorite trinkets he'd collected over the years, a notebook, and several pens. He'd decided it might be a good idea to try and keep a journal of their adventures. He didn't want to forget a thing they were about to experience.

"Thaddeus, you ready?" His father came to a stop in the door to his bedroom at the sight of Teofil sitting on the foot of Thaddeus's bed. "Oh, Teofil. I didn't realize you were up here."

"I'm ready now," Thaddeus said and hefted the backpack onto his shoulders. It was heavier than he'd anticipated, and he shifted it around until it felt more comfortable. Looking over at Teofil, he asked, "Are you ready, Teofil?"

"I am. My pack is downstairs."

They closed the windows and drew the blinds in the upper level, then all of them tromped down the steps to the kitchen where Miriam and two of Teofil's older siblings waited, along with Leopold.

"Ah, here they are," Leopold said with a smile and a knowing wink to Thaddeus. "All ready for their big adventure."

"Thaddeus, dear," Miriam said as she waved to the gnomes beside her. "After much discussion and arguing, Rudyard and I have agreed that Teofil's older brother and sister should accompany us. Do you remember meeting Fetter and Astrid?"

Thaddeus nodded to Teofil's brother and sister, and they nodded back. They were both a bit shorter than Teofil, about up to Thaddeus's chest, but looked as sturdy and strong as Teofil did himself.

"Well, then, if everyone is ready, let's proceed," Leopold said, and headed for the back door.

Only he didn't go out into the yard as Thaddeus expected. Instead, Leopold turned to walk down the steps into the basement.

"We're not going to the yard?" Thaddeus whispered to his father.

"Leopold has discovered a way to give us a head start," Nathan replied.

They gathered at the far corner of the basement where a narrow wooden door stood in the stone basement wall. Thaddeus frowned and turned in a slow circle to look around the basement, finally coming back to the door. He'd never noticed a door there before.

"Was there always a door here?" he asked his father.

Nathan grinned. "Welcome to a life of magic."

"Miriam, would you like to go first?" Leopold asked.

"Thank you, Leo, that's kind of you." Miriam inspected her three children with a discerning eye, then nodded once as if to assure herself they were all set before she faced the door again. "I'm ready."

"Be cautious, and be well," Leopold said.

"You, as well," Miriam replied.

Leopold turned a large key sticking out of a brass-plated keyhole set into the door. The lock clicked open with a loud rattle of tumblers, and then Leopold twisted the big, bright doorknob, and the door swung open. A meadow lay beyond, grassy and beautiful, leading up to a thick line of ancient trees, their branches reaching up toward puffy white clouds scattered about the bright blue sky. Off in the distance, many miles beyond the meadow and woods, stood a mountain range, peaks obscured by mist.

"Wow," Thaddeus whispered.

Miriam stepped through the door, followed by Astrid, then Fetter. Teofil smiled at Thaddeus, then followed after his family. Nathan looked at Thaddeus and gave him a single nod and a tight smile before he stepped up to the doorway and extended his hand to Leopold.

"Thank you, Leo," Nathan said. "I know I was harsh in my treatment of you when we met once again, and I apologize."

"Apology accepted," Leopold replied with a bow of his head as he shook Nathan's hand. "Be wise and wary on your journey."

"You too, my friend." He looked back once more at Thaddeus, then stepped into the doorway.

"You're next, Thaddeus my boy," Leopold said and waved him forward. "Don't be afraid. It doesn't hurt."

"I don't see them over there," Thaddeus said as he squinted and looked beyond the doorway into the meadow. There was no sign of the gnomes or his father, and he glanced at Leopold, mistrust blooming within him. "Where are they? Why can't I see them over there?"

"I've concealed your whereabouts for protection," Leopold explained. "Come along, Thaddeus, the door cannot stay open indefinitely."

Thaddeus looked from Leopold to the meadow, then back. He pressed his lips together, adjusted the pack on his back, took a breath, and stepped into the doorway.

The Well of Tears

For Fred, who makes every day feel like magic.

Acknowledgments

MANY THANKS to Lee Brazil and Havan Fellows who continually root for Thaddeus and Teofil. Mooshberry wine for everyone!

Chapter ONE

THADDEUS CANE knew he was still in the United States; he knew this as a fact with his heart and his mind. But the landscape he had been traveling through the last few days seemed intent on convincing him he'd been dropped into a magical world. Which made sense, seeing as how he reached this far point by stepping through a magical doorway conjured up in the wall of his basement.

They were currently crossing a wide plain, somewhere far removed from the town of Superstition. The grass was as high as his hips, and he ran his hands over the tops that bristled with seeds. Off in the distance, beyond a line of trees standing close together, a mountain range rose from the flatland, its peaks hidden by clouds. Their small but determined group of six was led by Thaddeus's father, Nathan, and included their neighbor—and, Thaddeus liked to think, his boyfriend, although neither of them had said the word yet—a handsome garden gnome named Teofil, as well as Teofil's mother, Miriam, and his brother and sister, Fetter and Astrid. They had no definite destination save for the mountain range in the distance. They were hiking across the land in search of signs of the Bearagon—a vicious beast that was a combination wolf, bear, and dragon—in hope it might lead them to the dragon that was, in actuality, Thaddeus's mother, Claire. The farther they traveled, the less Thaddeus felt like he was, to borrow a famous movie line, "still in Kansas."

He had a feeling he'd have to hitch a ride home once this quest was completed. That, or ride on the back of a dragon, which might be entirely possible.

"Doing all right?" Teofil asked.

Thaddeus looked over his shoulder and into Teofil's blue eyes. "I am. How about you?"

Teofil smiled and lowered his voice to whisper, "I like my view." Teofil dropped his gaze to Thaddeus's butt, then looked up at him again, grinning.

Heat rushed to Thaddeus's face and dropped down through his body, spreading out through his limbs and into his fingers and toes. Teofil seemed to have that effect on him, all of him, and it both scared and excited Thaddeus.

"Oh, well…," Thaddeus managed to say, before his foot caught on a rock, and he fell forward onto the path forged through the grass by his father. He felt a sharp pain in the heel of his left hand as it scraped along another rock hidden among the stalks, and then a numbness. A gasp of surprise rushed out of him, and he lay still a moment, taking stock.

What just happened?

"Thaddeus!" His father knelt beside him. "Are you hurt?"

Thaddeus pushed up to his knees, hissing at the pain in his hand, and the tug of the stitches in his leg, a result of his run-in with the Bearagon a few weeks before. He looked at his left palm and winced at the raw, red scrapes that dotted his palm, which had joined the scratches he'd received while yanking the drachen narcosis out of the ground in Leopold's yard. As he watched, blood welled up within the injuries, bright red against his pale skin.

"Dammit, you're bleeding," Nathan said, shrugging out of his backpack. "I've got a first aid kit in here somewhere."

Miriam stepped up beside Thaddeus and put a hand on his back. "Thaddeus, hold your hand still now. Try not to let the blood drip onto the ground."

Thaddeus held his left wrist with his right hand and looked up at Teofil's mother. "Why not?"

"The scent of blood is an easy tracker," Miriam explained. "If we're being followed, it would be just like planting a sign with an arrow that points in the direction we're walking. Hold still now, dear."

As she spoke Miriam rummaged through the pack she carried slung over one shoulder and now produced a handful of leaves. She added a swipe of some thick, wet, brown glop to the leaves and then firmly pressed the mixture against Thaddeus's injuries. Stinging pain seared Thaddeus's palm, and he sucked in a hissing breath as tears flooded his eyes.

"It hurts," he said.

"Aye, that it will, dear," Miriam assured him. "That means it's getting to work chewing up all the nasty germs trying to get inside you."

"Must be a hell of a lot of them," Thaddeus grumbled as the sensation intensified. "Really smarts."

"What is that you're using, Miriam?" Nathan asked as he finally pulled the first aid kit out of his backpack.

"Oh, just some plantain leaves mixed in with a bit of rose water, a touch of raw honey, and some comfrey leaf oil." She smiled at them each in turn. "When you've got as many children under your belt as I have, you pretty much keep things like this in constant supply."

To distract himself from the sting of the natural antiseptic mixture Miriam still held pressed against his wounds, Thaddeus asked, "How many children do you have?" He looked apologetically up at Teofil, then back at Miriam. "Sorry, I've lost count."

Miriam smiled. "No worries, dear. I lose track of them on occasion myself. I have been fortunate enough to have fourteen healthy, happy, beautiful children. You know Teofil, of course, and Fetter and Astrid here," she said, nodding to each of the gnomes in turn. "After that there's Seamus, River, Meadow, Rose, Violet, Robin, Martin, May, Stone, Iris, and young Flora." She looked around at her three children. "Did I remember everyone?"

Astrid nodded. "All of them, Mum. And in order. Much better than usual."

"Thank you, dear," Miriam said, then gently lifted a corner of the leaves to peek at Thaddeus's hand. "The wounds look good, but we'll need to keep the leaves and mixture on them for a while yet."

"I've got tape here," Nathan said, kneeling beside Thaddeus and opening the first aid kit. "How about your leg? Did you hurt that?"

Thaddeus shook his head. "No. Just pulled the stitches a bit when I fell, but it doesn't hurt as bad anymore." Thaddeus smiled up at Teofil. "Just clumsy me, having to make us stop."

"We were due for a break anyway," Nathan said, wrapping a long strand of medical tape around Thaddeus's hand.

They all settled on the ground and sipped from waterskins or canteens. Teofil sat beside Thaddeus and, after looking around to make sure no one else was listening, leaned in to whisper, "Sorry, I shouldn't have said that to you about liking the view."

Thaddeus blushed, again, and darted a glance at Teofil, whose expression was so serious he managed to give him a longer look. "Why do you say that?"

Teofil shrugged. "It flustered you and made you trip and fall. I should have kept my thoughts to myself."

"I'm glad you said it," Thaddeus assured him. "I just…. No one's ever said that kind of stuff to me before. It's tough to believe that someone could feel that way about me."

"I can't believe no one has ever said something like that to you before," Teofil said. "You're so handsome and caring and brave."

"Not as brave as you," Thaddeus countered. "Leaving your family to live on your own with a wizard and tend to his garden without knowing why."

"I guess we're just brave enough to be drawn together," Teofil said.

"I guess so."

Their gazes met and locked, and Thaddeus had to remind himself to breathe.

"How's your hand?" his father asked, pulling Thaddeus's attention away from Teofil.

Thaddeus winced as he flexed the fingers. "It's okay. Hurts, but not like it did when I first tripped."

"Your leg okay too? No stitches pulled out?" Nathan continued.

"My leg's fine," Thaddeus replied. "I'm okay, Dad."

"Think you'll be ready to move on soon?" Nathan looked out across the grassy plain toward the thick line of trees. "I'd like to get closer to the tree line by nightfall."

"We're going to camp in the woods?" Thaddeus asked, more than a little nervous. The Bearagon had stalked him through the woods by his house before it had attacked them at Leopold's house.

"Just outside of it, if we can," Nathan replied.

"That's the Lost Forest," Fetter said from where he sat a few feet away. He had thick dark hair pulled back into a ponytail and a neatly trimmed dark beard. He was Teofil's older brother, but shorter than his sibling by at least a foot. With a broad chest and thick, strong legs, Fetter was an imposing powerhouse of a gnome.

"Lots of travelers get lost in there," he continued. "That's why they call it that."

"Stop telling stories," Astrid scolded him and let out a heavy sigh. She turned to look at Thaddeus and Nathan, her blue eyes a shade darker than Teofil's and her dark blonde hair pulled back into a single braid that hung halfway down her back. She was broad across the shoulders and strong as well, and her nose was crooked in two spots, which indicated to Thaddeus it had been broken at least twice in the past.

"That's not why they call it the Lost Forest," Astrid continued, and Fetter grinned and shrugged one big shoulder. "They call it the Lost Forest because legend tells of a place hidden deep within its borders that contains a powerful magic."

"Really?" Thaddeus asked. "What kind of place? A temple or something?"

Astrid shook her head. "Nothing as fancy as that. None have seen it since the day it was built, but many know the stories."

"Oh, Astrid," Miriam said, standing behind her with her hands on her hips. "Are you on about that story again? I swear, you're going to start saying it in your sleep, you've been talking about it so much lately."

"The fairies told me about it, Mum," Astrid replied. "It's all true."

Thaddeus thought about the legend and wondered how many more of them he had yet to learn. Maybe the Superstition town library had a secret room of big, dusty books filled with tales of history and heroism within the magic community, a room that was watched over by Vivienne. Thoughts of the stern but kind red-haired witch who ran the Superstition library made Thaddeus feel a bit homesick, and he wondered how she was doing. Vivienne, Leopold, and Teofil's father, Rudyard, had agreed to remain back in Superstition and work on uncovering the assumed identities of Isadora and her supporters, then meet up with them once they'd reached the mountains. He hoped they were having better luck than him.

"Tell the story as we walk," Nathan said and picked up his backpack. "We're losing daylight."

They gathered their items and set off again, Astrid walking between Teofil and Thaddeus as she told the story of the Lost Forest. Though the day was sunny, and a warm breeze stirred the grass around them, Thaddeus felt a chill as Astrid related the tale. Suddenly, the rustling of the grasses started to sound like whispers, and the wind felt like the breath of Death itself.

"The Lost Forest was once filled with magical beings," Astrid explained. "Gnomes, fairies, elves, dwarves, witches, wizards, all of them living together, all out of sight of men. Even ogres and trolls and goblins, on occasion, though they're mostly bad and fond of eating others. Anyway, there came a great sickness that swept across the land. It infected those who lived in the forest and surrounding country, and it was quite deadly. Many died from it, and those who cared for their loved ones who were first infected caught it as well, until only a handful of survivors remained."

"How awful," Thaddeus said, his gaze cast down to keep a watch out for rocks.

"They never found out where it originated," Astrid continued. "And so they buried all the bodies in a long pit, somewhere deep inside the forest. After many years, the infected blood from all of those bodies found its way into the soil and, finally, the roots of the trees around the grave. Those trees grew darker and twisted, and bore fruit that tasted vile and sour. The foul fruit attracted evil into the forest, and as time went on, the magical creatures who had survived the sickness left the forest and the darker beings took over. The gravesite has since been lost, and any who have gone in search of it have never returned."

"Wow," Thaddeus whispered. "That's quite a story. And we have to go through this forest?"

"Just keep in mind that's what it is," Nathan said. "A story."

"Suit yourself," Astrid said. "But I've heard the story from more than one source."

"You forgot the best part," Fetter piped up.

"What do you mean?" Astrid asked, her voice edged with annoyance.

"About the well," Fetter said.

Astrid sighed, and Thaddeus glanced back in time to see her roll her eyes. "You and that ridiculous well," Astrid said.

"It's the best part of the story!" Fetter nearly shouted.

"Keep your voices down, both of you," Miriam scolded them gently. They all fell silent a moment, then Miriam said, "And you did leave out that part, Astrid."

"See?" Fetter immediately said. "I told you!"

"Shut up!" Astrid snapped.

"Oh, for the love of geranium, both of you keep still!" Miriam said. She marched up to get between Astrid and Thaddeus and lowered her voice as she told the part of the story Astrid had skipped. "You see, the people who lived within the forest had no idea what was making their loved ones so sick. It could be something they were eating, or maybe the water they were drinking. To be safe, they dug a new well far outside their village. At first, the water they pulled up from this new well was cool, clear, and plentiful, but soon it dried up, with no explanation or reason. Those who still remained would gather at the edge of the well and lower the bucket with hopes of finding just a little bit of fresh water, but there was none to be had. They cried as they circled the well, so very thirsty and still heartbroken from the loss of their loved ones, and soon their tears filled it up, but that was too salty for them to drink, so they had to move away."

Miriam gave a nod and adjusted her pack across her shoulders. "To this day, that well remains, somewhere deep within the Lost Forest, filled with the shimmering tears of a great number of magical beings. The magic contained within that Well of Tears is powerful indeed, because it's the collected power of all of the enchanted creatures."

"The Well of Tears?" Thaddeus whispered.

"That's what they call it," Fetter said from the back of the line. "Isn't it a great name?"

Astrid made a disgusted sound. "It's a horrible name. Ridiculous and romantic, and not even a good part of the story. No one's ever seen it, and do you know how many tears it would take to fill a well? It's not even possible!"

"Oh, and the infected blood from all the corpses getting into the trees and making them dark and twisted is possible?" Fetter said.

"Enough!" Miriam held up her hands. "I want you both to remain silent for the rest of this hike, until we stop to set up camp. Understood?"

"Yes, Mum," both replied in sullen tones.

"Good." Miriam took a breath, then smiled at Thaddeus when he looked back over his shoulder. "Gnomes," she said, shaking her head.

Thaddeus grinned and turned to face forward again. He followed his father, who forged a path through the tall grass, keeping an eye out for rocks. But more often than not, his thoughts strayed to a mass grave filled with the bones of magical beings surrounded by dark, twisted trees and a well filled with tears, and he wondered—not for the last time, he was sure—if he would ever stop being surprised by this strange new world he had discovered.

Chapter TWO

THE SMALL fire crackled and popped, and the wind carried the smoke across the fifty remaining yards of the grassy plain, then into the darkness that had gathered between the twisted tree trunks of the Lost Forest. Overhead, the stars winked and blinked down at them, and without the lights of a large city nearby, they appeared brighter and closer than Thaddeus had ever seen them.

"Beautiful, aren't they?" Teofil whispered.

Thaddeus smiled at him. "They look so close. I'm not used to seeing the night sky outside of a city."

Teofil smiled back. "City weaned."

"Pretty much," Thaddeus agreed.

Teofil looked back up at the sky and pointed. "See those stars there?"

Thaddeus followed Teofil's finger and saw he was indicating the Big Dipper. He decided to play dumb and asked, "Those bright ones?"

"Yeah, those. See how they're all in a box like that? That's Faux Flora."

"Faux Flora?" Thaddeus frowned at him. He started to respond, probably harsher than he would have intended, that it was the Big Dipper and ask where Teofil had learned his constellations. But then he noticed his father looking at him with raised eyebrows. Nathan shook his head slightly, which told Thaddeus he should keep quiet and let Teofil talk.

"Faux Flora," Teofil continued. He continued to gaze up at the sky and his eyes gleamed in the starlight. Thaddeus pushed aside his learnings and his ties to the human world and, instead, scooted closer to Teofil and listened to something from this magical new realm to which he had recently been introduced.

"Flora was a fairy princess who lived among the treetops," Teofil said. The soft, deep tone of his voice, the sound of the fire, and the cool breeze that carried the smoke off into the woods really set a mood. Nearby, Fetter and Astrid were settling beneath their blankets. Miriam knitted and smiled as she listened to her son. Nathan stretched out on the ground with his hands behind his head as he looked up at the stars.

"She was kind and loving, and watched over all the forest creatures and plants," Teofil continued. "But there were those outside of the forest who felt they deserved her love and protection as well. These Plains Dwellers tried to convince Flora to come down from the forest treetops and live with them on the grassy plains, but she refused. She loved the forest too much to leave it.

"Feeling slighted, the Plains Dwellers got together and decided to lure her down to the forest floor and capture her. They set fire to the edge of the forest, but Flora brought along a great rainstorm that doused the flames. Undaunted they next caught a number of the forest creatures, hoping she would come down to rescue them, but Flora instead sent larger forest creatures out from the cover of the trees. The Plains Dwellers were frightened and ran from the larger creatures, which then freed the smaller ones and led them back to the forest.

"Then the Plains Dwellers decided to knock Flora out of the treetops and capture her when she hit the ground. They talked about slingshots and catapults, but didn't want to injure or possibly kill her. They just wanted to take her captive. Finally, they decided to build a windmill, tall as the forest trees with large blades. The windmill would blow a hearty wind toward the forest and knock Flora from the treetops so the Plains Dwellers could grab her.

"They worked through the day and night, foregoing sleep they were so eager to have Flora among them. Finally, the windmill was ready, and they set it in motion. The blades spun faster and faster, directing the wind along the tops of the forest trees. Flora understood at once what was going on, and knew she needed to end this selfish plot. She quickly gathered some sticks and leaves from around the roots of the forest trees and built a likeness of herself. When it was ready, she lifted it to the treetops and let it go in the great blast of wind. The likeness spun and swirled in the strong current and, eventually, blew up into the sky where she resides now, a Faux Flora, watching over all the lands of the Earth."

Thaddeus let out his breath. His smile was plastered to his face, and he looked at Teofil's profile and wondered just how much more he could fall in love with him.

Before Teofil or anyone else could say a word, however, a tremor rumbled just below the surface of the ground. Nathan sat up, and Fetter and Astrid did the same, their blankets falling off them. Miriam's busy fingers stopped in the midst of her knitting, and she frowned as she looked toward the dark line of trees.

"Did everyone feel that?" Thaddeus asked, his voice a whisper.

"Was it an earth tremor?" Teofil wondered, and looked at his mother.

"I'm not sure," Miriam replied.

She set aside her knitting and got to her feet. They all followed suit, standing around the fire and looking toward the trees. In the darkness of the forest, something large and pale shifted within the soft glow of the starlight. Another tremor rumbled through the ground, and Thaddeus reached out to take Teofil's hand.

"Something's moving in the trees," Astrid said, her voice quiet.

"What is it?" Fetter asked.

The loud crack of breaking branches startled them all, and they took a few steps back as a group. One of the trees at the edge of the wood swayed and then fell to the ground with a great crash. Thaddeus felt the wind of its fall on his face a moment later and thought about the giant windmill built by the Plains Dwellers as his heart hammered.

A tall, wide creature stomped out from between the trees. It stood at least ten feet tall and had a round, bald head atop large, rounded shoulders. A pale, flabby stomach hung over the breeches covering half of the thing's short, thick legs. The creature sniffed the air and looked right at them before letting out a roar that sent chills through Thaddeus.

"Troll!" Teofil shouted.

"Troll?" Thaddeus asked, unable to take his gaze off the advancing giant.

"Weapons!" Nathan directed. "Take up your weapons!"

"We should run," Thaddeus said.

"It'll catch us," Nathan said. "And we're stronger as a group. Here!"

Nathan handed him a dagger, and Thaddeus gripped it tight. His palms were damp, and the scrapes on his left one burned, but he ignored the pain. A cool layer of sweat had broken out all over his body, and it made him shiver as he felt the beat of his rapid pulse echoed in the wounds on his leg and hands.

"Stay together," Miriam instructed, and Thaddeus looked around to see her take up a crossbow. "Go for the throat and the eyes."

"Oh my God," Thaddeus whispered as his stomach knotted and his supper threatened to come up. They were going to have to kill this thing charging toward them. He had never killed anything before—well, not on purpose. Except flies or mosquitos, but they were completely different from a massive beast like the one clomping toward them. He wasn't sure he would be able to deliver a death blow to another creature, not even one that plainly wanted to kill him.

"Stay with me," Teofil told him. "I'll protect you."

"Yeah, okay," Thaddeus said and adjusted his grip on the dagger.

Swinging a club made from a large branch, the troll came upon them. It stomped through their campsite, and they all dodged the club. Miriam stopped and shot the troll in a leg with an arrow. The troll roared with pain. It reached down to pluck the arrow out of its pale, flabby skin and tossed it aside. It sneered and came at them again, swinging its club, and they scattered. Thaddeus cried out when the club caught Teofil's heel and sent him sprawling. He turned back and grabbed Teofil's arm to pull him to his feet. Something whistled past his ear, and Thaddeus ducked, then turned to see a thin barb stuck in the ground behind him.

"What is that?" Thaddeus asked.

"Poison barb," Teofil explained. "Don't touch it."

"Where'd it come from?"

"Trolls have them beneath their tongues," Teofil said as he got to his feet. "They use them when hunting. Now run!"

Thaddeus turned and ran with Teofil by his side. Poison barbs thumped into the ground behind them. Thaddeus kept a tight grip on his dagger, the adrenaline in his system shutting down any pain he knew he should be feeling in his hands and leg. Teofil led him out into the tall grass and then in a wide circle around their campsite. The blades of grass slapped at his legs and hands as they ran, and Thaddeus's breath was hot in his throat. He could see the troll swinging its club and opening its mouth to shoot poison barbs at the others. Nathan swung his sword at the troll's leg. Miriam fired off more arrows, and Astrid flung rocks with her slingshot. Thaddeus couldn't see Fetter and worried that he might have been felled by a poison barb or struck by the club.

Ahead of him, Teofil turned to angle around behind the troll, and Thaddeus followed. They each held daggers, and without need for explanation, Thaddeus knew what Teofil had planned. They would attack the troll from behind and take it by surprise.

A painful shout from someone in their group sent a chill through Thaddeus. It had sounded like his father, but he couldn't stop to investigate. He needed to focus on attacking the troll, or all of them would be dead. He followed Teofil out of the tall grass onto the path his father had forged. He stuck the dagger into his belt to free both hands and somehow found the strength to run even faster. They closed the distance to the troll as the others distracted it. He jumped a few seconds after Teofil, and both of them landed on the troll's back. The pale skin was slick and greasy with sweat, and Thaddeus had to avert his face from the stench of the thing to draw in a fresh breath.

The troll roared in pain as Teofil jabbed his dagger into its back. It reached a big hand back to grab at him. Teofil dropped to the ground to avoid the troll's thick, dirty fingers, leaving his dagger in place.

"Stab it and drop!" Teofil shouted. "Hurry!"

Thaddeus clung to the troll's back with both hands. He couldn't seem to open his fingers for fear of falling beneath the thing's feet and getting trampled. The troll turned and twisted, reaching for the dagger in its back as well as Thaddeus himself. He heard it roar in pain again, and figured Miriam or Astrid had fired at it some more. Finally, the creature came to a stop and stood in place, its breathing wet and thick. Thaddeus released one hand and pulled the dagger from his belt. He lifted it high and brought it down hard, hearing the heavy pop of the blade breaking the skin and then feeling the warm splash of blood across his hand.

He let go and fell to the ground as the troll's roar turned to a shriek and, finally, it collapsed to the ground with a mighty crash.

Silence descended over them, and darkness. The troll had landed on top of their campfire, and all they had to see by now was starlight. Thaddeus got to his feet, swayed unsteadily a moment, then went to find Teofil.

"Are you hurt?" Teofil asked.

"No, are you?" Thaddeus replied, though his hand and leg were throbbing now.

"No." Teofil leaned in to kiss him quickly, then held his good hand as they walked around the fallen troll. Thaddeus refused to look at the troll's flat, ugly face, instead keeping his gaze forward, looking for his father.

"Dad?" Thaddeus asked, and Teofil followed it with, "Mum?"

"Here," Miriam called. "We're here. Are you two hurt?"

"No," Teofil assured her as they approached where she knelt on the ground. He stopped suddenly and said, "Oh."

Thaddeus couldn't quite put together what he was seeing. Then it became clear, and he dropped to his knees beside his father as tears flooded his eyes. "Dad? Dad!"

"He was struck by the troll's club," Miriam said. "And it appears he was grazed by a barb."

"Oh my God. No, Dad!" Thaddeus shook his father's shoulders as a sob burst from him. "Dad, no, not like this. You can't leave me now. Stay with me."

Nathan coughed and gasped, and the sound of it loosened the iron band that seemed to have tightened around Thaddeus's torso. He took a shaky, relieved breath of his own, and put a hand on his father's chest. Nathan's heartbeat was weak and fast, but his grip was strong when he took Thaddeus's hand.

"You hurt?" Nathan asked.

"No, I'm fine," Thaddeus assured him. "Keep quiet. Save your strength."

Nathan shifted position and grimaced, then flashed Thaddeus a weak smile. "I zigged when I should have zagged."

Fresh tears swamped Thaddeus's eyes, and he looked away to keep his father from seeing him cry. Miriam stood nearby with her arms around Astrid and Fetter, her expression grim and her own cheeks wet with tears. Teofil knelt beside Thaddeus, a respectful distance away to give them privacy, but close enough to provide support.

"Thaddeus," Nathan said, his voice weak. "You have to go on. You have to find your mother. Head to the mountains. That's most likely where she flew."

"I'm not leaving you," Thaddeus replied, shaking his head as he cried. "I won't."

"You have to." Nathan turned his head away and coughed before continuing. "Our mission depends on you now."

"Dad, I can't leave you," Thaddeus said. "Would you leave me if our roles were reversed?"

"That's different," Nathan replied. "You have to continue the journey. I'll rest here and wait for you to return."

"No." Thaddeus shook his head. "No. And that's final. Now, let's get you comfortable for the rest of the night."

"You have to keep going," Nathan said, but his voice was soft now, just above a whisper. "It's important."

"Dad?" Thaddeus watched Nathan's eyes slip closed, and a jolt of fear went through him. He leaned down to press his ear against his father's chest, then let out a relieved breath at the sound of his heart. His father was still alive, for now.

Thaddeus looked at Miriam. "We're not leaving him behind. Do you understand? We're not."

"Let's all rest tonight, Thaddeus," Miriam said, and sent Astrid and Fetter off to make a new campfire away from the dead troll. "We'll rest tonight and discuss it in the morning."

Thaddeus nodded and settled in beside his father, understanding the meaning beneath Miriam's words: If Nathan was still alive in the morning.

In the distance Fetter and Astrid bickered about how to properly arrange a campfire. Taking his father's hand, Thaddeus hung his head and fought back tears as he listened to Nathan's labored breathing.

Chapter THREE

A DENSE gray fog lay heavy across the grassy plain the following morning. Everything was damp from the touch of the mist, including Thaddeus himself when he started awake and sat bolt upright. He squinted into the heavy, roiling fog that surrounded him, then looked at his father who lay alongside him, shivering beneath blankets. Nathan's face was pale, and the flesh beneath his eyes dark and puffy. His dry, cracked lips were slightly parted, and Thaddeus could see that his tongue had paled as well.

"How is he?" Teofil whispered from Thaddeus's other side.

"Worse," Thaddeus replied.

"He looks worse than he is," Miriam assured him as she materialized from within the fog. She had fresh firewood in her arms and a handkerchief bulging with something that stained the material a bright yellow.

"Mooshberries!" Astrid said, apparently recognizing the color of the stain. She held out both hands and smiled eagerly. "Where did you find them?"

"The edge of the forest is a veritable field of them," Miriam replied. She dropped the firewood and poured a few plump, yellow berries into Astrid's hands. "Who else wants breakfast?"

Thaddeus held out one hand and sniffed the berries Miriam doled out to him. They smelled sour and acidic, and he gave Teofil a skeptical look. Teofil laughed as he popped three berries into his mouth.

"Don't give me the stink eye," Teofil said. "Just try one. They taste better than they smell."

Thaddeus bit one of the berries in half and was surprised at the sweet juice that filled his mouth. He quickly ate the other half, then finished off what he had been given. The berries were meaty and filling, but he was still a bit hungry and realized he should have taken another handful while he had the chance.

"Here," Teofil said with a smirk. "I took a little more than you did. You can have some of mine."

"Oh, you don't have to do that," Thaddeus said.

"It's okay, take these."

Thaddeus held out his hand, and Teofil tipped the berries into his palm.

"Thanks, Teofil."

"Gotta keep up your strength for our walk," Teofil said.

Thaddeus looked at his father again. "I'm not sure I can leave him."

"Nonsense," Miriam said, then looked at each of her children in turn. "Fetter, Astrid, Teofil, see to the fire."

"But we built the last fire!" Astrid whined.

"Astrid...." Miriam drew out her name in a low tone that left no room for argument.

The three gnomes moved off to the stack of wood and began to whisper in low grumbles. Miriam ignored them and lowered herself to the ground next to Thaddeus. For a short time, they watched Nathan sleep, and then Miriam spoke in a voice too low for her children to overhear.

"When I was about your age, Thaddeus, my father, Jozafat Peony, fell ill. He had always been a force of nature in the hollow where we lived, and his illness caught not just my family by surprise, but our entire tribe. He wasn't a leader, mind you, not in the official sense, but he was known by every gnome for miles around and well-liked and respected. When he first took ill, I spent all my time nursing him while my mother looked after my brothers and sisters. If you think fourteen children is a lot, my parents had twenty-two."

Thaddeus gasped. "You had twenty-one siblings?"

Miriam nodded, her gaze on Nathan's face. "A large family, to say the least. I was the middle child, number eleven, and I took it upon myself to nurse my father. For weeks I catered to him. I cooked for him and fed him and fetched him water and helped him up when he needed to move about. I let my studies slide... and my friends. All I could think to do was care for him.

"Despite all my attention, his condition worsened. Finally, one morning, he looked over to where I sat in a rocking chair darning socks for my mother, and he said, 'Miriam, I need something from you.'"

She smiled, and Thaddeus could see tears in her eyes as the conversation between Teofil, Astrid, and Fetter drifted to them from out of the fog.

"What did he need?" Thaddeus asked, not sure he wanted to know the answer.

"He said, 'I want you to go to the village center and get me some mooshberries.'"

Thaddeus smiled. "Mooshberries?"

Miriam nodded and laughed, glancing at him as she dabbed at her eyes. "Mooshberries. That man dearly loved his mooshberries. Now, mind you, I did not want to go and leave him on his own. So I told him I would send one of my siblings for them. But he was insistent, and he told me I was the only one who knew how to choose the sweetest, most perfectly ripe mooshberries. So I put down my darning and I went."

She fell silent, tears rolling down her face.

"What happened?" Thaddeus asked in a quiet voice. The fog thickened around them, sealing them off from the rest of the world. He rubbed his injured palm through the plantain leaves held in place by the medical tape his father had applied.

"I went to the center and gathered the freshest, ripest mooshberries I could find. When I got back, I rinsed them all at the pump and brought them inside. I couldn't find anyone about, which was unusual, so I dropped them into a bowl and picked the biggest, ripest one of the bunch and carried it into his room.

"My family was all in there, every single one of them gathered around my mother. She sat in the rocking chair I had just left only a few minutes before. She was holding my father's hand and crying. I saw his face, how still and pale and beautiful it was, and I knew he had sent me away on purpose."

"That's horrible," Thaddeus said. "You must have felt so guilty."

Miriam met his gaze, and Thaddeus was surprised to see her tears had dried. "I did at first. But I came to find out Rudyard had been at the village center that day, as well, and had caught sight of me inspecting the mooshberries. I had been so intent on finding the best, most perfect mooshberries I didn't notice him watching me. He said that first sighting was the moment he fell in love with me, and he had to know who I was because he wanted to marry me."

Flames from the freshly started campfire gave a yellow tint to the fog around them, and then Teofil materialized out of the mist and smiled down at Thaddeus.

Miriam reached up to take Teofil's hand and smiled up at her son as she said, "You see, Thaddeus, you can protect them, of course, and feed and clothe and teach them the values with which you were raised. You can share a life with them and support and encourage them." She looked back at Thaddeus. "Your father is a brave, good man. He loves you so very much. He knows not only what he means to you, but what missing your mother has taken from you. He's in a very tight predicament, Thaddeus, I hope you can see that. He's unable to continue the quest we all set out on, but it must not end here; it can't. The dragon, your mother, must be found before others get to her and use her for evil purposes. She knows your scent. We've already seen that when she was released from beneath Leopold's yard. This journey, and the fate of all of us, depends on you seeing it through."

Thaddeus hung his head. The fog left him damp and chilled, and he could hear his father's labored breathing. Teofil knelt beside him and placed a hand on his back, moving it slightly in a comforting motion, up and down his spine.

He knew Miriam was right, knew it deep inside his heart and his head. But a spot halfway between didn't want him to go on without his father. There was a place within him, interrupting the connection between heart and mind, that was afraid of being on his own without his father's guidance, without his leadership. Now that burden would fall to him, Thaddeus Cane, all of fifteen and just being introduced to this magical world that existed within the "normal" one he knew best.

Or was that the other way around? Did the "normal" one exist within the magical one?

Whichever way it was, Thaddeus was afraid to continue the journey without his father. Everything he thought he'd known about his life was a lie. He was a wizard, but he had no idea what that meant. And now he was supposed to hike for miles through dangerous places to find his mother, a cursed dragon.

But what choice did he have? His mother had to be found, and soon, before Isadora or one of her supporters found her first. It was up to him to finish the mission.

"Thaddeus," Miriam said in a soothing voice. "I will stay behind to care for your father. I'll make sure he's comfortable and fed, and receives the best remedies possible for his injuries."

"What?" Astrid and Fetter exclaimed together as they stepped out of the fog. Thaddeus noticed it had started to thin a bit as now he could see the hearty stack of wood Miriam had gathered and the dancing flames of the fire the gnomes had built.

"The three of you must continue with Thaddeus," Miriam said. "He'll need help navigating the Lost Forest and the lands beyond as you head to the mountains. Dragons feel safe high up in craggy peaks. They like to hide in caves and sleep, but can be dangerous if improperly awakened. All of you will have to work together to make sure you arrive safely. Do you understand?"

"Mum, but…," Astrid said and looked at Teofil and Fetter. "We're going to be on our own?"

"Oh, love," Miriam replied as she gathered Astrid into her arms. "You've got a wide, deep independent streak in you that rivals my own. You are a child of the Peony and Rhododendron tribes, all three of you are, and you are brave and smart and strong. Listen and talk with, not at, each other. I will be right here waiting for you to return." She looked at Thaddeus. "We both will."

A numbness stole over Thaddeus as Miriam talked to the others. He moved up to his father's side and took his hand, dismayed at how cold it felt within his own. Nathan snorted and sighed. Then his eyes fluttered open and he looked up at Thaddeus.

"Thaddeus," Nathan said, his voice dry and scratchy. "You should have left already."

"Too much fog right now," Thaddeus replied.

Nathan shifted his gaze around, and when he looked back at Thaddeus, he managed a weak smile. "Thank God for that. I thought I was going blind."

Thaddeus managed a gentle laugh and leaned down to kiss his father's forehead. "I'm going to leave soon with Teofil, Astrid, and Fetter. Miriam will stay behind and care for you."

"She should go with you," Nathan said, then turned away again as a fit of coughing overwhelmed him.

"We'll be fine on our own," Thaddeus assured him. "You need someone to stay and care for you, and Miriam has the best background for that."

"You be careful," Nathan said.

"I will. You get better."

"I will."

Thaddeus sat in silence and held his father's hand as the fog slowly burned away. Nathan had fallen asleep by the time it was clear enough for them to move on, and Thaddeus kissed his father's forehead once more before gathering his backpack and turning to face Miriam.

"I know you'll take care of him," Thaddeus said. "Just...." Words failed him as his voice broke.

"We'll be fine, dear," Miriam said, tears in her eyes as she pulled him into a tight hug. "You be safe and alert. Teofil will protect you."

"We'll protect each other," he promised her.

"Oh, you dear boy," she said with a sniffle, and then squeezed him once more before pushing him away. "I know you will. Go on now. I've packed some herbs and mooshberries for you all. Teofil, change that dressing on Thaddeus's hand every other day."

"I will, Mum," Teofil said.

Thaddeus watched the gnomes hug her once again. He cast one more look at his father's profile, so still and pale as he slept, and then turned away toward the dark, twisted trees of the Lost Forest.

Chapter FOUR

THADDEUS COULD see why they called it the Lost Forest. They were just a few hours into the continuation of their journey, and he didn't think he could find his way back if he wanted to. He was walking behind Teofil and in front of Fetter and Astrid and stopped to look back the way they had come. A strong part of him felt drawn in that direction, back to the safety of the world outside their dark and spooky surroundings, back to his father, and back to adults who made decisions for them. But even if that feeling flooded up and overwhelmed his senses, urging him to run back to his father's side, he would most likely become lost.

He was, indeed, on his own. But at least he was among friends.

"Thaddeus?" Fetter asked in a quiet voice. "You okay?"

Thaddeus nodded and gave him what he hoped was a reassuring smile. "I'm fine. Just wanted to see how far we'd come, but I can't even see the way back."

"The Lost Forest," Astrid said as she stepped around them to follow after Teofil. "Quite aptly named, don't you think?"

"Come on," Fetter said. "Let's keep up with the others."

Thaddeus walked after Astrid, and Fetter brought up the rear. They traveled for a time in silence. After a while, Fetter spoke up from behind Thaddeus, his voice low, as though he might be talking to himself instead of the rest of them.

"Shame about your dad. Troll poison is awful stuff. Powerful and deadly. Since he was just grazed by one of the barbs, though, there's a chance he'll pull through." Fetter fell silent, then said, "It's a slim chance, but I'm sure he'll still be alive when we get back."

Thaddeus fought back tears as he stepped around roots and over fallen branches and trees. There was no direct path through the Lost Forest. Teofil was picking the easiest route to traverse, and it was tricky.

"I hated leaving him," Thaddeus confessed. "Most difficult thing I've done."

"My mom will take good care of him," Fetter said. "But her skills are limited, especially against troll poison. There's only so much that can be done with rose water, comfrey leaf oil, and plantain leaves."

Thaddeus tightened his fingers around the leaves taped against his palm. "Surely she's got other ingredients with her."

"A few, I'm sure," Fetter agreed. "She carries a lot around in that pack of hers. But it will take something powerful to fight that poison."

Silence fell on them again, and Fetter's words pinged around inside Thaddeus's mind. They broke down the assurances he'd forced himself to believe about leaving his father's side, allowing concerns to fill the spaces left behind. They walked for a long time in silence, and then Teofil, still in the lead, came to a stop and the others gathered around him.

"How is everyone?" he asked and reached out to give Thaddeus's shoulder a gentle squeeze. "Let's take a break here. We've made some good progress."

Astrid looked at the leaning, twisted trees that stretched out around them. "How can you tell?"

They all chuckled at that, and Thaddeus felt his mood lighten just a bit as he settled on a moss-covered rock and sipped from his canteen.

"I can tell," Teofil replied. He approached Thaddeus and asked, "Is there room enough on that rock for two?"

Thaddeus smiled. "Might be a little crowded."

"I don't mind if you don't."

Thaddeus shifted over, and Teofil sat next to him with a contented sigh. Teofil's hip pressed against his, and Thaddeus felt a shiver of attraction shoot through him. The contact between them eased Thaddeus's troubled mind, and he relaxed a bit.

"We might want to camp here tonight," Teofil said.

Fetter looked straight up at the thick canopy of leaves. "I can't see the sun. Is it very late?"

"We've been walking a good number of hours," Teofil said. "And we left later than expected due to the fog. I think we might want to take advantage of what little light we have left to make camp and build a fire." He nodded off to one side, where Thaddeus could see a small clearing between a few trees. "Besides, I think that's a fairy circle over there, and I'd like to see if any wood fairies show up. I might be able to get some directions from them."

"Wood fairies?" Astrid squinted as she peered into the trees. "Can we trust wood fairies? They like to play tricks."

"That's what people say about gnomes too," Fetter said.

Astrid gave her brother a narrow-eyed look, and then asked Teofil, "I'm serious. Do you think we can trust wood fairies to give us proper directions? They might enjoy watching us stumble around in a circle."

Teofil smiled at her. "After living at Leopold's house with just the fairies for company, I've learned a few tricks about talking with them."

Astrid grunted and looked off into the trees again.

"Must have been tough for you," Thaddeus said. "Lonely."

"Just like it's been for you," Teofil replied.

Thaddeus nodded and looked away. "I had my dad to lean on, at least."

"My folks came by," Teofil said. "Not very often, but enough to let me know they hadn't forgotten about me. No one ever told me why I was staying at Leopold's house or tending to his garden. I just knew it was an important task, so that helped me from missing them too much. Besides, they had a lot to contend with on their end, raising the rest of my brothers and sisters." He smiled at Astrid and Fetter in turn. "They're kind of a handful, in case you haven't noticed."

"They sold you, you know," Fetter said.

Thaddeus looked at him, surprised at the flat, unemotional tone to Fetter's voice. He might just have said "I wish it was a sunny day," or "I had a mooshberry for lunch," instead of something so shocking.

"Sold him?" Astrid wrinkled her nose. "What do you mean?"

"They made a deal with Leopold." Fetter shrugged. "I was never clear what it was for, but I knew it was important. I overheard them talking just before they came to take you. You were always the best with the plants, and Leopold needed someone to keep his garden alive. It wasn't going to be a short-term thing, either. I could tell that much from what they'd said. And then Leopold handed over a bag of coins before he left.

"You were very young, if I remember. Two or three years old, but they could tell you had a special touch with garden plants. Anyway, the next day, Dad took you for a walk and you didn't come home. We asked about you, but all they said was you were away on a special mission. I asked and asked and asked about it, until Dad threatened to tan my backside but good if I mentioned you again. So, I stopped asking. And now, here we are in the Lost Forest, looking for a dragon. Funny how life works out, eh?"

Thaddeus looked at Teofil to see how he was handling this bit of information, but all he could see was Teofil's profile as he stared out through the twisted tree trunks. From the tight line of his lips to the muscle clenched in his jaw, Thaddeus figured this was new information to Teofil.

"Hey," he said in a low voice, and leaned in to bump his shoulder against Teofil's. "You okay?"

"Yes, I'm okay," Teofil replied with a single nod. He turned to flash a tight smile at Thaddeus before he pushed to his feet. "Let's get busy gathering firewood and try to find some leaves for bedding. It will be dark soon."

Finding his strength, Thaddeus got up. His wounded leg ached as if asking him to sit down again, just for a while.

Astrid came up to Teofil and put an arm around his shoulders. "So Mom and Dad sold you to a wizard to be his garden gnome, so what? I bet they got a good price for you."

Teofil laughed and hugged his sister tight, then leaned in to give Thaddeus a quick kiss before he knelt to start digging a fire pit. Astrid moved off into the trees to pick up sticks, and Thaddeus walked in the same direction but with a bit of distance between them. As he picked up branches and dried leaves for the fire, Thaddeus thought about Fetter's revelation. He wondered how he would react to finding out his parents had sold him off for a job. Granted, it turned out it had been a very important job—keeping the drachen narcosis alive so his mother in dragon form remained asleep—but when it came down to it, it still amounted to a kind of slavery, and child slavery at that.

And it wasn't as if secrets hadn't been kept from Thaddeus as well. Secrets like his wizard heritage and that he and his father had moved so many times because some members of the magic community wanted to kill them. And then there was the fact that his mother was still alive, but as a dragon who had been sleeping beneath the garden next door to their latest house. He was pretty sure there were still some secrets his father hadn't told him. He just hoped his father lived long enough to share them with him.

"I guess I upset Teofil."

Thaddeus started and turned to find Fetter standing near him, a pile of sticks in his arms.

"Oh, I don't know," Thaddeus said and went back to his own gathering. He was uncomfortable talking with one of Teofil's siblings about family and relationship matters. He was an only child and didn't know much about navigating waters with unknown depths such as the relationship between siblings in a large family. He wished Fetter had gone off with Astrid and left him alone for some time to think.

"I do that sometimes," Fetter said, then followed it up with, "Well, probably a lot."

Thaddeus gave up on wishing Fetter would move off into another part of the forest and instead asked, "Do what?"

"Say things I shouldn't," Fetter explained. "My family's told me that a lot since I was very small." He picked up a few more sticks. "I remember that day, you know."

Thaddeus frowned. "Which day? The day Teofil went to live with Leopold?"

"No." Fetter looked him in the eye. "The day of the attack on our village. I was only three, but I remember it clearly. Astrid was two, and Teofil was a year old."

"You were all there?" Thaddeus asked.

"We had to run for our lives," Fetter said. "I picked up Teofil and ran as fast as I could. One of the men caught us, a bad wizard named Azzo Eberhard. Mum and Dad told me about him later—said he had gained a lot of dark magic and was supposedly very close with Isadora."

"What happened?" Thaddeus asked. The sticks in his arms were forgotten as was the forest around them. All he could think about was young Fetter, only three years old, running for his life with his baby brother in his arms and how terrified they must have been.

"I got away somehow," Fetter said. "I remember kicking and screaming for help as Azzo dragged me off into the woods. I dropped Teofil somewhere along the way. After that it's a blur, and the next thing I remember is coming out of the woods with Teofil back in my arms."

"Oh my God," Thaddeus said in a quiet voice. "You must have been scared."

"Yeah, I was." Fetter nodded and stared off into the distance, his expression blank and unreadable. Then, just as suddenly, he looked right at Thaddeus and gave him a bright smile. "Anyway, that was a long time ago, right?"

"Well, yeah, I guess," Thaddeus said. Fetter's sudden shift in mood made him feel a little uncomfortable. He couldn't blame him for wanting to put the subject behind them, but the abruptness of the change made him uneasy.

They gathered sticks in silence for a while, and then Fetter spoke once again.

"I've been thinking of our conversation about your dad."

"Oh?" Thaddeus didn't want any more discussion of leaving his father behind. But he didn't want to be rude to Fetter, especially since they were all on this journey because of his family. So he kept quiet and let Fetter talk.

"Remember that story Astrid and I told you about the Lost Forest and the grave of magical beings and the Well of Tears that contains a powerful magic?"

Thaddeus nodded and picked up another stick. "I do."

Fetter moved closer to Thaddeus and lowered his voice. "What if we tried to get Teofil to ask the wood fairies for the location of the Well of Tears instead of a path through the Lost Forest to the mountains? We could take some of the water from the Well of Tears back to your father and heal him with it."

The idea exploded inside Thaddeus's mind like a supernova and filled him with an urgent sense of hope. He didn't know about magic, or levels of magic, but water from the Well of Tears sounded like it might be just the thing they needed to cure his father. Why hadn't he thought of that?

"Do you think it would work?" he asked.

Fetter shrugged. "I don't know. But it's worth a shot if it will save your father's life, isn't it?"

"Oh my God," Thaddeus said, his mind spinning now, imagining them finding the well, pulling up a bucket of its magical water, and then rushing back through the forest and across the grassy plain to his father's side. Tears swamped his eyes, and he barely managed to hold in a sob that, had it escaped, would have embarrassed him for certain.

"Are you all right?" Fetter asked.

Thaddeus nodded, not trusting his voice at that moment, and turned his face away. To distract himself, he picked up a few more sticks as he worked to get his emotions in check. When he was ready, he looked at Fetter again and said, "I don't know what to do. We're supposed to be finding my mom... er, the dragon. But my father is very sick. I'm not sure how to ask Teofil something like this."

Fetter smiled. "Let me take care of it. I'm the oldest after all."

"But, shouldn't I ask Teofil about it since it's my father and mother in the balance?"

"Teofil might not like the idea of going off course of our initial mission," Fetter said. "Do you want him angry at you so early in your relationship?"

Thaddeus shook his head. "Oh, no. I guess not." He'd never had anything close to a relationship before, and he'd never dreamed he'd find someone as unique and loving as Teofil. The thought of ruining what they had between them before it really had a chance to grow made Thaddeus feel ill. "You don't mind asking about it?"

"We're all in this together, right?" Fetter said.

Thaddeus nodded and smiled. "That's right."

"I'll ask once we get the fire going and have some food." Fetter tipped his head toward the place where Teofil worked on the fire pit. "Come on, let's take this wood back and look for leaves for bedding."

Thaddeus followed Fetter through the undergrowth. He clutched the sticks in his arms tight, and he was careful to watch where he stepped so he didn't fall again. His leg felt stiff, and his injured palm ached a bit. Now and then the mixture Miriam had spread over the wounds on his hand seemed to get deeper into his system and sting as it attacked more germs. But that was minor compared to his combined excitement and anxiety over the possibility of finding the Well of Tears. If only it weren't such a life-and-death decision between his father and his mother, Thaddeus might not be so anxious.

Teofil smiled at him when Thaddeus dropped his armload of sticks near the fire pit, and he tried to smile back, but he was a bit too nervous to pull it off. Instead, he went about gathering fern leaves to use for bedding as his thoughts went back and forth between trying to save his father and continuing the search for his mother.

Chapter FIVE

THE FIRE crackled and popped as the smoke curled up toward the heavy canopy of leaves. All around them, the darkness crouched as if just waiting for the fire to die down so it could fall upon them. Thaddeus shuddered at this thought and shifted a bit closer to Teofil. They ate the last of the mooshberries they had packed, and then Astrid brought out some wild carrots she had uncovered while looking for bedding, and they all munched happily.

Even as he filled his belly, though, Thaddeus was nervous. Fetter had promised to ask Teofil about changing the course of their travels to find the Well of Tears instead of getting through the Lost Forest and closer to the mountain range in search of his mother. It was a long shot, Thaddeus knew this, but if it meant his father would live, it was a risk worth taking, in his opinion. He only hoped Teofil would feel the same way.

A sliver of guilt slid into him at the idea of Fetter broaching the subject instead of Thaddeus himself. It might be better if he stepped up and took responsibility for the idea since it involved a choice between his parents, even though it might mean Teofil would be angry with him. When he thought it through, really considered how it had come to this point, he realized it had truly been Fetter's idea. As he sat crunching absently on a carrot, Thaddeus went back and forth between wanting to ask Teofil himself and hoping Fetter would just ask and get it over with.

"You're deep in thought," Teofil said.

"What?" Thaddeus asked, startled out of his contemplation. "Oh. Yeah, I guess I am."

"Care to share?" Teofil asked.

Thaddeus looked away. "Just thinking, that's all. Nothing important enough to say aloud." A muscle in his neck cramped, and he tipped his head side to side to stretch it out. He didn't think he'd ever get used to sleeping on the ground.

A tiny light zipped into view. It circled a foot or so above their heads a few times, then flew off through the trees in the direction of the clearing Teofil had noticed earlier.

"The fairies have arrived," Astrid said as she licked mooshberry juice from her fingers. She leveled a look at Teofil. "Don't get us lost, big brother."

Teofil smiled at her. "Have I led us astray yet?"

Astrid waved to the trees surrounding them. "No idea. Every stupid tree in here looks like every other stupid tree."

"Careful how you talk about the forest with wood fairies around," Fetter said. "If they hear you, they'll give us bad directions for sure. Or worse."

Astrid waved at him dismissively and then turned away to start putting together the leaves she had gathered for her bedding.

"Brother dear, a word if I may?" Fetter asked, pushing to his feet and brushing the dirt and leaves off the seat of his trousers.

Thaddeus watched Teofil stand, noticing the thin line of his lips and the muscle twitching in his jaw. Teofil was more than likely still sore at Fetter for his hurtful comment about their parents selling him to Leopold. Thaddeus wondered how Teofil would receive Fetter's request for a change in direction, and the mooshberries and carrots rolled within his nervous stomach. He swallowed hard and watched the brothers walk a short distance into the trees.

"You all right?" Astrid asked.

"What?" Thaddeus looked at her. "Yes. Of course. Why?"

"You look pale, and you're acting kind of twitchy and nervous," Astrid said. "Just wanted to make sure you felt all right."

Thaddeus let out a breath. "I do. Thanks." He looked over to where Fetter and Teofil were talking, saw Teofil fold his arms over his broad chest and narrow his eyes.

Astrid followed his gaze. "What are they talking about, I wonder?"

"Can't be sure," Thaddeus replied.

"Doesn't look like Teofil likes it, whatever it is," Astrid said.

"Yeah, it does look that way, doesn't it?" Thaddeus agreed.

"No!" Teofil said suddenly, his tone sharp and his voice loud.

"Oh God," Thaddeus said with a moan. He'd agreed to Fetter's suggestion, and now Teofil would know and be upset with both of them. He'd never wished harder to be able to take back a decision than at that moment. Why had he agreed to allow Fetter to broach the subject of switching the goal of their journey? The Well of Tears was a legend, for goodness' sake, a story passed down from generation to generation. No one even knew whether or not it really existed.

"What's wrong with you?" Astrid asked. She looked from Thaddeus to where Fetter and Teofil stood arguing and back again. "What's going on? You know something. Tell me."

"Fetter's suggesting that Teofil ask the wood fairies for directions to the Well of Tears instead of a route through the Lost Forest."

"What?" Astrid was on her feet in a moment. "When was this decided?"

Thaddeus stood up as well, holding his hands out to Astrid in an effort to get her to stop. Panic surged within him, making his heart pound and his breath come in short pants. "No, no, no. Astrid, you can't get involved. Let them figure it out."

"Forget that," Astrid said and stomped up to her brothers. "Hey! We should all have a say in where we go."

"Astrid, calm down," Fetter said.

"I'll calm down when I'm good and ready to calm down!" Astrid shouted at him. "And I'm not yet ready to calm down. Is what Thaddeus told me true?"

Thaddeus groaned and walked up to stand just behind Fetter, his arms tight over his chest and his gaze hopping around from place to place, looking at anything and everything except for Teofil. He didn't know if he could take receiving an angry look from him. Or, even worse, a disappointed one.

"I don't know what Thaddeus told you," Fetter said in a condescending tone of voice. "So I can't tell you if it's true."

Astrid glared at him a moment, then pointed at Thaddeus who hovered just behind Fetter's shoulder, causing Thaddeus to flinch. "He told me you're suggesting that Teofil ask the wood fairies to tell us how to get to the Well of Tears instead of how to get through the Lost Forest."

"Then, yes, it's true," Fetter said.

Astrid crossed her arms. "I think it's a bad idea."

"As do I," Teofil said. "We have to find Thaddeus's mother."

"But his father is dying," Fetter said, waving a hand toward Thaddeus. "We all know it. Why aren't we talking about it?"

Teofil's voice was low and cold as he replied, "Because we care about Thaddeus and don't want him to feel any more guilty than he already does about leaving his dad. We have a mission, Fetter, and an important one. In case you've forgotten, there's a dragon loose in the world, and Thaddeus is the only person who's lived through a face-to-face encounter with it."

"What?" Thaddeus peered around Fetter's shoulder at Teofil. "What do you mean?"

"Later, Thaddeus," Teofil said.

"Yes, Thaddeus," Fetter said as he glared at Teofil. "Let your boyfriend brush off your question as he makes his point about allowing your father to die a horrible, painful death from troll poison."

Teofil glared at Fetter, fists clenched at his sides. "That's not what I meant. You're twisting my words."

"Am I?" Fetter took a step closer to Teofil. "Or have you simply assumed the role of leader of our happy little band of travelers and started making our decisions because you were special enough to be sold off to Leopold?"

"Stop!" Thaddeus shouted and put up his hands as if he were being arrested. Silence thick with tension fell over them, and he took three long breaths before he found the courage to step around Fetter and face Teofil. "Fetter is right. I wanted to come ask you to talk to the wood fairies about directions to the Well of Tears. My father is very sick, and I know this may be difficult for you to understand, but he's more real to me than my mother. I understand the threat she presents to the world in her current form, I really do, but my father is dying."

Thaddeus's voice caught in his throat, and he dropped his gaze to stare at the ground until he had his emotions under control. When he looked back up at Teofil, he was glad to find that his features had softened somewhat. "We all know he's dying, Teofil, there's no denying it. And he's all I've got left. So if you ask me if his life is more important to me than tracking down a dragon that just happens to be my mother under some kind of spell, then I would have to say yes. His one life is more important to me than all of that. He's the only family I have."

Teofil looked at him in silence for so long Thaddeus started to worry his words might trigger a backlash of sorts, the complete opposite of what he'd intended. Finally, Teofil gave Thaddeus a nod, then looked at Fetter and Astrid.

"Do you agree with Thaddeus?" Teofil asked.

"I do," Fetter hastily replied. "The fairies are gathering in the circle, Teofil, we don't have much time."

Astrid looked off into the woods to where Thaddeus could see more of the fairies, glowing like fireflies, floating toward the small clearing. She looked at Thaddeus a moment, then at Teofil and gave a single nod. "I agree. If I stood where he stands, I would most likely choose the same."

"So be it." Teofil turned to stride off into the woods without a second glance at Thaddeus.

Thaddeus's heart raced as he watched Teofil make his way through the trees. He was concerned not just about his father—and his mother, for that matter—but also about this strange and precarious place he suddenly found himself: in a relationship. And not just any normal kind of relationship, but one with a gnome, of all things, surrounded by danger and close family members.

He was certainly out of his depth of experience. But as Teofil stepped into the clearing within the trees and dropped to one knee with his head lowered, a rush of attraction flooded Thaddeus, leaving him momentarily breathless. The simple gesture of Teofil paying his respects to the wood fairies was so gallant and chivalrous, it made Thaddeus appreciate him even more.

And he hoped, with every part of himself, that his insistence on seeking out the Well of Tears instead of his mother, and having Fetter ask for him instead of broaching the subject himself, hadn't lessened Teofil's opinion of him. Thaddeus didn't know what he would do if this exciting and amazing new relationship he had just discovered ended so soon because of something he did.

As he watched Teofil's broad back, just visible from the light of their campfire, the small glowing shapes of the wood fairies circled his head. Some zipped fast and angry, like disturbed hornets, buzzing past his ears and the side of his face. But Teofil held very still, head bowed, one arm resting across his upraised knee, waiting for the right time.

"The wood fairies look kind of angry," Astrid said in a quiet voice.

"He can do it," Fetter whispered. "He's got a lot of experience talking with fairies."

"He does," Thaddeus said. "I used to watch him from my bedroom window at night. The fairies would circle his head the whole time he worked in the yard. I thought they were fireflies at first."

"How could you confuse a fairy with a firefly?" Astrid asked.

Before Thaddeus could reply, a familiar sound came to him from the fairy circle, and it made him smile. Teofil was humming. It made Thaddeus think back to the nights before he'd actually met Teofil, when he would lie in bed and the sound of Teofil humming as he gardened would lull him to sleep. Now, the sound comforted him and made him feel as if, despite all the odds stacked against them, everything just might turn out all right.

The fairies stopped flying around Teofil and arranged themselves into a line in front of him. Astrid took Thaddeus's hand as they watched Teofil slowly lift his head to look at the fairies. This was it. Teofil was about to talk to the wood fairies and ask for directions to the Well of Tears. Thaddeus just hoped the wood fairies took enough pity on them not to lead them astray.

After what felt to Thaddeus like hours but was most likely only thirty minutes, Teofil returned to the fire.

"Well?" Fetter asked.

"What did they say?" Astrid added.

Teofil looked at them, then fixed his gaze on Thaddeus. "They've given us directions to the Well of Tears."

Thaddeus let out a relieved breath and a laugh. Fetter clapped his hands together and smiled at Thaddeus. Even though he was glad to be doing something to help his father, Thaddeus still felt anxious as he wondered if Teofil would be angry with him.

Teofil sat to Thaddeus's right, leaving a little space between them. He didn't say anything, just stared into the flames, lost in thought.

"Hey, are you all right?" Thaddeus asked.

Teofil nodded. "I am. It's just…." He looked up at him, and his expression was so sad Thaddeus felt a cold blade of regret push into his gut. "I wish you had felt you could talk to me about the change of direction."

Thaddeus glanced across the fire to where Astrid and Fetter seemed to be trying not to listen in. He scooted closer to Teofil and lowered his voice. "I'm very sorry for not asking you myself. I should have, I know that. But the risks that come with the change and the newness of what we have between us made me doubt myself."

"Not just yourself but me too," Teofil said. "As if you didn't think I would hear you out."

Thaddeus dropped his head and closed his eyes. Regret built within him, brick by remorseful brick. He took a breath and lifted his head to look into Teofil's beautiful blue eyes. "You're right. I didn't put faith in you as well as myself. I apologize."

Teofil nodded as he held Thaddeus's gaze. "You're very important to me. I want you to be able to trust me."

"I want that for both of us," Thaddeus replied. "I'm sorry."

Teofil's smile was small, but it filled Thaddeus with hope and relief. "Apology accepted," Teofil said.

Thaddeus smiled back and turned his gaze to the fire. A host of emotions swarmed him, and he doubted he would be able to get much sleep that night.

"Are you two all made up now?" Astrid asked with a smile.

"Never you mind," Teofil replied. "Pass me a mooshberry if you haven't eaten them all."

"Not many left," Astrid said as she handed him a berry. "We should try to save a few."

"We'll find more," Teofil said. "And we'll need our strength for where we're going."

"Oh?" Thaddeus asked and felt a chill go up his spine. "Dangerous?"

Teofil nodded. "The fairies weren't specific but told me some of what we can expect."

"And?" Fetter asked.

"It's going to be harder than finding a path to the other side of the Lost Forest," Teofil replied. He looked at them each in turn, finishing with Thaddeus. "We should all try to get some good sleep tonight."

"You're scaring me a bit," Thaddeus said with a nervous laugh.

"Good," Teofil said. "We'll all need to be cautious. I'll take first watch and the rest of you can get some sleep."

They were silent as they stretched out on beds of fern leaves and moss. Thaddeus listened to the crackle of the fire and the sounds of small animals moving among the trees. His heart pounded and his mind raced as he imagined all sorts of dangerous creatures waiting for them deeper in the Lost Forest. Thaddeus fell into an uneasy sleep where animals with sharp claws and long fangs stalked him from the shadows of the woods.

Chapter SIX

"IT'S LIKE a never-ending dream," Fetter said as he squeezed between two tall trees coated with black bark. "It just goes on and on and on."

Thaddeus didn't think he could fit between the trees, so he stepped around the side of one of them and right into a slick, messy pocket of mud. His foot became trapped, and he had to brace himself against the moss covered tree to keep from falling on his face.

"Oh, gross," he said.

Teofil and Fetter stopped ahead of him and turned to look back.

"What's wrong?" Teofil asked.

"My foot's stuck," Thaddeus said. He tried to pull it free, but despite his best efforts it remained locked in place. "It's like a suction or something. I can't get it out."

Teofil crouched and inspected the dark, thick substance Thaddeus had stepped in.

"What is it?" Astrid asked from over Thaddeus's shoulder. "Ugh. It stinks."

"I don't think it's just a simple mud puddle," Fetter said.

"I think you're right," Teofil agreed. "It's something else."

"Is it tree sap?" Astrid asked. She walked around the tree, looking closely at the moss and bark. "This isn't the right type of tree for something like that."

"It's not like any tree sap I've ever seen," Teofil said.

"Okay, so we've ruled out tree sap and mud," Thaddeus grumbled. "Can we maybe get my foot out of it and then figure out what it is?"

Teofil looked up at him and grinned, and Thaddeus relaxed somewhat and grinned back.

"Getting a little spooked having your foot stuck in there?" Teofil asked.

"Not funny," Thaddeus replied.

Teofil got up and bent at the waist. He wrapped his big hands around Thaddeus's calf and tugged on it.

"Lean on my back," Teofil instructed.

Thaddeus put one hand on Teofil's back and the other on the trunk of the tree. He could feel the muscles of Teofil's back tighten and release as Teofil pulled on his leg. Fetter joined in, and then Astrid, and, finally, with a great shout of effort from all four of them, Thaddeus's foot pulled free of the sticky substance. He stumbled backward and fell on his butt, his teeth clicking together hard enough to make his eyes water.

"Are you hurt?" Teofil asked as he knelt beside him.

Thaddeus shook his head. "No. Just a little unsteady. What the heck is that stuff?"

"It's definitely something unusual," Fetter said as he inspected it. He looked up at Thaddeus. "Did your shoe come off?"

"No, thank goodness," Thaddeus said, shaking his foot. It was coated with a heavy layer of the sticky stuff and felt twice as heavy as the other. "It's just covered with that gunk."

"Quiet a moment," Astrid said. She stood very still, her arms extended and palms held up toward them. "Listen."

They all stopped, and Thaddeus strained to hear something, but the woods were silent.

"I don't hear anything," Thaddeus whispered.

"Exactly," Astrid said, looking at Teofil with wide eyes. "No bird song or animals moving through the underbrush. It's all silent."

"Astrid's right," Fetter said and looked around. "Something's wrong."

Teofil reached down to help Thaddeus to his feet and put an arm around his waist to support him. Thaddeus took comfort from their connection and leaned against him as he wiped his shoe back and forth along the ground in an effort to clean off the sticky residue.

"Something is out there," Astrid said with a tremor in her quiet voice.

Thaddeus stopped moving his foot, and they all stood very still, listening. Then he heard it. From a short distance away, he could hear the muffled sound of someone crying for help.

"Someone's in trouble," Thaddeus said.

"I heard it. This way!" Astrid ran off through the trees.

"Astrid!" Teofil shouted. "Wait!"

"I'll go after her," Fetter said. "Stay here with Thaddeus."

"I'm fine," Thaddeus assured Teofil. "Go after them."

Teofil looked off to where Fetter sprinted after Astrid, then back at Thaddeus. "Are you sure?"

"Yes, I'm sure. Go."

Teofil gave Thaddeus a quick kiss on the lips, then ran off. Thaddeus's lips tingled from the kiss as he listened to Teofil run through the underbrush. He sat on a log and inspected the gunk covering his shoe, then collected a handful of fern fronds and tried to wipe it off. A good portion of the gunk came off onto the fern leaves, but his shoe was still sticky with it.

As he reached for another handful of leaves, Thaddeus heard Astrid scream and got to his feet. Before he knew it, he was running in the direction he had seen them all go. After he'd run about thirty yards, he came to a sudden stop when he heard something big roar from deeper within the forest directly ahead of him.

"What the hell was that?" he said to himself as chills prickled across his scalp.

Fetter bounded out from between a couple of trees, his eyes wide and his face pale as he ran toward him. "Run!"

Thaddeus took several steps back but continued facing him. "Where are Teofil and Astrid?"

"Run!" Fetter shouted again, hurrying past him.

"Teofil!" Thaddeus called. He took a step forward but hesitated. Then, with a curse, he ignored Fetter's suggestion and started running toward the spot where he had last seen Teofil and Astrid.

The roar came again, louder now, and up ahead he could hear Teofil shouting at Astrid to move.

"He's not free yet!" Astrid shouted back.

"Go!" Teofil yelled. "Now!"

Thaddeus made his way through a thick grouping of trees and stopped. Teofil and Astrid knelt beside a small, pale man who seemed to have both feet stuck in the same sticky gunk that had trapped Thaddeus. They each held one of the man's legs and were pulling up as hard as they could. Somewhere deeper in the forest, Thaddeus heard the crack of trees snapping and the roar of whatever was approaching.

He clenched his fists, swallowed hard, and ran up to them. "Let me help."

"Thaddeus!" Teofil shouted up at him. "You shouldn't be here."

Thaddeus dropped to his knees behind the pale man and grabbed him under the arms. He felt a snap, and a tingle shot through him when he touched the man, making Thaddeus jump a bit. Another roar sounded, and Thaddeus put aside his surprise and grabbed the man under the arms again to start pulling. Slowly, painfully slowly, the pale man's feet began to pull free of the thick, sticky goo.

Looking down at the top of the pale man's head, Thaddeus noticed his fine blond hair hanging halfway down his slender back and his pointed ears, and thought *I'm holding on to an elf,* just as the elf's feet came free and they all tumbled backward.

"Thank you," the elf said. "Oh, thank you."

"Thank us later," Teofil said. "Everyone run!"

They all got up and started to run, but the elf cried out. "My feet are sticking to the ground!"

Astrid ran back and turned around so he could jump on her back. Holding him piggyback style, she ran ahead of Teofil and Thaddeus just as something big pushed down the last of the trees that stood between it and them.

The air left Thaddeus's lungs in a rush, and his feet seemed rooted in place as he stared at the monstrosity before him. Pale and soft-bodied, it was ten feet tall and twice that wide. Small eyes, black as pitch, stood out in contrast to its white body. The mouth was a beak, serrated along the edges, and tiny hands stuck out from the slick flesh beneath it, pushing against trees and grabbing at everything in its path. It was like a giant maggot with the beak of a squid and small, pale hands.

"Reaper grub," Teofil said, grabbing Thaddeus by the hand and pulling him along. "Killers."

"I've never seen anything like it," Thaddeus said as he ran behind Teofil. He glanced back to see the reaper grub slithering through the underbrush after them, black eyes shining and beak parting to emit its deep, terrifying roar.

"They pretty much stay here in the Lost Forest," Teofil explained. "Sunlight burns their skin. They can burrow a hole crazy fast, and stories say they've wiped out entire villages. That's how they got their name."

"It's still coming after us," Thaddeus said after another look back. "We'll never outrun it."

"You won't have to." Astrid stepped out from behind a tree. She held her slingshot and swung it high over her head, her face set in grim determination as she watched the reaper grub approach.

Thaddeus and Teofil stopped a dozen feet behind her and turned to watch as they caught their breath. Movement in the underbrush to Thaddeus's right caught his attention, and he looked over to see the elf they had rescued hanging by his legs from a tree branch, a bow and arrow in his hand.

The reaper grub closed in on them. Just when Thaddeus was about to shout at Astrid to get out of the way, she let the rock in her slingshot fly. At almost the same time, the elf fired his arrow, and both shots hit their marks. Astrid's rock punctured the reaper grub's right eye, while the elf's arrow took out the left. The roar that followed nearly deafened them, and Thaddeus dropped into a crouch and covered his ears. The reaper grub flailed, banging against trees and bringing down leaves and branches on itself. A large branch snapped right above the reaper grub's head. It fell, splintered end down, and impaled the monster. With a shudder that shook its entire fleshy body, the reaper grub collapsed and heaved a final, horrible-smelling breath. The tiny arms beneath its gnashing beak trembled, stiffened, and then went lax.

"Wow," Thaddeus said, straightening up and staring at the mammoth grub not twenty feet away.

"Those things smell awful," Astrid mumbled as she turned to them. "You stepped in its spit, you know."

Thaddeus sneered and looked down at his foot. "I did?"

"It leaves puddles of it around to trap prey," Teofil explained. "Then follows the scent of its spit on a continuous circuit." He looked at Astrid and shook his head. "I never even thought of a reaper grub."

"Me neither," she said. "I've never seen one before, only heard tales of them."

A throat cleared from behind Thaddeus, and they all looked to find the elf standing there. He stood only as high as Thaddeus's waist, about three and a half feet, and his blond hair seemed to gather what little sunlight managed to make its way through the heavy canopy of leaves, shimmering like spun gold. His eyes were brilliant green, and tiny specks of light sparkled within the wide irises.

"I give you thanks a many for saving my life," the elf said sweeping into a deep bow, his hair piling on the leaves beneath him.

"You are quite welcome," Teofil said. "I am Teofil, of the garden gnome Rhododendron clan. This is my sister Astrid, and my boyfriend Thaddeus."

Thaddeus's heart seemed to jump at Teofil's introduction, but he managed to keep his wits about him enough to nod to the elf once he had straightened up. Never before had someone called him "boyfriend!"

"I am Dulindir," the elf said. "Son of Tulusdir and Celeblaswen."

"What tribe do you belong to?" Teofil asked.

Dulindir dropped his gaze and clutched his hands together before him. "I have been cast out of my tribe."

"Cast out?" Astrid stepped closer. "What for?"

"I fell in love with a non-elf female," Dulindir admitted.

Astrid and Teofil exchanged a "so what?" look, and then Astrid asked, "They banished you for that?"

Dulindir lifted his gaze and nodded once. "It is not permitted within elf culture. There are strict rules."

"I guess we gnomes have it easier than I thought," Astrid said and waved toward Thaddeus and Teofil. "These two are in love, and Thaddeus is a human. Well, a wizard. But still, he's not a gnome."

"Love?" Thaddeus said, his cheeks and ears burning. "Well, I don't know about that. I mean, we like each other."

Astrid waved his protests aside, and Thaddeus risked a glance at Teofil, surprised to find him blushing as well. Could Astrid have been right? Did Teofil love him? Did he love Teofil?

Before Thaddeus could pursue that thought much further, Astrid's next question to Dulindir gathered his attention.

"Have you been on your own very long?" Astrid asked.

"One hundred years," Dulindir replied.

"Oh my God," Thaddeus blurted. "That long?"

Dulindir nodded. "It has been a long time. And I do get lonely."

Before any of them could say another word, Fetter stepped out from behind a tree and gasped at the sight of the dead reaper grub. "You killed a reaper grub?"

"Dulindir and I did," Astrid replied. "No thanks to you."

"What?" Fetter asked.

"You ran off without helping us get him free," Teofil said, frowning at Fetter.

"I thought you said run," Fetter explained. "So I ran."

Teofil shook his head and looked at Dulindir. "You're welcome to join us if you have a mind to. We're traveling to the Well of Tears."

Dulindir's green eyes widened. "The Well of Tears? Whatever for?"

"My father has been poisoned by a troll," Thaddeus said. "I want to take some of the water back to heal him."

"Troll poison is very powerful," Dulindir said. "How long has it been?"

"Three days," Thaddeus replied.

"You're running short on time." Dulindir shook his head. "Very short. Which way are you going?"

Teofil turned and pointed. "The wood fairies told us to continue in this direction—"

"You listened to wood fairies?" Dulindir asked. "They love tricks and misdirection."

"Isn't that what they say about elves?" Fetter asked.

"Elves are mischievous, yes," Dulindir replied. "But not when someone's life is at stake." He turned in a slow circle, scanning the thick trunks of the trees that surrounded them.

"Well?" Astrid asked. "Did they trick us?"

"I don't believe so," Dulindir replied. "But I can lead you there as repayment for saving my life."

"It's not necessary," Teofil said. "But we would be grateful if you would."

"Have you been to the Well of Tears?" Astrid asked as Dulindir struck out in roughly the same direction they had been heading before Thaddeus got his foot stuck.

"I was born and raised in the village near there," Dulindir replied.

"What?" All four of them said at once.

Dulindir turned to face them and gave a single, grave nod. "I was banished before the illness took hold of the village and before the Well of Tears was built. I haven't been back since, but I remember all too well the way home. Come, it will be dark soon, and we have far to travel."

Thaddeus exchanged a surprised look with Teofil and then fell in step behind Astrid as Teofil followed him, and Fetter brought up the rear.

Chapter SEVEN

IT SEEMED as if the rain would never stop. It fell so hard it made its way through the heavy canopy of leaves and onto the five of them as they picked a path through the undergrowth and around the trees. The rain drenched their hair and dribbled down the backs and fronts of their shirts. It soaked them through until Thaddeus was shivering as he walked.

"This is miserable," he muttered. "I don't think I've ever been this wet. Not even in a shower."

Teofil chuckled from behind him. "You're funny."

Thaddeus snorted. "Thanks. But I'm kind of serious."

"It's a heavy storm, all right," Dulindir called back from the front of their group where he led them through the trees. His long blond hair lay plastered to his head and around his pointed ears.

"The sun's gone down already, hasn't it?" Fetter asked from the rear of the group behind Teofil. "Are we going to stop for the night?"

"What's the point?" Teofil asked in response. "We can't light a fire in all this rain; there's no dry wood. We might as well keep walking."

"It's going to be very dark soon," Fetter said. "How will we see?"

"I can gather the starlight and project it around us," Dulindir offered. "That should provide us enough illumination to continue our quest."

"Great," Fetter grumbled. "Starlight from an elf. In the rain."

They walked for a bit longer until it was so dark Thaddeus could not see a foot ahead. He realized just how dark it had become when he walked into Teofil, who had come to a stop in front of him.

"Sorry," Thaddeus said.

"It's okay." Teofil fumbled for Thaddeus's hand and squeezed it. "How about some of that starlight, Dulindir?"

"It takes a moment," Dulindir called from a short distance ahead. "You mean gnomes can't see as well in the dark as elves?"

"We can grow a hell of a nicer garden," Fetter replied.

"Not much help out here, is that?" Dulindir responded in a snarky tone.

"Now, now boys," Astrid said, and a moment later, Thaddeus heard her sigh as she sat down. "Take a load off while Dulindir conjures up the starlight."

Thaddeus hesitated before sitting down. He was already wet from the rain, but did he really want to sit on the drenched ground and let the cold soak into him? As if reading his thoughts, Teofil tugged on his hand and directed him to a fallen log a few feet away.

"Can you see very well in this dark?" Thaddeus asked.

"Better than you can, I think." Teofil put an arm around him and pulled him close. Thaddeus sighed at the warmth of Teofil's touch soaking through his wet jeans and shirt. "There's a spell to conjure up a floating ball of light, you know."

"Oh yeah?" Thaddeus let out a sigh. "I've got a lot to learn. I can't even begin to imagine casting a spell."

"You're smart. You'll pick it up quick," Teofil said.

Thaddeus nodded, then remembered how dark it was and said, "I hope so."

"You'll get it," Teofil assured him. "Why so unsure?"

"It's just that I've only recently learned this about myself, you know? And the one person who might be able to teach me how to conjure spells is my father, and he's really sick right now. For all we know, he could have died already and this side trip is just a distraction." Sudden, hot tears surprised Thaddeus, and he wiped stubbornly at his eyes. "Sorry. I didn't mean to get all emo on you."

"What's emo?" Teofil asked.

Thaddeus couldn't help a smile. "It's short for emotional. Basically I was acting more than a little emotional. Sorry."

"You're not a bit emo," Teofil said, pulling him into a hug. "And you're allowed to be scared. I'm scared, and I bet, if Astrid and Fetter were truthful, they would tell you they're scared as well."

"He's right," Fetter said from not very far away on Thaddeus's side.

"We are," Astrid added from Teofil's side.

Thaddeus groaned at the knowledge Teofil's siblings had been listening to him but managed to mumble, "Thanks," in spite of his embarrassment. He considered that the worst part of a journey—perhaps even more than the need to sleep outdoors in any weather condition, go to the bathroom in the woods, and find their own food—was the lack of privacy. He and his father had always given each other their own space, and with no siblings to share his room or his father's attention, he'd had it pretty easy. While on one hand it was nice to have been included in Teofil's family so quickly—and he was grateful to them for accompanying him on this journey his family had brought about—it was also more than a little overwhelming to deal with the high emotions that ran between Teofil, Astrid, and Fetter.

And now they'd added an elf to their group, and Thaddeus had discovered that elves and gnomes appeared to be a bit standoffish with each other.

As he thought about Dulindir, Thaddeus suddenly realized he could see Teofil beside him, Fetter off to his right, and Astrid to Teofil's left. The humid air around them seemed to be alive with light, and he could now see the fern fronds quivering beneath the rainfall.

"I can see!" Thaddeus exclaimed.

"Hey, me too," Astrid said.

They looked to where Dulindir stood a bit farther off. His blond hair shone in the dark, and Thaddeus realized the light was being emitted from the elf's long locks.

"You're projecting starlight from your hair?" Thaddeus asked, feeling just a bit ridiculous at the question.

"I am," Dulindir said with a smile. "It's a little trick we forest elves have kept secret. Our hair is our source of power."

"Like Samson," Thaddeus said.

"Who's Samson?" Teofil asked.

"Is he a wizard?" Astrid followed up.

Thaddeus was surprised for a moment at their lack of knowledge of the Bible, then remembered they were not human. His father had not raised him to be at all religious, but Thaddeus had picked up Bible stories from the few friends he'd had as he'd grown up in the different towns where they'd lived. He could still recall the surprised expression on some of their faces when they found out he didn't attend church and had never read the Bible. For some of them, that had marked the end of their friendship, and that never failed to make Thaddeus feel like more of an outcast than usual.

"It's a Bible story," Thaddeus said. "Samson's strength came from his hair."

"What's a Bible story?" Astrid asked.

Thaddeus took a breath and tried to think of a way to describe it. Then he decided he was too tired to try. "I'll explain that another time. Now that we can see, should we continue walking?"

Fetter and Astrid groaned, but Teofil got them on their feet, and they resumed following Dulindir through the wet forest, the light from his hair like a beacon among the dark trees.

Some time later Thaddeus realized the ground he stepped on felt spongy and soft. Then his next step rewarded him with a splash and water up to his ankle.

"It's flooding," he said, coming to a halt. Ahead of him, Astrid stopped and looked down, her eyes heavily lidded, and Thaddeus assumed she had been half asleep as she walked. Teofil came up behind him, and Fetter followed a moment later.

"Great," Fetter said. "The forest is flooding?"

"It's not the forest," Dulindir called from a few yards ahead. "It's the Wretched River coming over its banks."

"The Wretched River?" Fetter repeated. "We're way the hell out of our way, aren't we?"

Guilt tried to flare up within Thaddeus. They were lost, and it was all because he'd wanted to take this detour. He tamped down the guilt, for now, and made himself focus on the issue at hand. There were more important things to deal with, like how they were going to ford a flooded river—especially one named the Wretched River—in the dark.

"How deep is the river?" Thaddeus asked.

"Come up here and see for yourselves," Dulindir replied.

Moving slowly, Thaddeus waded to where Dulindir stood on a large rock staring into the darkness. They clambered up beside him and peered ahead. At first Thaddeus had no idea what he was seeing. The dark ground ahead of them seemed to be shifting and moving in the starlight that Dulindir was reflecting. Then something pale coasted past—surely not a living thing—and Thaddeus realized he was looking at the swiftly moving waters of the Wretched River.

"Oh my God," Thaddeus whispered. "That's all water?"

"We'll never make it across," Fetter said. "It's moving too fast."

"Can we wait it out?" Astrid asked. "It's got to stop raining soon, right?"

"The water's been rising even as we've stood here on this rock," Teofil pointed out. "We'd have to backtrack a long ways to make sure we would be safe before we could wait it out."

"Then how do we cross it?" Thaddeus wondered.

"We swim," Dulindir stated.

"We can't swim across that!" Fetter exclaimed. "We'll be swept away by the current!"

Dulindir turned to him and smiled. "Exactly." Then he jumped down off the rock and strode through the rapidly rising water back the way they had come.

"What does that mean?" Fetter asked. He looked at each of them in turn, and Thaddeus could only shrug in response.

"Let's find out," Teofil said, then jumped down with a splash and started off after Dulindir.

They followed Dulindir until he stopped at a mooshberry bush.

"Oh, good, I'm starved," Astrid said, and she pulled off a big, ripe berry that was as large as her head.

Dulindir snatched the berry out of her hands.

"Hey!" Astrid exclaimed. "That one's mine!"

"Yes, and it's going to keep you from drowning," Dulindir explained. "Not many people know this, but—"

"Mooshberries float!" Teofil finished with a laugh.

Dulindir grinned, and the starlight emanating from his hair seemed to brighten. "We stuff mooshberries into our clothes and float with the current, swimming until we get to the opposite bank."

"But that will put us downriver," Fetter said. "Isn't that out of our way? We'll just have to walk back once we reach the other side."

"We're actually quite a ways north of where we need to be," Dulindir replied as he handed the mooshberry back to Astrid and picked one from the bush for himself. "So this is a good solution."

"Hmph," Fetter said, and even though he didn't look convinced, Thaddeus couldn't help smiling when Fetter reached for a mooshberry of his own.

Not long after, Teofil pulled a length of sturdy vine rope from his pack and they tied themselves together with five feet between them. Thaddeus followed after Dulindir, Astrid, and Teofil as they walked back toward the river. His arms stuck out from his sides due to the many mooshberries he had slipped inside his shirt, and he would have laughed at himself had he not been so scared of what was about to come. The river had spread out even farther from its banks and he found himself wading sooner than expected into the fast-moving water of the Wretched River.

"Prepare yourselves!" Dulindir shouted back to them. Thaddeus could see the glowing sheen of the elf's hair as he waded deeper into the river. "The ground is very soft beneath your feet, and the current is strong. We will be pulled away very quickly."

As if to prove Dulindir's point, the current swirled harder around Thaddeus's legs as he stepped deeper into the water. He forced himself not to consider the dirt and silt finding a way into the wound on his leg, while ahead of him, Dulindir wobbled and pinwheeled his arms in an effort to stay on his feet. The current proved stronger, however, and Dulindir was swept away, his glowing head bobbing along in the black water.

"Dulindir!" Astrid shouted.

"Brace yourselves!" Teofil shouted.

Thaddeus planted his feet, but it was too late. Astrid was pulled into the water and swept away, her scream echoing through the trees. Teofil was able to hold his ground for the span of a few breaths, but the current was too strong, and soon he was pulled off his feet, followed by Thaddeus, and then Fetter. They bounced off tree roots, boulders, and other debris as the water rushed them along. Thaddeus went under several times, but the mooshberries brought him back to the surface, sputtering and coughing. They spun around one another, the vine sometimes tangling in their limbs, and one time becoming caught as Thaddeus and Teofil went to either side of a young sapling. The water tugged at them, filling their mouths and rushing through their clothing as they all dangled in the current, snagged on the tree. The young tree bowed slowly under the force of the current, and foot by foot, the vine slipped up its slender trunk. Branches bent and snapped beneath its progress until, with a great lurch, the vine finally slipped free and they once again spun off downriver.

The glow from Dulindir's hair had lessened somewhat now that they were in the water, but it provided enough illumination for Thaddeus to catch quick glimpses of what he thought was the opposite bank of the river, which was their destination. Trees stood tall and close together, and occasionally Thaddeus saw an animal standing and watching: a deer one time, antlers tall and proud; and a pair of rabbits another time, ears swiveling as they perched on a rock above the rushing water.

"Try to make your way to shore!" Dulindir instructed.

Thaddeus watched as Dulindir began to swim crosswise with the current, his glowing head angling toward solid ground. He tried to direct himself toward shore as well, but the current seemed to have other ideas. Each time he thought he was making progress, he was pulled back to the center of the river.

Then he felt something touch his ankle, and it startled a shout out of him. It had been different than the sensation of branches and undergrowth he had become used to since stepping into the river. This had been the touch of something alive.

"Something's in here," he said. "Under the water with us."

Fetter bounced off a rock and turned to face him, his face pale in the diminished glow of Dulindir's starlight. "I've felt it too. Something's trying to grab me under the water."

"Water sprites!" Dulindir shouted back to them. "Very dangerous! Keep alert!"

Before Thaddeus could call out a question, Dulindir was suddenly pulled beneath the water. With the source of their light swallowed up by the Wretched River, the night pounced on them, leaving them blind as the current spun them farther south.

Chapter EIGHT

THE WRETCHED River had Thaddeus now. It had all of them, really, and in the grip of its strong current, he bumped from tree to tree, the mooshberries inside his clothing bringing him back to the surface each time he went under. The mooshberries absorbed many of the impacts of his journey downriver, keeping his preexisting injuries from suffering worse harm and saving him from fresh bruises or, worse, broken bones. With each bump, however, they became less buoyant and Thaddeus began to struggle to keep his head above water.

"Dulindir!" Astrid shouted from the darkness ahead of him. "Where is he?"

"Something pulled him under," Teofil called out from close to Thaddeus's right.

They were all still bound together with the vine rope, but they weren't close enough to touch. Still, if they could find each other in the darkness and cling together, maybe they could make it to shore.

"Teofil! Grab my hand!" Thaddeus shouted, waving his hand in the dark. He hoped for all of their sakes that gnomes could truly see as well in the dark as Teofil had implied.

"Almost there," Teofil said.

Just as Teofil's fingers grazed his own, Thaddeus felt cold, thin fingers wrap around his ankle. He opened his mouth to shout a warning but was pulled beneath the surface before he could manage it.

The water was murky with dirt, leaves, and other debris. Thaddeus hadn't had a chance to take a proper breath, and his lungs ached as he was carried along underwater. He tried to pull free of whatever held him, but its grip was too strong, and he remained under; not even the mooshberries could get him to the surface now. He looked down but could see nothing in the clouded water. Kicking with his free foot at the fingers around his ankle, Thaddeus tried to pull himself above the surface with his arms, but he wasn't strong enough. Blood pounded in his temples, and he knew that soon, very soon, he would need to open his mouth and try to take a breath. But all he would be able to do was fill his lungs with the cold black water of the Wretched River.

A pale face appeared directly in front of Thaddeus and a shout of surprise nearly ended him. The creature's face was white and smooth, with no nose or ears. Long, pale green strands of hair floated around the head like seaweed, and its lips were a blue slash in its white face. Large, black eyes blinked at him, and gills on the side of its neck pulsed as it breathed.

It was a water sprite, Thaddeus figured. It stared at him as it floated just inches away, its long, limber arms slowly moving back and forth to keep it in place. Thaddeus could still feel fingers around his ankle holding him down, so there were at least two of them. The water sprite in front of him opened its mouth to expose rows of small, sharp teeth, and the smooth, white brow furrowed with anger.

Thaddeus jerked back from it and lifted his free leg to kick out at the water sprite. He caught it in the chest and pushed against it, shoving the sprite away and pushing himself back. The fingers around his ankle loosened, and he managed to pull free. But the water sprite below and out of sight was quick, grabbing for him again, long nails snagging his shoelace and pulling him down as he thrashed for the surface. His lungs burned, his mind and body screaming for air. He could feel his fingers break the surface of the water above him, but he couldn't get his face up high enough to breathe.

Panic fluttered in his chest like a frightened bird. The water swirled around him, dirt and debris stinging his eyes, and he wished he could see well enough to fight back. If only he had a light. His heartbeat banged in his temples as he struggled to keep his mouth closed against the Wretched River. Just when he thought he was done for—that he would drown here and his father would die from the troll poison and his mother would stay forever a dragon—his palms grew warm where they stuck up out of the water, and a sudden light bloomed above him. In the new glow, he could see a water sprite hovering just a few inches away, staring directly at him as if it was just waiting for him to drown. The light that reached down beneath the gloomy surface of the river made the sprite flinch away, and the one holding him loosened its grip enough that Thaddeus was able to yank his foot free.

He broke the surface and drew in a deep breath, coughing and spitting. Someone grabbed the collar of his shirt. He gasped as he coughed, then relaxed when he found Teofil floating beside him.

"Hold on to me," Teofil instructed.

Thaddeus nodded and put an arm around his shoulders, holding on as Teofil tried to paddle closer to shore. Thaddeus had lost track of which shore they needed to be on, so he focused on getting his breath back and trying to help move them forward as much as possible. He could see the vague outline of trees ahead, the flooded river water parting around them.

When he realized he could see some of the shore, Thaddeus looked around, expecting to find Dulindir nearby, his glowing hair lighting their way. But there was no sign of any of the others, and Thaddeus's heart sank. What had happened to Fetter, Astrid, and Dulindir?

He looked up, then did a double take and stared a moment, his hands floating idle as Teofil continued to swim. A glowing ball of light, about the size of a basketball, hovered above them, illuminating their way.

"What is that?" Thaddeus asked.

"I was going to ask you," Teofil replied. "You conjured it."

"What?" Thaddeus stared at him. "I did that?" The brush of a water sprite's fingers along his leg made him kick out, and the movement propelled them closer to shore.

"Keep kicking!" Teofil said, gasping for breath. "We're close. Come on, kick with me."

They clung together and kicked, frothing the water as they angled toward the shore. The ball of light followed along, maintaining a discreet distance about ten feet overhead.

"Where are the others?" Thaddeus asked, pausing for breath between words.

"I don't know," Teofil replied. "One of the water sprites chewed through the rope."

A cold ball of grief spun to life inside Thaddeus, high in his chest, as if it wanted to claw its way up his throat and push out between his lips as a scream. He fought it back and stared up at the light, amazed at what he had conjured and wondering if he could ever do it again. It must have happened when his palms had grown so warm. But he hadn't said any words, just wished for light to be able to see the water sprites. Was that all it took for him to conjure magic? Maybe he did possess magical abilities after all.

But that was small compared to those missing. Once they were on land again they would be able to find the others and pull them from the water. He couldn't even consider that Fetter, Astrid, and Dulindir were dead. Not after all they'd been through. They'd been separated and swept farther downstream, that was all.

It took a long time for them to reach shore, kicking to keep the water sprites away and measuring out their arm strokes. Thaddeus's muscles were burning, especially in his injured leg. The plantain leaves had come off the wounds on his palm, and he'd pretty much given up hope of ever standing on firm ground again when his hand struck a tree branch. He grabbed on to it and directed Teofil to it as well. They pulled themselves from the water, gasping and grunting, helping each other climb over fallen trees and wade through sucking mud until Thaddeus finally fell onto solid ground, panting as he caught his breath.

"Astrid!" Teofil was up on his feet and shouting out over the swiftly moving dark water. "Fetter!"

Thaddeus pushed to his feet and joined him, the ball of light above illuminating the river for a good twenty feet all around them. "Astrid! Fetter! Dulindir!" He pulled the smashed mooshberries from inside his shirt as he shouted out their names, his skin tacky from the berry juice left behind.

"Astrid was swimming toward the spot where Dulindir went under the last I saw them," Teofil said. His voice sounded tight and tense, and Thaddeus wished he could reassure him somehow.

"We'll find them," he said. "They're both really smart and really stubborn."

That got the small smile he was hoping for, and Thaddeus reached out for his hand. "Come on. Let's walk downriver and call out to them some more."

The ball of light followed along with them, hovering over the river as they picked their way around trees and ponding river water on their way downstream. Now and then, Thaddeus looked up at the ball of light, still amazed that he had produced it.

"I was as shocked as you are," Teofil said, catching him staring up at the light. "I didn't know where any of you had gone to, then this ball of light erupted from the water, and I saw your hands splashing the surface. By the time I got to you, your head had popped up." He stopped and tugged on Thaddeus's hand so he would come to a stop as well. "I thought I'd lost you."

Thaddeus nodded. "Me too," he said, hugging him tight. They clung to each other a moment, the light illuminating them.

"Teofil!"

The voice startled them both, and they pulled apart. Astrid and Fetter were carrying Dulindir around a fallen tree. Dulindir's feet dragged and his head hung down. His wet hair was like a thick curtain that obscured his face.

"Astrid!" Teofil shouted. "Fetter!"

"You're okay!" Thaddeus chimed in.

The ball of light he had conjured flickered a few times, then went out. Its glow went with it, leaving them in darkness again, relieved now only by the low glimmer of Dulindir's hair.

"Why'd it leave?" Thaddeus asked, more of himself than Teofil.

"We must not have needed it anymore," Teofil replied. He smiled and took Thaddeus's hand. "Come on, let's go meet them."

They hurried through the trees, and tears filled Thaddeus's eyes as he watched Teofil hug first Astrid and then Fetter. Thaddeus was surprised when Astrid grabbed him in a strong hug, and he wrapped his arms around her as well. When she pulled away, Fetter came up and gave him an uncomfortable hug, which Thaddeus awkwardly returned. It was odd, but still made him feel good.

"How is he?" Teofil asked. He knelt beside Dulindir where Astrid and Fetter had carefully laid him on the soft, wet ferns.

"He's been unconscious since we found him washed up on the shore," Astrid replied. "If his starlight hadn't kept going, we might have walked right past him."

"Will he still be able to direct us to the well, do you think?" Fetter asked.

Teofil looked up with a frown. "Let's just get him awake first and see how he's doing, okay?"

Fetter nodded and shuffled his feet. "I was just asking for Thaddeus's father's sake." He glanced at Thaddeus, and then looked back at Teofil. "We've taken longer than expected to get to the well."

"We know, Fetter," Astrid said. "But we can only do so much. Dulindir could have died."

"All of us could have," Thaddeus added and shivered when he remembered the water sprite floating just inches away, staring dispassionately at him as if waiting for him to drown.

Teofil went through his bag that, miraculously, hadn't been swept off downstream, and handed some berries and leaves and oils to Astrid to tend to Dulindir. Thaddeus still had his backpack as well, and he wondered if the things inside would ever dry out as he let it fall off his shoulders and set it aside before sitting on a log. Teofil came to sit beside him, holding plantain leaves and the dark, thick stuff Miriam had given them.

"Let me see your hand," Teofil said.

"It's fine," Thaddeus said. "See to Dulindir."

"Astrid is doing that," Teofil said. "Let me see it."

Thaddeus held out his hand, and Teofil angled it toward the faint glow of Dulindir's hair as he inspected it.

"The abrasions are better, but they're still open and raw. We should cover it again."

Teofil's touch was gentle, and Thaddeus smiled as he watched him work on his injury.

"You're good at that," Thaddeus said. "Your mother taught you well."

"He didn't spend enough time with our mother to learn that from her," Fetter said casually from where he sat leaning back against a tree a dozen feet away. He saw the looks Thaddeus and Teofil both gave him and flashed a sheepish smile. "Sorry. Private moment. I'll stay out of it."

"Too late," Teofil muttered, then went back to Thaddeus's hand.

"Where did you learn this?" Thaddeus asked. "If not from your mother?"

Teofil shrugged as he finished securing the plantain leaves around his hand with a thin piece of vine. "Leopold, I guess. Or maybe the fairies."

"Well, wherever you learned it, you're good at it." Thaddeus inspected the leaves and smiled at him. "Thank you."

Teofil kissed him quickly. "Glad to do it." He smiled back, then looked at Astrid. "How's Dulindir?"

"Coming around, I think," Astrid said.

"Is he speaking?" Fetter asked, jumping to his feet.

"No, but his hair is brighter," Astrid replied, pointing.

Thaddeus looked, and sure enough, Dulindir's hair was glowing brighter. "That's gotta be a good sign, right?"

"Who knows with elves," Fetter replied. "Could be his dying breath."

"Fetter!" Astrid and Teofil said together.

"What?" Fetter asked, seeming as if he were genuinely surprised by them yelling at him.

"It's not my dying breath," Dulindir said, his voice weak but steady. "So you can put away the party poppers and bunting, Fetter. I'm going to pull through."

Astrid knelt by Dulindir and helped him sit up. She sat beside him, an arm around his shoulders, and hugged him tight against her.

"You take your time and warm up," Astrid said, rubbing her hand up and down his arm. "Get your strength back."

"Yes, indeed," Fetter said. "Get your strength back. You'll be needing it to lead us the rest of the way to the Well of Tears." He paused, then asked, "How much farther, do you think?"

"For Flora's sake, Fetter!" Teofil shouted. "Let the poor elf wake up before you start badgering him about the well. If I didn't know better, I'd say you were the one we were traveling to the well for instead of Thaddeus."

Before Fetter could reply, Dulindir pointed off away from the river. "No worries, Teofil. I shall keep my word and lead you to that accursed place." He looked at Fetter. "It's not much farther now. Just a day's walk is all. We shall be there before the sun sets tomorrow."

Fetter nodded, glanced guiltily at Teofil and Astrid, then said, "Well, that's good to hear. And… I'm glad you're coming along, you know, healthwise. Good show."

Astrid rolled her eyes and pulled Dulindir tighter against her side. "You're impossible, Fetter."

"What did I say now?" Fetter asked, looking at each of them in turn. When his gaze came to Thaddeus, he could only shrug and shake his head, not wanting to get involved in a family dispute.

"We'll need a fire," Teofil said. "To help dry us out." He turned to Thaddeus. "Want to help me look for firewood?"

Thaddeus nodded, eager to be away from Fetter and the tensions he brought out in the others. "Yeah, of course."

"I'll dig a fire pit," Fetter offered.

"Sounds good," Teofil said without looking at him. He reached out for Thaddeus's hand and said, "Let's go."

Thaddeus let Teofil lead him off into the trees, thankful to have some time on their own, even if it was for just a few minutes, to gather firewood.

"Are you okay?" Thaddeus asked when he felt they were out of earshot of the others.

Teofil shot a glare back toward the others. "I don't understand what Fetter's problem is. He's always been kind of disruptive and demeaning to the rest of us, but lately he's been taking things a bit far, even by his standards."

"Not to stick up for him or anything," Thaddeus said, "but we are in a very high-tension situation here, you know? It can magnify the worst aspects of people." He stooped to pick up a branch that seemed dry enough to burn, then grinned at Teofil. "Or gnomes, I guess."

He received a wan smile in response but was heartened by it.

"I guess so," Teofil agreed, though it sounded reluctant. "It's too dark this way to continue. Let's circle back and find wood on the way. Once we get a fire going, we'll all feel better."

"Agreed," Thaddeus said, then took Teofil's hand and tugged him close. "One more thing." He kissed him. It felt good to have space away from Teofil's family members for a bit, and Thaddeus wanted to take advantage of it, reestablish the connection they'd had back when Teofil had been living next door to him.

Their kiss deepened, and Thaddeus felt Teofil's tongue press against his lips. He opened to him, their tongues twining and stroking as Teofil pulled him up close. When they finally broke the embrace, Thaddeus needed a moment to catch his breath. His head spun and his thoughts were scattered as he stared into Teofil's blue eyes, dark now with passion.

"I've never kissed someone like that before," Teofil admitted, and even in the diffused glow from Dulindir's starlight-infused hair, Thaddeus could tell he was blushing. "Honestly, I've never kissed anyone before you."

"Me neither," Thaddeus said. "It was really nice."

Teofil grinned. "Nice?"

Thaddeus rolled his eyes and swatted Teofil's strong shoulder. "You know what I meant."

Teofil leaned in close, his breath warm against Thaddeus's cheek when he whispered, "Did you mean sexy?"

Furious heat bloomed in Thaddeus's cheeks. "How do you know about all this stuff?"

Teofil pulled back and cocked his head. "What stuff?"

"Relationship stuff," Thaddeus said. "All the subtle stuff that goes on between two people. The teasing, the word choices. I have a tough time with it, and I grew up watching TV and interacting with other kids. But you grew up with just Leopold, who I can't see having those kinds of talks with you, and from what I gather, no television. How do you do it?"

Teofil shrugged. "It just comes to me. It must be because of how I feel about you." He bent over to pick up the sticks he had dropped when they kissed, then fixed Thaddeus with a meaningful look. "I don't need other people to tell me how to act around you. I just know that you're a good person, I trust you, and I want to become better acquainted with you. With all parts of you." He winked. "Come on. Let's get back."

Thaddeus stood rooted to the spot for a moment, watching Teofil's broad back as he returned to the others. His heart pounded and his brain buzzed pleasantly. This strange journey he had suddenly found himself on, and the family secrets he had recently learned, seemed small in comparison to the—dare he say it?—love he had discovered with Teofil. Everything they had gone through, and everything yet to come, felt possible because of him, and Thaddeus almost couldn't recall what his life before Teofil had been like.

"Come on, Thaddeus," Teofil called over his shoulder. "Don't tarry, the Lost Forest is home to lots of things, both friendly and unkind."

"Coming!" Thaddeus replied, then bent to grab an armload of sticks. Even though his feet squished in his wet shoes, and everything he owned was soaked through, he had a smile stuck on his face as he hurried after Teofil.

Chapter NINE

THE FIRE had burned down to a few glowing embers when Thaddeus awoke the next morning. The air was damp following the heavy rain from the day before, and he could feel it sitting in his sinuses. He sat up and stretched, once more missing his bed back home, as well as his laptop, cell phone reception, and most of all, the bathroom. He'd at least brought along his toothbrush and toothpaste, although he didn't look forward to rinsing his mouth with water from the Wretched River.

Teofil snored quietly to his left, and Thaddeus sat looking at him for a moment. His handsome face was calm and still as he slept, and Thaddeus noticed how much his dark blond beard had filled out during their journey. He reached up and scratched at his own scraggly whiskers, wishing once again for things back home he'd never thought to bring along. He'd only just started shaving, and now the patchy whiskers were itching enough to drive him mad.

"I'm done talking about it!"

Dulindir's sharp tone surprised Thaddeus, and he turned to see him stomp back into the clearing where they had set up camp. When Dulindir saw Thaddeus sitting up, he stopped in surprise, glanced back over his shoulder, and then nodded to him.

"Good morning, early riser," Dulindir said, his tone clipped and cool.

Thaddeus lifted a hand. "Good morning. I wasn't aware it was that early."

"Dulindir, look—" Fetter walked out from the trees and stopped when he saw Thaddeus sitting up. "Oh, good morning. My, you're up early."

Thaddeus got to his feet. "That seems to be the consensus. Excuse me for a moment. Nature calls."

Dulindir cocked his head and looked around. "I didn't hear anything."

Despite the strange tension between the three of them, Thaddeus couldn't help a smirk. "No, it means I need to use the bathroom."

"Bathroom?" Dulindir repeated with a frown.

Thaddeus sighed. "I have to piss, okay?"

"Oh, I see. By all means, then." Dulindir waved toward the trees.

As Thaddeus moved off through the bracken and undergrowth, he wondered just what Fetter and Dulindir had been discussing, and why Dulindir had ended the conversation so abruptly. It hung in the back of his mind as he peed, and when he finished, he sighed with relief, then made his way back to camp. He was happy to find Teofil and Astrid had awakened during his absence and were both sitting up and yawning.

"Good morning," Thaddeus said to Teofil and leaned down to kiss the top of his head.

Teofil smiled sleepily and ran a hand up and down Thaddeus's uninjured leg. "Good morning. Sleep well?"

"As well as can be expected when sleeping on a bed of leaves on the wet ground," Thaddeus replied, stretching his arms overhead.

Teofil and Astrid walked off into the trees to relieve themselves, and Thaddeus got busy gathering his belongings he'd set out to dry overnight. The humidity had prevented his few changes of clothes from drying out very much, even with the fire they'd managed to start, and he reluctantly rolled up the damp clothes and stuffed them into his backpack.

"We weren't talking about anything bad," Fetter said from just behind him, and Thaddeus jumped and turned.

"You startled me," he said with a nervous laugh. "I didn't hear you come up."

"Dulindir and I," Fetter continued as if Thaddeus had not said anything. "We weren't discussing anything bad. We just went into the trees to keep from waking you three up while we talked."

"Okay," Thaddeus said, unsure what Fetter wanted to hear and wishing Teofil and Astrid would return. "I wasn't concerned."

"It's just that you had a funny look on your face when you walked out into the woods," Fetter explained. "I didn't want you to think Dulindir and I were plotting against you three or anything."

"I wasn't thinking anything like that until you just mentioned it," Thaddeus said. Then, with his ire up a bit and his courage following suit, he met Fetter's gaze. "If you're so concerned with what I might be thinking of the conversation you had with our guide while we were all sleeping, then maybe you should tell the three of us just what it was you and Dulindir were talking about."

"He wanted to know if there was a shortcut to the village," Dulindir said as he approached from the river.

Fetter glared at him, then looked back at Thaddeus and nodded. "He's right. I was asking if we could find a shorter route to get to the well more quickly. I am concerned for your father's health. It's taken us longer to get this far than expected."

"Well, I appreciate it," Thaddeus said, suddenly uncomfortable and missing his father even more than he had to this point. So much had happened, it was difficult to understand just how long they'd been apart. "I want the same thing you do, Fetter. But I trust Dulindir is leading us along the fastest path he knows. Right, Dulindir?"

"You are correct," Dulindir replied. "We will be at the village—" He looked at Fetter. "—and the Well of Tears, before sundown tonight."

"Did I hear correctly?" Astrid asked as she stepped out from around a tree. "We'll be there tonight?"

"Precisely," Dulindir said. "If we get underway quickly."

"If that was directed at me, I'm here and ready to go," Teofil said as he stepped into the clearing. "I just need to pack up my bag, and we can leave."

"What about breakfast?" Thaddeus asked with an embarrassed blush. "I know we're in a hurry, but we need to eat."

"There are mooshberry bushes off in that direction," Astrid said and pointed. "Isn't that the way we need to go?"

"Mooshberries?" Thaddeus repeated with a sigh. "Again?"

"What's the matter?" Teofil asked with a grin as he loaded up his pack. "Tired of mooshberries already?"

"Sort of." Thaddeus managed to grin back at Teofil as he put his arms through the straps of his backpack. "Okay, let's hit the dusty trail."

"It's rained far too much to be dusty," Dulindir pointed out.

Thaddeus waved it away. "Sorry, it's an expression from old movies. My dad likes Westerns, and I've had to watch a lot of them, and…." Tears welled up in his eyes, sudden and embarrassing. "Sorry. Not sure why this is happening. Maybe I'm just as damp as the ground around us with all the rain and everything."

Teofil took his hand and squeezed it. "It's okay. You're worried about your dad, that's all. We'll be at the well tonight, get the water and get back to your dad quick. Ready?"

Thaddeus wiped away tears and nodded. "Ready."

"Let's go, then. Dulindir, you lead the way."

As if Dulindir had been able to see the future, they reached the edge of the village with some light left in the sky. Something had felt off about the last half mile they walked, but Thaddeus didn't understand what it was until Astrid pointed it out.

"So quiet," she said in a low voice. "No birds or insects, nothing."

"Feels like even the wind has stopped," Teofil added.

"The village is near," Dulindir said from the front of their single-file line. "Not much farther."

"The very air feels…." Fetter stopped, seemingly at a loss for how to describe it.

"Sad," Thaddeus finished for him.

"Yes, sad," Fetter agreed. "Thank you, Thaddeus."

"It's making me feel sad," Astrid said. "I just want to sit down and cry."

"Don't do it," Teofil said. "You make an ugly face when you cry."

Astrid stopped to punch him in the arm, then turned to follow Dulindir once again as Teofil and Thaddeus laughed.

A short distance later, they came upon the remains of a trail. It was barely visible as it had been reclaimed over the decades by the Lost Forest. Dulindir produced a long, gleaming blade from a scabbard around his waist and cut a path through the overgrowth. They followed, ducking their heads and pushing aside dangling vines and branches. Thaddeus noticed long, pointed thorns along one branch and paid close attention to the placement of his hands as he made his way beneath the heavy green canopy of foliage.

They came out of the trail into a large clearing and stopped behind Dulindir. A village, or rather what remained of a village, stood before them. The houses had all fallen into ruin, most now just a pile of rubble. Of those that remained standing, Thaddeus could discern the care and craftsmanship that had gone into their construction. Stones stacked tight together formed the walls, and thick, thatched roofs sat atop. Trees had grown around, beside, and within most of the structures, bursting through the roofs and pushing out the walls. Pottery, dishes, and personal belongings lay strewn about, and Thaddeus was struck by the complete silence of the scene before him. No birds called; no animals ran away from them in fright. Even the wind seemed to have died down to a respectful breeze as it played with a stained and torn lace curtain at a dark window.

"Oh my God," Astrid whispered. "It's so heartbreaking to see this."

"Here, my friends, is the village of Bower's Grotto," Dulindir said in a somber tone. "Slowly being taken back by the Lost Forest this last century. Few survived the illness that rushed through its streets, and even fewer have set their eyes upon the ruins you see before you." He turned away from the village where he had lived before being cast out and looked at each of them in turn. "Take nothing with you as we walk these streets. And touch only that which you are required to touch. Though the village looks and feels void of life, these ruins have attracted many dark things to take shelter here. We must be cautious."

Thaddeus tried to take in everything at once as Dulindir picked a path along the main road into Bower's Grotto, and they all followed. He was overwhelmed, and not just by the sight of so many buildings in ruins around them, but also the very air itself was tainted with a sense of loss. A few of the personal items strewn about stuck out to him. A woman's shawl, made of delicate, handwoven lace, fluttered in the slight breeze where it was snared on the branch of a dark and twisted tree that grew from the center of a house. A wagon made of heavy wood, whatever color it had been painted long peeled away, lay on its side in the road. The collar and leash for what must have been a beloved pet.

"It's so tragic," Thaddeus whispered. "So many lost."

Dulindir stopped a few minutes later, and they gathered behind him. Up ahead, Thaddeus could see a long, low mound of dirt that stretched off into the forest to either side. That had to be the mass grave. Dark green, almost black vines grew out of the mound of dirt, and a cold, icy spot opened up within Thaddeus at the thought of all the lives lost and the bodies buried together. The vines had wrapped themselves around the twisted trunks of trees that grew along the edge of the grave, their bark almost black and branches weighed down with dark, foul-looking fruit.

"That's the grave?" Fetter asked, his voice low and surprisingly reverential.

Dulindir nodded. "My family is buried somewhere inside it. I never got to say good-bye."

Astrid put a hand on Dulindir's shoulder, and Thaddeus noticed a tear trembling on the edge of her eye. He had sensed the friendship between Astrid and Dulindir deepening and was glad to see it, but he wondered what Teofil and Fetter would think of their gnome sister being involved with a forest elf.

Pushing aside those thoughts for the time being, Thaddeus cleared his throat. "I really hate to ask this, but is the well on the other side of the grave?"

Dulindir turned his head to look at him and gave a single nod. "It is."

"And why did they build the well in such a location?" Teofil asked. "Didn't they need to go over the grave to get to it?"

Dulindir was quiet a long moment, his gaze cast down. Then he looked at each of them in turn before focusing on Teofil. "Those who travel on their own through the woods like to share tales they've heard along the way when they come upon another traveler. I have heard many stories in this manner about what happened to the village where I once lived. Some tend to exaggerate certain details, but after meeting many travelers and hearing many different versions of the same story, I believe I have been able to find the kernel of truth within them all." He took a deep breath.

"The grave started out as two mass graves, originally, in the forest outside of the village. But as more and more villagers perished from the illness, they had to extend it closer to the village as the trees deeper in the forest were too close together to allow them to dig. The well was dug when the graves had not yet met in the center of the street. By the time those few left alive needed to bury the last of the ill, they had abandoned the well altogether so it did not matter that the grave blocked the main road." He shrugged. "It was a matter of convenience. They knew they were about to leave Bower's Grotto for good." He faced the grave again and straightened his shoulders. "It is the most expeditious route to walk over the grave. We shall be quick and fleet of foot. Do not tarry. For safety's sake as well as respect to those who lie within the grave. Come. The Well of Tears is not far now."

Chapter TEN

THADDEUS TOOK Teofil's hand as they followed Dulindir along the overgrown main road of the abandoned village. He stepped around a baby carriage, long ago claimed by dark and twisted vines, and set his gaze on the mass grave they needed to cross in order to get to the Well of Tears. Now, one hundred years later, vines with broad, dark leaves and red spots had taken root in the poisoned soil.

"What was that?" Astrid asked, coming to a sudden stop in front of Thaddeus.

Dulindir frowned. "Did you hear something?"

Astrid looked right and left, her gaze moving slowly along the full length of the grave. "I thought I heard something move."

"I haven't heard anything," Fetter said. "Come on, let's keep on while we still have the light."

Thaddeus watched Fetter stride up to the grave and stop. The vines had twisted together and lay at his feet in a clump, leaves looking black in the low light. Fetter lifted his foot to place it on the grave, then stopped and looked back at them.

"Aren't you coming?" Fetter asked.

"I've got a bad feeling about this," Thaddeus whispered.

"Me too," Teofil whispered back. "But we don't have a choice, do we?"

Thaddeus shook his head. "No, we don't."

The four of them walked up and stood in a line to either side of Fetter. They all looked down at the closely packed vines.

"Try not to break the branches," Dulindir suggested. "Just nestle your foot inside them, like this."

He used his foot to nudge aside a few of the vines and slipped it beneath them until he met solid ground, then did the same with his other foot.

"Just move slowly and be cautious," he said.

"Elves," Teofil muttered. "They walk lighter than any other being, and expect everyone else to do the same."

Thaddeus released Teofil's hand and took a breath as he stared down at the vines. With slow movements he carefully placed his foot in among the vines. The reaction was instant, and before he knew what had happened, a vine had wrapped tight around his ankle and yanked him off his feet. He cried out as the vine lifted him into the air, five, ten, twenty feet up. The wound on his leg pulled and stretched as he swung back and forth above the ground. His backpack slid off and fell to the ground away from the grave and the reach of the vines. The others were similarly grabbed and hoisted off their feet, the vines waving them about as more of the plant's creepers rose from the ground. A second vine grabbed Thaddeus by the wrist and tugged his arm so violently he cried out.

"Be still!" Teofil shouted. "Don't struggle!"

"They're around my throat!" Astrid shouted. Thaddeus twisted around until he could see her clawing at a vine that steadily tightened around her neck. "It's choking me!"

"They're angry," Teofil said. "Relax. They're angry from having grown in this poisonous soil for all these years. Let me try something."

"Hurry," Astrid said with a wheeze. "Hard to breathe."

"I am unable to speak to them, Teofil," Dulindir said, the vines spinning him in the air so his blond hair fanned out. "They're refusing to listen to me."

"Let me try," Teofil said, and he closed his eyes. Teofil's lips moved as he spoke quietly, and Thaddeus wondered what he was saying.

The vines holding Thaddeus's ankle and wrist stopped swinging him through the air with a suddenness that made his joints crackle and pop. The wound on his leg reopened, and he hissed in pain. Another creeper, thinner than the vines that held him, snaked up out of the thick growth below and slipped around his neck. Thaddeus felt the rough glide of the vine against his skin and swallowed hard. Blood rushed to his head as he was still hanging upside down. He slowly, carefully turned to look over at Teofil who had his eyes closed and was moving his lips as though speaking to himself. He didn't want to interrupt him, but he was scared—no, terrified was more like it. Beyond Teofil, the vines held Astrid by her ankles, and she desperately pulled at the one coiled around her neck.

"Teofil!" Fetter shouted from where he hung beyond Astrid, being swung back and forth by two vines around his wrists. "Work your backyard magic a bit faster, please."

Thaddeus's blood pounded in his temples, and he closed his eyes. He tried to think back to the Wretched River and how he had felt when he had conjured the ball of light. If Teofil's influence over the vines failed, Thaddeus wanted to be able to help as much as possible so they could all escape the plants. He just didn't know what he would do or how he would do it. He had the ability to cast magic; he had found that out already. It was simply a matter of being able to do it at will, and knowing what spell he could cast that would help. The ball of light had been easy, in retrospect, but what could he possibly conjure up in this situation? A large hedge trimmer? A flamethrower?

The vine around his neck loosened and unspooled. Thaddeus drew in a deep, grateful breath and heard Astrid let out a relieved sob. All of them were lowered to the ground on the side of the mass grave opposite the ruins of Bower's Grotto.

"Is everyone all right?" Teofil asked as he got to his feet. "Thaddeus? Astrid?"

Thaddeus smiled shakily. "I'm fine. Was that your doing?"

Teofil nodded, and then looked around. "Astrid?"

"I'm okay," Astrid said as she sat up, rubbing her throat. A red streak marred the pale skin, and Thaddeus figured his throat had a similar mark.

"Where's Fetter?" Dulindir asked.

"Here," Fetter practically shouted, and extricated himself from a mooshberry bush, heavy with overripe fruit. As he struggled out of the thick branches, the berries burst and splattered him with dark yellow juice.

Thaddeus joined Teofil, Astrid, and Dulindir in laughing at Fetter's stained hair, skin and clothes.

"Very funny," Fetter snapped at them. "I could have been killed, and here you all are laughing."

"We all could have been killed, brother dear," Astrid said, pulling a handkerchief from her pocket. "Here, wipe yourself off."

Fetter scrubbed off as much of the berry juice as he could, grumbling quietly to himself as the rest of them gathered their belongings that had been scattered about. Thaddeus leaned in to kiss Teofil on the cheek and asked, "What did you say to the vines?"

Teofil shrugged as he put items back in his pack. "I just let them know we were sorry for all they had gone through and all that had been lost. I explained that we are lost ourselves, and we wanted to try to make some things right. I guess it worked."

Thaddeus looked at the vines, now nestled back into place along the mass grave. "You do have a way with plants, don't you?"

"Better than some," Teofil said. "But far from perfect." He slung his pack over his shoulder. "Dulindir, which way do we go?"

"Through those trees," Dulindir said, pointing to a narrow path. "Not far now."

"You keep saying that," Fetter grumbled as he set off in the lead. "And yet here we are, still walking toward the well."

Teofil glanced at Thaddeus, sighed, and shook his head before following Fetter into the trees. Thaddeus followed Teofil, and Astrid and Dulindir brought up the rear. They'd walked long enough for Thaddeus to start worrying that Fetter was going to ask yet again how much farther it was to the well, when they stepped out into a small clearing. Fetter stood transfixed, staring at the stones stacked in a low circle in the center. The five of them stood side by side in a line, just gazing at the simple assembly of stones. The air within the clearing felt even more still to Thaddeus than that within the deserted village. He looked at the moss-covered stones and couldn't help feeling a little let down. He'd imagined something a bit more grand, but then again, the townspeople had dug this well at their lowest time. They wouldn't have put more effort into it than was necessary.

Fetter, of course, was the first of them to begin walking toward the well.

"Fetter, wait!" Teofil called. He hurried up and put a hand on his shoulder. "Let's take it slow, all right? There are many stories about this well, and we don't know the truth from legend."

Thaddeus moved to stand behind Teofil. He forced himself to look away from the well and at Fetter's face, startled to see his angry expression as he glared at Teofil.

"We didn't journey all this way to be cautious now, Teofil," Fetter said. "We need to draw a sample of water from the well and rush it back to Nathan to cure him." He nodded, his head bobbing up and down in a manic rhythm as he looked around at them all. "And we should take extra too, in case the troll poison has gotten into his blood or organs. Just so we have enough."

"That's a good idea, Fetter," Teofil said in a gentle voice. "But let's be cautious as we approach the well, for all our sakes. Who knew the vines at the grave would be so angry? Let's keep our wits about us and our eyes and ears open."

Fetter nodded, but Thaddeus saw a muscle in his jaw tighten as Fetter clenched his teeth.

"Good." Teofil looked at each of them. "Let's go up there together. We'll spread out to surround it on all sides and walk up slowly."

They dispersed in a rough circle around the well. A portion of the wall had collapsed, the stones lying in a heap on the ground and now covered by moss and small, brightly colored wildflowers. To his left, Teofil flashed him a quick, reassuring smile, then took a step closer. They all followed suit. Nothing happened, and Teofil took another step and the rest of them did as well.

Fetter stood across the well from Thaddeus, clenching and releasing his fists as they slowly approached the stones. Thaddeus could almost feel the impatience rolling off him, and it set his nerves on edge. Fetter was unpredictable during his best behavior, but being in such close proximity to the well seemed to be making him act even more erratically.

When they all finally stepped up to the well, they leaned in as a group and peered down the stone-lined shaft. Darkness stared back at them, a deeper darkness than Thaddeus had ever seen.

"Is it empty?" Astrid asked.

"It can't be," Fetter insisted. "The stories have all said there's water in it. Though the stories are different, that's the one similarity. All of them have stated there's water down there. There has to be water."

"Let's find out," Dulindir said and stooped to pluck a small stone from alongside the well. He held it out over the opening, looked at each of them in turn, and then let it drop.

Thaddeus held his breath and strained to listen. Just when he started to expect the worst, a quiet splash echoed up to them, and they all cheered.

"But, how do we get it up?" Astrid asked. "There's no bucket."

"Oh," Teofil said as he looked around. "Astrid is right. There's no rope or bucket."

"You have rope in your pack, don't you?" Thaddeus asked Teofil.

He nodded and dropped to one knee, rummaging in his pack and pulling out the rope. "I do. It should be long enough. Now we just need a bucket."

"Or a volunteer," Dulindir said as he removed his sword, quiver of arrows, and bow. He set the items aside and removed his green jacket to reveal a white shirt beneath. "You can lower me down, and I'll fill a waterskin."

"Why you?" Fetter asked.

Dulindir met his gaze. "I'm the lightest. It's the best solution." He raised his eyebrows. "Are you afraid I will run off with the water from down inside the well?"

"What? No. That's crazy." Fetter laughed, but it sounded stilted to Thaddeus and edged with anxiety. "Of course not. You're right, of course. You're the lightest."

"Tie this around your waist," Teofil instructed as he handed Dulindir one end of the rope.

Once Dulindir had secured the rope around his waist, he emptied a waterskin and tucked it inside his shirt. With that done, he sat on the edge of the well and turned to dangle his feet over the opening. Looking back at Teofil, he said, "Don't drop me."

"I won't," Teofil assured him.

Thaddeus draped the slack of the rope around his waist and stood behind Teofil, letting it play out slowly as Teofil lowered Dulindir into the well. Across the opening from them, Fetter paced with his hands clasped behind his back. Astrid peered down into the well, her expression pensive as she watched Dulindir descend. After a few moments, her face softened with a sudden smile and she looked at Teofil and Thaddeus.

"His hair is glowing again," she said. "I can see the water beneath him."

"Really?" Fetter asked, and leaned in over the well. "Where?"

The stones shifted beneath Fetter's hands, and Thaddeus's heart banged in response.

"Careful, Fetter!" Thaddeus shouted. "That wall isn't stable."

Fetter looked up at him, and in the space of a breath—too fast for Teofil and Astrid to see as they were distracted keeping Dulindir safe—Thaddeus saw an expression of pure, frightening hatred flash across Fetter's face. It startled him so much he nearly lost his grip on the rope but managed to hang on as he looked away. When he had worked up the nerve to look at Fetter again, his expression had softened to one of contrition and embarrassment, and he nodded to Thaddeus.

"Sorry," Fetter said to all of them at once. "Just excited, that's all."

Thaddeus wondered if that was really all it had been. He couldn't focus on that at the moment, however, as he was too busy helping Teofil lower Dulindir into the well.

"Let us know when he's close to the water," Teofil said, and Astrid nodded in response.

"He's almost there," she said. "Not much farther. Easy does it. Easy. There! Stop!"

The rope shifted and tugged in Thaddeus's grip as Dulindir worked to fill the waterskin. Sweat ran down Thaddeus's back, and the wounds on his palms ached and throbbed under the pressure of the rope. The reopened wound in his leg seemed to answer in kind, but he clenched his jaw and held tight to the rope. Dulindir was depending on them to keep him safe, and his father's life depended on them returning with this water, so a small thing—like a scraped hand or some gashes in his leg—wasn't much in comparison to that.

"Okay, he's ready to come up!" Astrid said. "Pull him up!"

Thaddeus and Teofil strained to lift Dulindir out of the well, finding that it was much more difficult than it had been to lower him. The rope slipped a few times along Thaddeus's injured palm, tearing away the plantain leaves and exposing the raw wounds. He hissed in a breath but maintained his grip as sweat dripped down his face.

"Fetter!" Thaddeus shouted. "Help us!"

Fetter looked startled at being asked to participate, but to Thaddeus's relief, he recovered quickly and hurried over to take up the slack behind Thaddeus. The extra pair of hands was just what they needed, and together the three of them hauled Dulindir up until he extended his hand to Astrid. She pulled him out of the well and hugged him tight.

"You were amazing," Astrid said to Dulindir.

"*He* was amazing?" Teofil said in a half-joking tone of voice. "We're the ones who did all the work."

Astrid grinned at Teofil, then hurried over to throw her arms around his neck and hug him. She planted a kiss on Teofil's cheek, then Thaddeus's, and finally on Fetter's. "You're all amazing. How's that?"

"I don't believe I received a kiss," Dulindir said.

Astrid was about to walk back to him when Teofil reached out to take her hand. "And maybe we'll wait on that for a few more days, hmm? Or years."

Astrid rolled her eyes and shot Teofil a glare, but Thaddeus didn't think there was much weight behind it.

"Is there very much water down there?" Fetter asked, stepping around Teofil and Thaddeus to approach Dulindir.

Dulindir took a step back from Fetter and tightened his grip on the waterskin. "There is still water down there. But it is lower than I had expected." He looked at Thaddeus and Teofil. "We won't have much room for mistakes."

Fetter looked at Teofil, his brow furrowed and anger flashing in his eyes. "I told you we needed to hurry. This may be our only chance to get this water."

"And get it back to Nathan," Teofil added. "Right?"

Fetter straightened his back and glared at Teofil. "You've been making snide comments for a while now, Teofil. I'd like to know why."

"Because you've been acting more than a little obsessed about this well," Teofil replied. "Would you care to explain why?"

Fetter's glare faded and a smile spread across his features. It was a cold, sinister smile, and Thaddeus shivered at the sight.

"I'll do better than explain it," Fetter said. "I'll show you."

He turned and reached for the waterskin. But Dulindir seemed to have been expecting the move and threw the waterskin with unerring precision right to Thaddeus. Reflexively Thaddeus caught it, surprised he didn't fumble and drop it. A horrifying vision flashed through his mind of the waterskin falling to the stony ground and splitting open to spill the precious water. He clutched it tight to his chest and, as he squeezed it, some of the water seeped out of the imperfect seal and dribbled over his injured palm. The water bubbled and sparked when it touched the open wounds, and a buzz traveled up and down Thaddeus's arm. He cried out and dropped to his knees, still grasping the waterskin in his uninjured hand as he raised the other to his mouth to suck at the water. The buzz traveled through him, spreading out through his limbs until it focused in his hand and leg as a tingle that could almost be labeled a burning sensation.

"Thaddeus!" Teofil knelt beside him. "What's wrong? What's happened?"

"I don't know," Thaddeus said as he gasped. "The water touched me, and it burned or something."

"Where?" Teofil said and reached for his clenched hand. "Let me see. Open your hand."

Thaddeus met his gaze. "I don't know if I want to. I'm scared."

Teofil gently took Thaddeus's hand, which he still kept closed tight in a fist. "Let me have it. Come on."

Thaddeus hesitated and took a breath. The pain had subsided, and now that he thought about it, it hadn't really been pain he'd felt at all. It had been more of a sensation in his hand and in his leg, and it had been startling instead of painful. Teofil slid the waterskin from Thaddeus's grasp and handed it off to Dulindir. Thaddeus watched from the corner of his eye as Dulindir accepted it and then moved to the other side of the well, away from Fetter.

"Okay, I know it's tough, and I know you're scared, but I need to see your hand," Teofil said. "Show me."

"Okay." Thaddeus closed his eyes and slowly relaxed his fingers.

Teofil gasped.

Thaddeus opened his eyes and gasped as well.

The wounds on his palm were completely healed.

Chapter ELEVEN

"IT WORKED," Thaddeus whispered. He looked at Teofil, and they laughed together. "It worked!" Thaddeus shouted. He sat down and pulled up his pant leg. He was only able to lift it partway over his knee, but it was enough to reveal that the wound he'd received from the Bearagon was gone. As he tugged at his pant leg to see more of his leg, the loose threads of the stitches tumbled out onto the grass.

Joy burst to life within him, filling him with hope, sunshine, blue skies, and long summer vacations from school. The well water had healed his hand and leg. Now they would take the rest of the water back to his father, and he would be cured. Astrid came over to peer down at his hand and leg and join in their laughter. It felt, for a moment, as if nothing bad could ever happen again.

But then everything changed.

"No! Let go!" Dulindir shouted.

"Hey," Teofil called and got to his feet. "Fetter, let him go!"

Thaddeus stood as well and gasped at the sight of Fetter grappling with Dulindir over the waterskin. Before they could all get around the well to help Dulindir, Fetter had managed to wrest it from him. Fetter ran to the edge of the clearing and turned to face them.

"Stay back or I'll slit this skin open and spill every last drop," Fetter shouted as he held the point of a small knife to the waterskin.

"Fetter, don't!" Thaddeus said, holding out his hand. "Please. You're holding my father's life in your hand. Please don't waste it."

"Yes, your father's life does depend on this, doesn't it?" Fetter smiled, but there was no humor in the action, only malice.

"What's gotten into you?" Astrid asked. "Why are you acting even worse than usual?"

"You have no room to be speaking to me about acting worse than I have before," Fetter said with a sneer that made Thaddeus flinch, and which, he could tell by her expression, hurt Astrid deeply. "For all these years I've put up with you. You, all our brothers and sisters, and our doting mother and stern but loving father. It's enough to make me sick.

Do you have any idea how many long nights I lay awake in bed, wishing I could just murder all of you in your sleep? Countless."

"Fetter!" Teofil shouted, his fists clenched and anger flashing in his eyes. "Enough of this foolishness. Hand the waterskin back to Thaddeus and let's be done with this nonsense."

"Oh, this is not nonsense, my special little brother," Fetter said. "No, no, no. Not by a long shot. This is years of planning. Over a decade. This is patience finally paying off."

"This is ridiculous," Teofil said. He walked around the well and headed for Fetter.

"Stop where you are, Teofil," Fetter said in a calm voice. "Or I'll be forced to make you stop."

"You can't do magic!" Astrid exclaimed. "You couldn't even grow a garden!"

A blast of light hit Teofil in the chest and knocked him off his feet. Thaddeus cried out and ran to kneel next to Teofil where he lay sprawled on the ground. He was relieved to hear Teofil moaning and helped him sit up.

"Are you all right?" Thaddeus asked.

Teofil squinted at him. "Yes, it just knocked me off my feet. Help me up?"

Thaddeus helped Teofil to his feet and held his arm when he wobbled on unsteady legs. "Okay?" he asked.

Teofil nodded. "Okay."

"Stay here," Thaddeus instructed, then turned and marched up to within ten feet of Fetter. Thaddeus stood with his chin thrust out as he glared at him. "Give it back to me."

Fetter smiled and held the waterskin out to him. "This is what you want?"

Thaddeus stood in place, not trusting him. "You know it is. Why are you doing this?"

"I'll show you why I'm doing this, young Thaddeus Cane," Fetter said. "Don't blink now. I've been waiting for this moment for a long, long time, and I wouldn't want you to miss a single second of it."

Fetter cut the bottom of the skin and held it up, opening his mouth wide to swallow every drop.

Thaddeus shouted, "No!" and started forward, but stopped when Fetter let out an anguished scream and collapsed to his knees. The waterskin fell to the ground beside him, and Thaddeus's gaze dropped to it, a cold spot opening inside his chest at the sight of its flattened, empty shape. All of the magical water was gone, and with it any chance his father might have to live.

Anger flared within him, starting hot in the center of his chest and burning away the cold spot that had formed. It ran through his body and pushed a furious scream from his lips as he clenched his fists. Before he knew it, he was rushing at Fetter, still screaming, the anger controlling him now as everything that had happened the past week caught up to him.

But then Fetter's body contorted in a violent and unnatural way. The sight of it stopped Thaddeus in his tracks. Fetter's left leg jutted out to the side, and, as Thaddeus stood and stared, slack-jawed, Fetter bent backward. His arms stretched toward the sky, fingers twisted into claws. Thaddeus had never seen anything like it. Fetter released a high-pitched scream, and it made Thaddeus jump and take a few steps back, his anger dissolving into a low-grade fear.

"What's happening?" Astrid asked, coming up beside Thaddeus. He glanced down at her and saw tears running down her cheeks as she watched Fetter convulse.

"I don't know," Thaddeus said.

Teofil stood on Thaddeus's other side. "It's changing him, I think."

"It looks very painful," Dulindir said from where he stood next to Astrid.

Just when Thaddeus noticed that Dulindir and Astrid were holding hands, Teofil took his and squeezed it tight.

"Is he dying?" Astrid asked. "Should we go to him?"

Fetter thrashed, his arms flying and legs kicking out as his head whipped side to side and he continued to scream.

"It's too dangerous," Teofil said. "He could injure us if we get too close. We'll have to wait and see what happens." He lowered his voice as he continued. "He knew what he was doing. Now he's got to live with it."

As Thaddeus watched Fetter shudder and spasm before them, he realized Teofil was correct: the water was changing him. He could now discern differences in Fetter's appearance. His hair had lengthened, and from what he could glimpse between movements, his facial features had shifted. It was difficult to tell because of the positions his body kept assuming, but it also appeared Fetter was growing a bit taller.

With a final, wince-inducing shriek, Fetter turned away from them and fell to the ground, heaving a few times before throwing up what little he'd had to eat. Then he lay with his back toward them, sides lifting and falling as he caught his breath.

"Is it over?" Astrid asked in a quiet voice.

Before any of them could answer her, Fetter spoke up. But it was no longer Fetter's voice; it was now a woman's voice.

"No," Fetter said. "It's just beginning."

Fetter pushed to his feet, keeping his back to them as he wavered unsteadily. His hair looked different: fuller and darker than the light brown it had been. His shoulders had narrowed, and his hips had more curve to them as he tipped his head side to side to crack the tension from his neck. After a final steadying breath, Fetter turned to face them, and they all gasped at the sight of the human woman standing before them.

"Who are you?" Teofil asked.

"Fetter?" Astrid's voice quivered with emotion when she said his name.

The woman who used to be Fetter smiled at Astrid, but her expression contained no joy or goodwill. It was a cold smile, full of dark, moonless nights and bitter winters.

"Fetter is gone," the woman said. "He has been for a very, very long time."

"Who are you?" Teofil repeated.

"For the love of Flora," Dulindir said, his voice a dry whisper filled with fear. "It can't be."

The woman looked at Dulindir, and her smile broadened and became even more chilling.

"Hello, my friend," she said. "Remember me?"

"Dulindir…?" Astrid asked, looking at him. "Who is she? Where's Fetter?"

"It's her," Dulindir replied. He took a step back, his gaze locked on the woman before them. "It's Isadora."

"What?" Thaddeus, Teofil, and Astrid all shouted together.

"How can that be?" Astrid asked. "Where is he?" She took a step toward Isadora, but Teofil reached out to grab her arm.

"Don't," Teofil said.

"Where's Fetter?" Astrid shouted. "What have you done with my brother?"

Isadora sighed. "Growing up with you all these years, I've always known you were a little slower than the rest of us, Astrid. But really, this does take the cake."

"It's been you all this time," Teofil said, his voice low and laced with an undercurrent of anger. "All these years, ever since the attack on the village."

"Oh, the special gardener wins the prize," Isadora said, then took a few steps toward them.

Teofil moved forward and put his arms out, shielding Thaddeus and Astrid.

Isadora stopped and tipped back her head to laugh. Then she fixed him with an icy glare and put her hands on her hips. "Always the noble one, aren't you? Mum and Dad's favorite, the one they shipped off to live with that doddering old fool Leopold. I wanted to slit his throat so often over the years. I lay awake some nights devising how I could get away with it too. But then I realized I'd never find out the secret he was so careful about, the secret we all discovered last week. Finally, after so many years, it's all out in the open that he had hidden a dragon beneath his yard. It was a secret he kept even from you, Teofil, his pet gnome who tended to his garden so dutifully for so very long."

"All these years?" Astrid said, her quiet voice full of grief. "All these years we grew up together were a lie?"

"All. The. Years," Isadora said slowly, savoring every painful word as she stared at Astrid over Teofil's shoulder.

"You are the most awful, wicked person I've ever met," Thaddeus said.

"Oh, look who pipes up. The dragon's child." Isadora took another step closer, and Teofil moved up a step to put himself between them.

"It's okay," Thaddeus said as he placed a hand on Teofil's back. "I'm okay."

"I don't trust her," Teofil said.

"And you shouldn't," Dulindir added.

Isadora leaned in toward Thaddeus, meeting his gaze and holding it. "I tried to kill you back on that fateful day. And if it weren't for these friends of yours, and the fact that I needed this well water to change back to my true form, I would have killed you out here in the forest. Nice and slow."

"Stay back," Teofil said with a growl.

"I could still do it," Isadora continued as if Teofil hadn't spoken. She continued to hold Thaddeus's gaze. He couldn't look away as his heart pounded and his breath came in shallow gulps. "But it would ruin all the fun of having you watch me control your mother and command her to blast you with fire. Then I'll listen to you scream while your skin turns black and crisp and your organs boil inside you."

"How?" Astrid asked in a quiet voice. "When?"

Isadora turned her gaze from Thaddeus, and he felt a shiver of relief to no longer be pinned down by her cold, black eyes.

"That day when I led the attack on the village, I was cornered," Isadora explained. "I knew I needed a way out. Your brother happened by on the path, carrying Teofil, and I had Azzo Eberhard bring him to me. I assumed Fetter's appearance and went home with Miriam and Rudyard. She's a horrible cook, by the way. Everything she served was bland or burned to a crisp. Anyway, it had been so many years since I'd changed, I became stuck in his form." She sneered and ran her fingers through her hair. "Living among you, smelling you, eating your slop, listening to your banal conversations, it nearly pushed me over the edge."

"That's why you could never grow a garden," Astrid said. "You weren't a true gnome."

Isadora glared at her. "I was gnome enough to share a room with you all that time, and you never suspected a thing. I think I did all right."

"Why?" Teofil asked.

"Why? I had to escape, first and foremost. And then I realized I was in the perfect position to find out the secrets," Isadora replied. "I wondered sometimes if it would be worth it in the end, but when I saw the magnificent beast Claire had become, I knew I would get my just rewards." She smiled at Thaddeus. "And finally end the Cane bloodline once and for all."

"Enough!" Dulindir shouted. "Stand back, you evil witch."

Isadora glared at Dulindir. "Or what? You'll throw a stone at me?"

"No," Astrid said, and Thaddeus turned to see she had stepped out from behind them and now swung her slingshot high over her head. "But I will."

Astrid released the stone, and it hit Isadora square in the forehead. She cried out and put a hand to the wound as she stumbled back. Blood ran down her face and into her eyes, blinding her.

"You evil little troll!" Isadora shouted. "I'll skin you alive for that!"

"I'm a gnome," Astrid shot back as she seated another stone in the slingshot. "I would have thought after living with us for so many years you would have figured that out. Talk about being slow."

The second shot glanced off Isadora's temple, and she spun around and fell onto the ground.

"Get her!" Teofil shouted and drew his sword.

Before any of them could advance, however, something big crashed through the undergrowth and into the clearing. It snarled and roared as it shook its big, furry head, and terror ran like ice through Thaddeus's veins.

"The Bearagon!" Thaddeus shouted. "Look out!"

Dulindir let an arrow fly, but the Bearagon swatted it aside. Astrid flung a stone, but it had no effect on the Bearagon's thick hide. It roared again as it stood between them and Isadora, not attacking them, but shielding the witch.

"It's protecting her," Teofil said.

"Of course it is," said Dulindir. "It's her servant."

"I knew him as Lucas back at my job," Thaddeus added. "I wonder who he really is."

Isadora pulled herself up and glared at them over the Bearagon's broad back. Blood streaked her face and matted her hair. She grabbed a handful of the Bearagon's fur and pulled herself up until she sat astride the beast.

"I'm not going to kill you where you stand," she said. "I'll just leave you stranded here. And you'll be left knowing you're the ones who led me straight to this place and allowed me to return to my true, fully powerful form. I guess I should thank you, but I've never been considered a gracious guest, so instead, I'll just do this."

She gestured toward the well, and the stones collapsed into the shaft.

"No!" Thaddeus shouted. Teofil held him back as he tried to run toward the ruins of the well.

"And now, Nathan will die a long, slow, agonizing death," Isadora said, looking right at him. "But maybe you can make it back in time to hold his hand when he takes his last, painful, blood-soaked breath. Shame he won't be able to share any more family secrets with you." She flashed that cold smile once again. "I'll tell your mother you said hello."

Isadora dug her heels into the Bearagon's sides, and with a final growl aimed at them, the monster turned and bounded off into the forest.

Thaddeus fell to his knees, and Teofil crouched down with him, holding him tight as he cried. What had Isadora meant by that? What other family secrets were waiting for him to uncover? Not far away, Thaddeus heard Astrid sobbing, and he mentally pulled himself together. There had been deeper betrayals revealed than those that affected him personally, and Astrid needed Teofil now more than he did.

"Go to her," Thaddeus said, nodding to where Astrid knelt a few feet away. Dulindir was on his knees beside her, rubbing her back.

"Are you sure?" Teofil asked.

"I'm fine, really. Dulindir and I will look at the well. Astrid needs you."

Teofil kissed him quickly on the lips before hurrying over to gather Astrid into his strong arms. She leaned into his chest and sobbed harder, saying incoherent things while Teofil stroked her back and made quiet sounds of comfort as he cried with her, both of them grieving their brother.

Dulindir joined Thaddeus, and together they approached the well. They inspected the damage and carefully picked at a few of the stones. Many of the stones had collapsed into the shaft and sealed it.

"It's gone," Thaddeus said in a quiet voice. "We'll never get to the water now."

"I don't think it's completely sealed up," Dulindir told him.

"What do you mean?"

"These larger stones appear to have wedged inside the shaft. Some of the smaller ones fell into the water at the bottom, yes, but most were caught by these larger ones stuck up top." Dulindir pointed them out. "See? If we carefully remove the smaller stones from on top of the larger, I may be able to slip past the blockage and retrieve more of the water."

"That sounds dangerous," Thaddeus said. "Those larger stones could fall in at any moment. Any small movement could bring them down."

Dulindir looked up at him, and Thaddeus saw the determination in his expression. "I'll not let anyone else die by her hand. I refuse."

"What happened all those years ago?" Thaddeus asked. "When she attacked the village?"

"It's a long story," Dulindir said and looked away. "And we don't have time for it right now. Ask me again another day."

"All right," Thaddeus said with a nod. "Let's get to work, then, shall we?"

Chapter TWELVE

THADDEUS HELPED Dulindir lift another stone and drop it a few feet away from the well. Astrid and Teofil had joined them a short time ago, and now all four stood staring into the dark, narrow opening.

"It's going to be tight." Dulindir looked up at Thaddeus with grim resolve. "But I'm willing to try it."

"Are you sure?" Thaddeus asked. "I can't ask you to risk your life for me to be able to take some magic water back to my father. For all we know, he might already have died."

"Stop talking like that," Teofil scolded him with a scowl. "Let's get the rope and lower Dulindir into the well."

"What will he use to bring up the water?" Astrid asked. Dark circles had formed beneath her puffy eyes. Each time Thaddeus looked at her, he just wanted to pull her into a tight hug and tell her how sorry he was about everything. Though she and Fetter had had their differences, most likely caused by Isadora herself, Thaddeus could tell Astrid had felt close to him. He couldn't imagine how deeply the sense of betrayal had cut her. And to have it combined with the unknown fate of Fetter himself most likely magnified the pain. They hadn't thought to ask Isadora whether Fetter was alive or dead. But Thaddeus figured that if Fetter had been killed, Isadora would have happily offered up that fact before leaving them.

Right now, however, they had no time to sit and discuss the possibilities. They needed to get the water and hurry back to his father.

"Oh yeah," Teofil said. "He—sorry, *Isadora* cut the waterskin."

"Didn't we have more than one?" Thaddeus asked. "I thought we did."

"It was in Fetter's—" Astrid stopped speaking, the words catching in her throat as tears welled up in her eyes. She shook her head and angrily swiped them away. "Stupid. I'm acting stupid. Sorry."

"It's okay, Astrid," Teofil said in a quiet voice and put an arm around her. "We're all a bit stunned about what happened. It will keep sneaking up on us for a while."

"Here!" Dulindir shouted from the other side of the clearing, and he held up Fetter's pack with a triumphant smile. "I found his pack."

He trotted back to them, long blond hair flowing behind to reveal his intricate, pointed ears. Thaddeus was heartened to see a faint blush color Astrid's cheeks as she watched Dulindir approach them. He wondered if Teofil had noticed Astrid's growing attraction, and what he thought of her having such feelings for an elf.

Teofil took the pack from Dulindir and squatted down. He hesitated a moment, the strap of the pack wrapped loosely around his hand. It all seemed so odd and dreamlike.

"You okay?" Thaddeus asked.

Teofil looked at him. Tears shone in his eyes, but he smiled and nodded. "I will be." He opened the bag and pulled items out, setting them aside. A couple of shirts, a pair of pants, some socks, and a small frayed and battered notebook lay on the grass. Then Teofil pulled out the canteen that Thaddeus had had with him at the beginning of the trip.

"Hey!" Thaddeus shouted and pointed. "That's my canteen. I thought I'd lost it in the Wretched River."

"Why would Isadora have stolen Thaddeus's canteen?" Astrid wondered.

"Maybe to fill it with water from the well," Dulindir suggested. "Is there anything in it?"

Teofil opened the top and upended the canteen, but nothing came out. "Dry as stone."

"Or a bone," Thaddeus muttered.

"What did you say?" Astrid asked.

"Nothing," Thaddeus replied with a shake of his head. "Just a weird saying people use."

Dulindir took the canteen from Teofil and hooked it onto his belt. He tied one end of the rope around his waist, and Teofil and Thaddeus wrapped shirts around their hands and took hold of the middle section. Since Thaddeus's hand had been healed by the water, he felt more confident in his ability to keep Dulindir from falling. He wasn't as sure, however, about the stability of the stones around the lip of the well.

Astrid stood back a bit, and Thaddeus heard her say softly to Dulindir, "Be careful."

They lowered him slowly into the shaft, Astrid giving them updates as she watched his progress. Just when Thaddeus thought he had to be getting close to the bottom, she called out "Stop!" and held up her hands.

Thaddeus and Teofil held the rope still. It spun and trembled in their hands as Dulindir shifted position at the bottom of the well, working to fill the canteen with water.

"Is there much left?" Astrid called down.

Thaddeus heard Dulindir's shouted reply, and his heart sank. "Not much! Some of the stones have fallen into it and are taking up space. It's difficult to get the canteen into a spot deep enough to fill it."

"Oh no," Thaddeus whispered.

"It will be all right," Teofil said assuredly, glancing at him over his shoulder. "You will see."

"I wish I had your confidence about it," Thaddeus said.

"So do I," Teofil replied, smirking.

Thaddeus couldn't help a smile, then both of them returned their focus to the rope as it shifted even more than before in their hands.

"What's he doing?" Teofil called to Astrid.

"He's trying to move to the other side of the well," Astrid replied. "To get to more water."

"Follow me," Teofil instructed Thaddeus. "But slowly."

They moved to the left, the rope sliding over the stones at the edge of the well. Thaddeus felt the thrum of the movement along the rope. His muscles burned now, and he felt a line of pain stitch its way up his back, across his shoulder, and on into his neck.

"He's going to need to finish soon," Thaddeus said. "And why does he feel so heavy? He's the shortest of all of us."

"Elves are weird that way," Teofil replied. "They are light on their feet but have a heavy center of gravity to keep them steady."

"Well, that makes perfect sense," Thaddeus grumbled.

It happened so fast, Thaddeus didn't have time to react. He saw the rope fray where it scraped across the rocks two seconds before it snapped. He and Teofil fell backward, sitting down hard as the rope piled on the grass around them. Astrid let out a cry and leaned against the well as she stared down the shaft.

"Dulindir!" Astrid shouted.

Thaddeus scrambled to his feet and ran with Teofil to peer into the well.

Dulindir's glowing hair provided enough light for them to see him at the bottom. He stood with his legs apart and feet planted on two stones that had fallen during the collapse. The severed rope lay in a pile between his feet, and he stared up at them with a surprised expression.

"The rope broke!" Teofil called.

"You don't say," Dulindir replied.

"Are you hurt?" Astrid asked.

"No, I landed perfectly on these stones," Dulindir said. "I can reach enough water to fill the canteen, but how do I get back up? Is there enough rope on your end?"

Teofil ran to check the length and came back with a long face. "No, there's not."

"Curse Isadora," Dulindir said, his voice echoing up from the bottom of the well.

"There's no other rope?" Thaddeus asked, looking around the clearing. "None at all?"

"I just had the one length," Teofil replied.

"What about the vines?" Thaddeus asked. "We could cut some of them—"

Teofil gave him a shocked look. "You can't cut those vines! They're living creatures."

"Oh, sorry," Thaddeus stammered. "I just thought... I've seen it in movies and stuff, so I thought it would work."

"Movies?" Astrid asked. "What's that?"

Thaddeus blew out a breath. "I'll explain later. Okay, the vines are out of the picture. Maybe there's rope back in the village?"

"No, wait, you might be right, Thaddeus," Teofil said and ran off toward the path that led back to the grave.

Thaddeus watched him go, then frowned at Astrid. "Did you understand what he meant?"

She shook her head and shrugged. "Not at all."

They waited a few minutes. Then Thaddeus couldn't take it any longer and had to find out what Teofil was up to. He walked quickly across the clearing and was about to step onto the path when a rustling sound brought him to a stop. His heart pounded and gooseflesh prickled along his arms. With all the strange, magical creatures lurking in the Lost Forest and the abandoned village not far away, Thaddeus's imagination ran amok. He was about to turn tail and run when Teofil appeared from the depths of shadow. Thaddeus let out a breath at the sight of him, then blinked in surprise when he saw a long vine slithering along the ground at Teofil's side.

"What is that?" Thaddeus asked.

Teofil smiled. "One of the vines. I asked if they would help us out, and they agreed. This is the longest vine of the group. I'm just hoping it reaches."

Thaddeus fell into step on the opposite side of Teofil from the vine. He kept casting nervous glances at the thing as it snaked through the fallen leaves and dirt.

"Did you promise it anything?" Thaddeus whispered.

Teofil looked at him from the corner of his eye. "I had to promise it something in exchange for its help, yes."

Thaddeus frowned. "What?"

"They want us to take only what water will fill the canteen," Teofil said. "The rest of the water belongs to them."

"What?" Thaddeus exclaimed. He stopped in his tracks and reached out to grab Teofil's arm. "How could you agree to that?"

"What will fill the canteen will be enough to heal your father," Teofil said. "We won't need any more water."

"But, we'll need it to be able to change my mother back," Thaddeus protested. "And what if one of us is injured again? What if another troll attacks us, or something worse?"

Teofil put a hand on his shoulder and squeezed. "Your father will only need a small amount to heal him. Look what a splash did for your hand and leg. We should have enough left to bring back your mother. As for future injuries, we'll have to take that risk. Just like all the others who have done brave things. Come on, we're losing the light."

Thaddeus wasn't happy with the deal Teofil had made to get the vine's cooperation, but what choice did they have?

The vine slithered up to the well and disappeared down the shaft. It proved to be long enough, and Thaddeus stood back a few feet, watching it pull back up. In moments, the vine had lifted Dulindir. It set him on his feet on the ground nearby, then twisted around and crawled back toward the path.

"Here you go," Dulindir said, handing Thaddeus the canteen.

Thaddeus felt the weight of it, and was glad to find Dulindir had managed to fill it completely. "Thank you."

A drop of rain landed on his hand as he clipped the canteen to his belt. Dark clouds had moved in while they had been working to get the water. More drops of rain fell, and then a heavy shower started. They ran back along the path, careful not to step on the vine as they slipped and slid in the mud. They clambered over the vine-covered mound of the mass grave, moving slowly so as not to break any. The vines tolerated their passing without so much as a rustle of leaves. Thaddeus thought perhaps the heavy rainfall was proving to be a distraction.

"We need to take shelter," Teofil shouted over the rain as it fell even more heavily. "In one of the houses."

"Ew, that's creepy!" Astrid said.

Lightning blazed in the dark sky, followed close by a loud boom of thunder.

"Right, then," Astrid said, "old abandoned house it is!"

They ran along the main street of the village, squinting through the downpour as they inspected the shops and homes that lined the road. Just when Thaddeus thought they might have to try to build a shelter out in the trees, Dulindir let out a whoop of joy and ducked into the dark doorway of what had once been a small shop. The rest of them hurried in after and stood in the center of the room, wiping rain from their faces and shivering in the gloomy chill. A long counter ran the length of the far wall, and a few tables and chairs lay scattered about the room.

"Ugh, smells like onions," Astrid said with a wrinkle of her nose.

"Old onions," Teofil added.

"But it's got a dry floor and a solid roof," Dulindir said. "And a fireplace."

"Is there wood?" Thaddeus asked.

"Let's break up some of this furniture," Teofil said, and they all got busy.

Soon a fire crackled and popped in the fireplace, and they sat huddled around the hearth. Teofil had run out into the heavy rain to gather some mooshberries and herbs to heat over the fire for a flavorful broth. With his belly full, clothes dry, and finally feeling warm, Thaddeus stretched out on the floor, the canteen tucked in tight against him.

"I miss seeing Faux Flora," Teofil said as he leaned in the open doorway and stared out at the rain. "I miss the open sky and all the stars."

"We'll be back to that soon," Thaddeus said with a yawn. "Back to the plains."

Astrid groaned and leaned back against a table that had been tipped on its side. "It'll take us days to get back to Mum and your dad."

"I wish we could fly there," Thaddeus said, his eyes growing heavy and his thoughts spinning off in different directions. "Just flap our arms and fly up over the trees."

Thaddeus heard Dulindir say, "That would be nice," before he slipped off to sleep.

He dreamed he was gliding over the treetops of the Lost Forest. The wind was cool and fresh on his face, and Thaddeus felt happy, free, and untethered to any concerns. He had no idea how he was flying, but it felt good.

Someone laughed from nearby, and he looked to find his father soaring along with him. Nathan looked good, not sick, and he smiled and laughed with Thaddeus as the very top leaves of the trees brushed their toes and fingers, and the wind brought the smell of flowers and fresh-mown grass to them.

Something in the fire popped, waking Thaddeus. As the dream faded, he chased it, but it proved too fleet of foot. Instead, he lay staring up at the ceiling layered with cobwebs, watching them sway in the heat from the fire. Around Thaddeus the others lay sleeping, Teofil close by his side. Thaddeus checked to make sure the canteen was safe, then got up and stared out the open doorway at the heavy rain. He wondered how his father was doing and hoped Miriam had enough of her special herbs to keep him well and comfortable. The long road back concerned him, and though he tried to put the useless worry aside, he knew time was running out. He just wished there was some faster way for them to return.

Chapter THIRTEEN

THADDEUS LOST track of time amid the steady fall of rain as he stood in the doorway. Thunder rumbled in the distance, and behind him, the fire popped. He heard someone stirring but didn't look around to see who. Concern about his father gnawed inside him, leaving him restless and edgy.

Arms slipped around his waist. Despite his mindset, Thaddeus smiled and leaned back against Teofil's strong frame.

"Is it letting up at all?" Teofil asked, his breath warm against Thaddeus's ear.

"Not really," Thaddeus replied.

"Worried about your dad?" Teofil asked.

"Yeah. It's going to take us days to get back." Thaddeus sighed and dropped a hand to the canteen on his belt. "I hope he's doing okay. I mean, I know your mom is doing everything she can to keep him well, but…."

"I know." Teofil kissed his neck and pulled him closer. "We'll figure something out."

Thaddeus felt Teofil's chin shift from one shoulder to the other. "Not even a break in the clouds yet?"

"Not yet," Thaddeus replied. "Don't worry, your Faux Flora is still up there waiting for you."

Teofil chuckled and turned Thaddeus to face him. "Are you mocking my admiration of Faux Flora?"

"Are you sure it's admiration?" Thaddeus asked with a grin. "Sounds a bit obsessive at times."

Teofil leaned in for a kiss, then whispered, "You're the only one I'm obsessed with."

"Ugh. This is what I wake up to?" Astrid sat rubbing her eyes. "And, Teofil, Thaddeus has a point, you do go on about Faux Flora an awful lot." She yawned and stretched and got to her feet. "All you do is talk about Flora making the fake likeness of herself from sticks and leaves and getting blown up into… the… night… sky."

Astrid's voice slowed as she spoke. Her eyes widened, and a bright smile bloomed, softening her grief-sharpened features and putting a rosy blush in her cheeks. Thaddeus knew if Dulindir had seen her like this, he would have fallen in love with Astrid in a heartbeat. But Dulindir was still curled on his side, sleeping soundly near the fire, blond hair lying over his shoulder like a shawl.

"Oh my Flora, that's it," Astrid whispered. "Do you see?"

Teofil and Thaddeus looked at each other, then back at Astrid. "No," Teofil said. "We don't. Tell us."

"What are you thinking?" Thaddeus asked.

"We build Floras," Astrid said. "Not her, exactly, but something like her. And we take them up to the tops of the trees and fly back to Mum and Nathan."

The peaceful dream of flying with his father over the trees of the Lost Forest slipped through Thaddeus's mind. He shivered as he took a moment to wonder if his subconscious had been trying to tell him the solution before Astrid had come up with it. Either way, it didn't matter, as long as they got back quickly.

And safely.

Thaddeus looked at Teofil and found him smiling at Astrid. "Will it work?" Thaddeus asked.

Teofil looked at him, back at Astrid, then at him again. "I think it might."

"Might?" Thaddeus repeated. "We're going to need to be a bit more definite than 'might.' We're not going to be able to help anyone if we plummet to our deaths."

Teofil laughed and pulled Thaddeus into a quick hug. "We're not going to plummet to our deaths. This is the perfect solution. Astrid, you're a genius!" Teofil hurried across the room and grabbed her in a hug, lifting her up and spinning her around. Astrid let out a squeal of laughter that woke Dulindir, who sat up, fully alert, and looked at each of them a moment.

"Why the celebration?" Dulindir asked.

"Astrid came up with an idea for our way home," Teofil replied.

Dulindir smiled at Astrid. "Tell me."

Astrid explained her idea, and Dulindir nodded along. When she had finished with her explanation, he was quiet for a moment, long enough for Thaddeus to ask, "Well? Do you think it would work?"

Dulindir smiled. "I do. The kites will need to be large, but the wind above the trees is strong enough to carry us."

Thaddeus took a breath and rested a hand on the canteen fastened to his belt. "Okay, how do we start?"

They scavenged pieces of walls and ceilings from the shop where they had spent the night and the structures that surrounded it. Dulindir had brought the broken length of rope from the bottom of the well with him, and Teofil had gathered what had remained up top, so as the rain lessened outside, they crouched inside by the fire and cut the rope into sections to be used to bind pieces of gliders together. Large fronds from the trees in the forest made up the wings of the gliders. By midafternoon, they had almost finished assembling two odd-looking aircraft.

"This will work," Teofil said as he stepped back to inspect their creations.

They had only found enough material to make two gliders, so they would have to buddy up. Now, their finished work lay on the floor nose to nose, wings stretched from one wall of the shop to the other.

"Uh-oh," Astrid said.

"What?" Teofil asked, frowning as he looked at the gliders. "Did we miss something?"

"Yeah," Astrid replied. "Like how we're going to get them out of the shop."

They all groaned as they looked between the narrow door and the large wingspans of the gliders.

"For Flora's sake," Teofil grumbled. "Can't anything be easy?"

"We could take a wing off each one," Thaddeus suggested. "And angle them out the door."

"We'll have to take off both wings," Astrid said. "They're too broad to fit any other way."

A loud rustling followed by the thump of a wall falling away caused them all to jump. Dulindir stood at the front of the shop, sword in hand and the front wall lying on the wet ground outside.

"Sometimes there's a simpler solution," Dulindir said.

"Elves are really surprising," Teofil said with a grin.

"In a good way," Dulindir added. "Right?"

"Of course," Teofil said, then stooped to grab one edge of a glider wing. "Let's move them out!"

They carried the gliders out of the shop and set them on the road. Thaddeus was impressed by the design, but still concerned about the ability of the gliders to stay aloft. What if they pushed off from the top of the tallest tree they could find only to plummet back to the forest floor? He shuddered at the thought and looked at the trees that stood around the outskirts of the village.

"Hey," he said, still looking up. "How are we going to get the gliders to the top of a tree?"

The others also looked up.

"That just rankles the grouse monkey," Astrid said with a sigh.

"Grouse monkey?" Thaddeus repeated.

She raised her eyebrows. "Yeah. A grouse monkey. Everyone knows what a grouse monkey is."

"I don't," Thaddeus said.

Astrid smiled and shook her head. "You really are from another planet, aren't you?"

"Not another planet, Astrid," Teofil interjected as he paced between them. "He was raised in the human world. He doesn't know about our magical beings and creatures. They stay hidden from humans."

"Sounds dull," Astrid said.

"It was," Thaddeus assured her before looking up into the trees again. "So, back to the gliders. How can we get them up there?"

"We used all of the rope," Dulindir said.

"Anyone know any levitation spells?" Teofil asked.

"Not for something that big," Dulindir replied. Thaddeus wondered just what he might be able to levitate, but decided not to derail the conversation any further than he already had asking about the grouse monkey.

"Look around everyone, see if you can find some other rope," Teofil instructed.

Thaddeus slogged across the muddy street and entered a small house. The air inside was heavy with dust and damp rot, and he shivered at the sound of rodents scurrying through the walls. A tree had taken root in a back room of the house and torn through the roof in its quest for light and water.

"Kind of extreme," Thaddeus whispered as he looked up along the trunk of the tree. He decided he needed to focus on the task at hand and not survey the damage to one house in an abandoned village. He turned away to look through the few belongings the previous owner had left behind.

After opening several drawers and cabinets and finding nothing that could help them raise the gliders, he searched a few more houses with the same luck. When he returned to the spot where they had left the gliders, he found the others standing there, all of them empty-handed as well.

"No luck?" Thaddeus asked.

"Same as you, it seems," Astrid replied.

"What about the vines?" Dulindir asked, looking at Teofil. "Do you think they would do us one more favor?"

Teofil glanced over his shoulder at the vines covering the grave mound at the end of the road, then looked at Thaddeus. "We have nothing left to offer them. We've already agreed to leave the water in the Well of Tears for them. It would just be asking a favor."

"Do you think they would do us a favor?" Thaddeus asked. "I mean, you've been very good to them, even though they're a little... well, a little crazy." Thaddeus felt a little crazy himself, talking about vines as if they were living beings. But, he had to be open-minded to all things, especially here in the Lost Forest.

"I can ask," Teofil said. He squared his shoulders and walked toward the mass grave.

"Should we move the gliders closer to the vines?" Astrid wondered.

"Couldn't hurt," Thaddeus replied. "Plus that tree down there looks to be the tallest in the area."

The three of them carried one glider down to within ten feet of the mound as Teofil stood facing the grave, arms outstretched, vines wrapped around his arms and hovering in front of his face as if listening. Thaddeus shuddered at the memory of the vines grabbing him and hoisting him off the ground. Turning away, he followed Astrid and Dulindir back to the second glider and carried it closer.

When they set the glider down, Teofil approached and said, "They agree to help us this last time. But they want a guarantee."

Thaddeus's stomach tightened at this news, and he asked nervously, "What kind of guarantee?"

"That we will never return not only to the well, but to the village or this area of the forest ever again."

"I think I can safely say that is one guarantee I'll be happy to keep," Astrid said.

"I second Astrid's response," Thaddeus added. "I'll stay as far from here as I can."

Dulindir was quiet, turning to look around the village.

"Dulindir?" Astrid asked. "You okay?"

"I was born here," Dulindir replied. He gestured off into the trees. "Back in the forest a bit, but I lived here for years before I was banished. I knew this road and these people." He gazed at the burial mound covered with vines. "My family is buried somewhere within that grave."

Astrid stepped up and touched his arm. "I'm sorry, Dulindir. I keep forgetting this used to be your home. But it's in such a ruined state. You can't ever want to come back to this place, can you?"

Dulindir looked at her, took a breath, and smiled. "No. Not anymore." He lifted his gaze to Teofil. "I promise to never return."

Teofil nodded. "So be it. The vines will—"

A number of thick vines slithered beneath the gliders and lifted them into the air. Thaddeus watched them rise, then shouted with surprise when a vine wrapped around his waist and lifted him off his feet. He kept a hand on the canteen at his belt as he rose higher and higher into the trees. Not wanting to scare himself, Thaddeus resisted looking at the ground. Instead, he focused on tipping his head back and forth to avoid being scratched by the branches of the tree as the vine lifted him.

In minutes Thaddeus grabbed the uppermost branches of the tallest tree and held on tight as the vine unwound from his waist and dropped away. His palms were damp with sweat, and his scalp tingled with fear as he made slight adjustments to his stance. The branch swayed beneath him, but he put that out of his mind and looked up to where the gliders rested above the leaves, almost within arm's reach. He would have to climb the last few feet, but they were almost there. He couldn't back down now.

"Thaddeus!" Teofil called.

Thaddeus looked around and found Teofil clinging to a branch not far away. He smiled and pointed toward the gliders. "Climb up!"

With the agility of a squirrel, Teofil climbed into the uppermost branches of the tree and began strapping himself into a glider.

"Okay, here we go," Thaddeus said to himself. "You can do this. Your father is depending on you."

Slowly, so very slowly, Thaddeus climbed toward the gliders. His sweaty palms were slick on the thin, rough branches. Astrid and Dulindir climbed past him and were now talking with Teofil about the seating arrangements in the gliders. Thaddeus could see the leaves stirring in the strong wind, and every now and then the gliders shifted, as if eager to lift off.

Finally, Thaddeus poked his head up through the last of the leaves and looked around. The sun was bright above the forest, and the wind blew strong and steady along the tops of the trees. He drew in a deep breath of the fresh air and then met Teofil's gaze.

"Hi," Teofil said.

"Hi," Thaddeus said back.

"Can you make it up the last foot?" Teofil asked.

Thaddeus nodded, then noticed Dulindir strapped into the glider beside Teofil. "Oh, we can't be together?"

Teofil shook his head. "We're the heaviest. Astrid's waiting for you."

Thaddeus looked to the other glider and saw Astrid reaching out to him. "Give me your hand, Thaddeus. I'll pull you up."

Reluctantly, he released his grip on the thin branch and extended a hand to Astrid. The branch he was using to support himself cracked, and Thaddeus's heart pounded as his blood turned to ice. For the span of a few heart-stopping seconds he felt weightless, poised hundreds of feet above the forest floor, and then Astrid clasped his hand and steadied him.

"I've got you," she said. "You're okay."

With Astrid's help, Thaddeus climbed into the glider. They had constructed the gliders so they could lie with their feet extended toward the tail, like a hang glider pilot. He slid his feet into the rope loops and tied himself in next to Astrid. He checked each binding three times, verified the canteen was firmly attached to his belt, then nodded to her.

"I'm ready."

She smiled. "You're going to love this." Astrid called out, "We're ready. Go ahead and take off."

Teofil looked over his shoulder to smile at Thaddeus, and Dulindir smiled at Astrid. Then the two pushed off from the top of the tree, and the wind took them. Thaddeus watched them go, marveling at the grace of the glider as it floated over the tops of the trees.

"Wow, they're really flying," he said with a smile.

"Our turn," Astrid said. "Hang on."

She released the branch she had been holding on to, and they pushed off with their feet. The wind slipped beneath the wings of the glider and pushed them aloft. The fronds rattled in the wooden frames but held, and Thaddeus caught his breath as he watched the trees fly by beneath them, only a foot or so away.

"This is amazing!" Astrid shouted. "Here's to Flora!"

Thaddeus laughed. "To Flora!"

They caught up with Teofil and Dulindir and pulled alongside them, all of them laughing together as they adjusted their rudders and gently turned the gliders west, into the setting sun and back to Miriam and Nathan.

As the wind ruffled his hair and clothes, Thaddeus hoped they wouldn't be too late.

Chapter FOURTEEN

THE TREETOPS swayed beneath them as Thaddeus and Astrid soared above. They each held on to the stick in the center to control the rudder as well as a support post to the side. Just ahead, Teofil and Dulindir shared the second glider, cruising along above the trees as they all headed for the plains and Nathan and Miriam.

"Look, unicorns!" Astrid pointed into a clearing as they soared past.

"What?" Thaddeus caught a glimpse of a pair of white horses and thought he might have seen horns on their heads, but they were well past the clearing before he had a chance to really look.

"Unicorns?" he asked Astrid. "I didn't think they existed."

She smirked. "You didn't think gnomes existed either, but you're flying above the Lost Forest with one and are in love with another."

"Good point," Thaddeus replied.

He looked ahead at the bottoms of Teofil's boots, the rounded swell of his butt inside his trousers, and his dark blond hair waving in the wind. A pleasantly nervous squiggle of attraction and anticipation went through him, and he looked away, down at the leafy treetops beneath them.

"Isn't this amazing?" Astrid asked. "I've never flown like this before."

Thaddeus was about to ask her how she had flown prior to this, but then movement to his left caught his attention and he turned his head. A large bald eagle coasted along on the breeze beside them. Wind ruffled the bird's white-feathered head, and its long wings stuck out at least five feet across. Thaddeus stared at the raptor floating in the air alongside him. He was stunned. He'd never seen an eagle up close before.

"Look!" Astrid said.

Thaddeus pulled his gaze away from the eagle and looked to where she was pointing. A large area of leaves off to their right had turned black, and Thaddeus squinted as they flew past. Just beyond the patch of blackened leaves, bare branches reached for the sky, stripped clean.

"What is that?" Thaddeus asked.

"That area's been burned," Astrid said.

Thaddeus met her gaze. "Burned?"

She nodded, her expression solemn. "In a long strip, see? Like it was burned from above."

"Dragon," Thaddeus said, staring at the long, burned ribbon of the forest, his voice a near whisper as a chill raced up his spine.

"Dragon," Astrid agreed. "I'm sorry. I know it's difficult for you."

"I want to see it again," Thaddeus said, reaching for the rudder.

"We can't!" Astrid exclaimed and put both of her hands around his. "We'll lose the wind!"

"But it's my mother," Thaddeus said. "It has to be. It could give us a clue as to where she was headed."

"I know, Thaddeus, but we need to get back to your father."

Thaddeus closed his eyes, still holding on to the rudder control, Astrid's hands wrapped around his. Through the rudder control, he could feel the thrum of the wind as it pushed them along. All it would take was one slight adjustment to the rudder's setting for him to circle the glider back around so he could get a better look at the burned patch of forest. But Astrid had a point. If they turned into the wind, they could lose altitude and crash into the trees, and then he certainly wouldn't get back to his father in time. As it was, he was afraid he still might not make it soon enough despite them flying back to where they'd left their parents.

He nodded, eyes still closed, tears threatening to spill. Slowly he released his grip on the rudder and allowed Astrid to take over.

"I'm sorry," Thaddeus said, unable to look at her.

"There's no need to apologize," she assured him, coaxing the rudder a bit to move them out from behind Teofil and Dulindir. "You've got a lot of pressure on you. We've all lost someone now, so I understand how you must be feeling."

He watched the trees flow past beneath them, felt the wind in his face, drying his tears. Up ahead, Teofil looked back and met his gaze, a broad smile on his face and his hair in disarray from the wind. Thaddeus smiled in response, and the heavy feeling inside his chest lightened. He wished he could have shared a glider with Teofil, experienced this flight alongside him.

Beside Teofil, Dulindir's long blond hair rippled in the breeze, streaming over his back like a soft golden wave. Watching the wind ruffle Dulindir's silky strands soothed Thaddeus's troubled mind. He let the concerns about his father's health and finding and changing his mother from a dragon slip away. Dropping his gaze from Dulindir's flowing hair, he took in the scenery below. It was a beautiful view of the forest, stretching out beneath them in all directions. The leaves ruffled in the wind, and now and then Thaddeus caught a glimpse of the twisting, shimmering line of what he assumed was the Wretched River. From this height, as the sunlight sparkled off the surface of the water, it looked more beautiful than dangerous. But then again, most dangerous things looked beautiful from a distance.

Shouts from ahead brought Thaddeus back from his contemplation of the forest below. Teofil and Dulindir were waving and pointing ahead. When he looked in that direction, stomach tight with nerves at whatever might be coming at them, he was surprised to see the trees end abruptly at the edge of the grassy plains. From this height, it looked as if some giant being had drawn a knife between the two parcels of land, sharply delineating forest from plain.

"We made it!" Thaddeus said with a laugh. "We've reached the grass plain!"

"Thank Flora," Astrid said. "Now we just have to fly along the edge of the forest to where we left Mum and your father."

Thaddeus checked to make sure the canteen was still clipped tight to his belt. "Any idea how far that is?"

"None," Astrid replied as she slowly, carefully, adjusted the rudder.

The glider banked in a gentle arc, following Teofil and Dulindir's as they soared above the line of trees. Birds flew out of the treetops, startled by the shadows the glider cast as they floated overhead. Thaddeus looked back and was able to see a few bare tree branches sticking up out of the leaf canopy, another place where the dragon—his mother, he knew it; why couldn't he admit it?—had burned the patch of forest. He tried to fix the spot in his mind, but it was difficult to judge distance and direction from their altitude.

"There!" Astrid shouted, bringing Thaddeus's attention back to the land ahead of them. "The tree in the plains, remember it? I see it way up ahead in the distance."

Thaddeus saw the tree as a vague shape on the horizon, and his heart pounded. He hoped they were not too late. They couldn't be too late, they just couldn't be.

"We traveled on foot a long ways," Thaddeus said.

"Makes sense now why my feet hurt so much," Astrid said, and they both laughed.

"Ahead!" Teofil shouted back to them, and pointed toward the tree.

"We already saw it!" Astrid yelled back. "You're too slow!"

Teofil smiled and shook his head, pointing at his ears to indicate he couldn't hear her.

"Just like a younger brother," Astrid said with a sigh. She looked over at Thaddeus and asked, "Are you ready?"

Thaddeus looked at her, wide-eyed. He hadn't even thought of how they were going to bring the glider back to earth.

"Did we build it for landing?" Thaddeus asked.

"Jeez, have a little faith in us, eh?" Astrid replied, but then she frowned. "It might not be the smoothest of landings, but it'll get us on the ground."

Thaddeus craned his head around to look up at the wings. "Did we build spoilers into the wings?"

"Spoilers? Not sure what those are, but we do have these flaps to help us slow down. See?" Astrid tugged a short piece of rope, and the glider dropped twenty feet as its speed decreased.

"Too fast!" Thaddeus shouted, fingers tight on the supports near him. "Ease up, Astrid, ease up!"

She adjusted the flaps a bit more, and the glider continued forward, though lower now. They were flying below treetop level, the forest zipping past to Thaddeus's left rather than beneath them.

"We have to descend slowly or we'll crash," Thaddeus explained.

"Where were you when we were building the wings?" Astrid asked in a grumpy voice.

"Probably building this compartment we're in," he replied. "Just be easy with that rope next time."

"Aye, aye, Captain," she said in a snarky tone of voice.

Ahead of them, Teofil and Dulindir started to descend as well, a little smoother than Thaddeus and Astrid had. Astrid gently pulled on the rope, and the flaps came up, dropping them slowly toward the ground. The plains rushed past beneath them, and Thaddeus feared they would crash nose first into the ground, causing injury and possibly spilling the precious water from the Well of Tears.

He kept quiet, however, as Astrid brought them lower and lower.

"We're going to need to release our feet," Thaddeus said as they neared the ground. The tree they had been aiming for was approaching fast, but he couldn't see any sign of Miriam or his father, and tension twisted around his guts like barbed wire.

"Let me know when you're ready for that," Astrid said. "I'm going to bring us down a bit more."

They were five feet above the tops of the tall grass and had passed the tree beneath which they had taken refuge after the troll attacked them. It zipped past so fast Thaddeus didn't have time to look and see if his father still lay in the tree's shade. Instead, he focused on pulling loose the ropes that held his and Astrid's legs up. Their feet dropped, skimming along through the grass, Thaddeus wincing as the edges of the tall stalks of grass smacked against his jeans. The ground came up, and he and Astrid ran as fast as they could once their toes touched down, but the glider proved to be too heavy for them to keep aloft, and it spun them around, the tip of the wing on Astrid's side digging into the dirt and bringing them to a jarring halt.

Thaddeus took a few moments to catch his breath and let his equilibrium return. He brushed stalks of grass out of his face and untied the rope around his waist. He slipped out of the glider supports and stumbled back a few steps before sitting down hard on the ground, crushing some of the grass beneath him. He made sure the canteen was still clipped on his belt, and then he struggled up to his feet and circled the glider.

"Astrid?" He pushed through the tall grass, grimacing at the sting of the rough blades against his bare arms. "Astrid, are you okay?"

He came up on her side of the glider and had to crouch to see beneath the bent and broken wing. Her head hung down, hair obscuring her face.

Panic flared inside him, and he reached out to gently shake her. "Astrid!"

She lifted her head and smiled at him. "By Flora, that was fun. I want to do it again!"

Thaddeus let out a breath and shook his head. "Once is enough for me, thanks. Let's get you out of there."

Once Astrid was free of the restraints, they made their way through the waist-high grass toward the tree standing tall and alone on the plain.

They were about fifty yards from it, and off to his left, Thaddeus could see Teofil and Dulindir walking in a diagonal line to intersect with them.

"You both okay?" Teofil asked when they met up a few yards from the tree.

"It was great!" Astrid exclaimed. "I wanted to do it again, but Thaddeus refused."

Teofil grinned and shook his head. He caught Thaddeus's gaze and said, "Gnomes."

"I agree with that statement," Thaddeus said, leaning in for a quick kiss. He took Teofil's hand and tugged him toward the tree. "Come on. Let's go find my dad."

Chapter FIFTEEN

A BAD feeling settled into Thaddeus's stomach. It had crept in when they were approaching the single tree a short distance out from the closely packed forest. This tree looked to Thaddeus as if it stood guard, maybe as a sentry for the rest of the forest. Or an outcast. Either way, it was their landmark, and as they'd soared overhead, he'd managed a quick look at the ground beneath the tree where they had left his father, but no one was there. There was no sign of Nathan, Miriam, or for that matter, the body of the large troll they killed before setting off on their quest.

Now the bad feeling spread through him, making his fingertips and scalp tingle.

"It's quiet," Astrid said.

"Too quiet," Thaddeus agreed. He released Teofil's hand and hurried ahead, parting the tall grass more and more frantically. "I didn't see my dad or your mom from the air."

"We'll find them," Teofil assured him.

"I don't know," Thaddeus said quietly. He chewed his lower lip and broke into a jog toward the tree.

They came out of the tall grass and onto the wide path that parted the plain for miles. The tree grew on the south edge of the path, its leafy branches spread wide and offering all travelers a place to rest out of the sun before they plunged into the dark, dank forest a few yards away.

"Dad!" Thaddeus called.

"Mum!" Teofil and Astrid shouted together.

There was no response but the grasses whispering in the wind.

"Where are they?" Astrid asked, her voice low and small, childlike.

"Maybe they went into the forest?" Dulindir suggested.

"But the troll's body is gone too," Thaddeus said, turning to look for the spot where they had finally brought the thing down. "I didn't see it when we flew over."

"Do you think another troll came along?" Dulindir asked. "Your parents might have had to leave in a hurry, if that were the case."

"Fan out," Teofil directed, pointing all around. "Don't go far; stay in shouting distance."

They called out to both Miriam and Nathan as they split up. Thaddeus headed for the tree, occasionally calling his father's name. He found beneath the tree a number of mooshberry stains, some plantain leaves, and a bit of brown gunk that Miriam would have surely used to dress a wound. He circled the trunk of the tree, searching for any other sign of his father and Miriam, but there was nothing. No note weighted down with a rock. No instructions carved into the tree. Nothing.

"Dad," Thaddeus whispered to himself, turning to look at the close-packed trees of the Lost Forest. "Where are you?"

"Here!" Dulindir shouted from off in the grass.

Thaddeus started running before he could even see Dulindir, not caring about the sharp edges of the stalks of grass. He overshot where Dulindir had called from by a dozen yards and had to circle back, following his hand waving above the tops of the grass. When he finally stepped into a clearing of matted-down grasses, Thaddeus found Teofil crouching near a dark stain that looked frighteningly like blood, while Astrid stood beside Dulindir with her arms crossed tight, watching her brother.

"What is this?" Thaddeus asked, then pointed at the stain. "What is that? Is that… is it blood?"

Teofil looked up, his expression solemn as he nodded. "It is. It's the spot where we brought down the troll. See?" He gestured to the grass matted and broken all around in a wide shape. "We were a bit away from the tree when it happened."

Relief flooded through Thaddeus. The blood was from the troll, not from his father or Miriam. "Oh. Yeah. Okay, I see it."

"But where is the troll?" Astrid asked. "Mum couldn't have carried it off herself."

"Something came by and dragged it away," Dulindir said. "See how the grass is bent all the way to the forest's edge?"

"Another troll, probably," Teofil said and stood up beside Thaddeus. "Maybe Mum had to hide your dad because more trolls came by looking for the one we killed?"

"But why didn't they leave a note or anything?" Thaddeus asked, hating the whine he heard in his voice but unable to help himself. He just wanted to see his father again. He'd been through so much to get back to him, and with the water from the Well of Tears no less.

"They didn't think we'd be coming back," Astrid said in a quiet voice. "We were supposed to go on to the mountain to look for your mum."

Thaddeus nodded. "Maybe your mom got my dad up and hid him in the forest. Let's look near the mooshberry bushes."

They walked as a group toward the forest, following the trail of broken and matted-down grasses left by whatever had dragged away the troll's body. Thaddeus kept a hand on the canteen fastened to his belt to reassure himself that once they found his father he'd be able to deliver a serving of the healing water as soon as possible.

The familiar feeling of being in the forest closed over Thaddeus as he followed the others into the trees: the air was heavy with moisture, warm and close. A quiet sensation of oppression snuck up and wrapped around him.

"I liked being in the glider much better," Teofil muttered to him.

Thaddeus gave him a thin smile and nodded. "I wish we had been able to fly in one together."

Teofil took his hand and squeezed it, giving him a smile. "Me too."

Astrid was in front, picking out the easiest path to take them along the edge of the forest in search of Miriam and Nathan. As she stepped around a tree, she suddenly jumped and gave a shout, then laughed and squealed one word with more joy than Thaddeus had ever before heard anyone manage: "Mum!"

"Mum?" Teofil said, a quiver in his voice as he kept tight hold of Thaddeus's hand and pulled him along toward Astrid.

As they got closer, Thaddeus could see Astrid hugging Miriam tight, laughing and crying as Miriam held her close. Almost every inch of Miriam's exposed skin had mud smeared over it. Her clothes were dirty and disheveled, her blouse torn in some places, and a scabbed-over scratch ran the length of her left arm.

"Did you do it, then?" Miriam asked as Teofil and Thaddeus approached, and she looked up at them. Thaddeus noticed she quickly looked away from him, not meeting his eyes, and a sense of dread formed low in his belly.

"Did you find the dragon so quick?" Miriam asked. She pulled Teofil into a hearty hug. "Did you find her?"

Teofil pushed free and looked around at them all, then back at his mother. "Well, we, um, we kind of took a detour."

Miriam flicked her gaze between Teofil and Thaddeus, touched on Dulindir a moment with a frown, and then searched the forest behind them.

"Where's Fetter?" Miriam asked. "Where's your brother?"

Astrid took Miriam's hand. "He's gone, Mum," she said in a small, sad voice. "All this time it wasn't him."

"What?" Miriam looked at them in turn again. "You're not making sense. And who's this elf that's with you instead of Fetter?"

"I am Dulindir," he said, as if stating his name offered explanation enough.

Miriam looked at Dulindir blankly a moment, then turned her attention to Teofil. "Are you telling me that your brother is dead?"

"We're not sure, Mum," Teofil replied. "Like Astrid said, it wasn't him at all. Since the day of the attack when Fetter was carrying me to safety, it's been Isadora."

Miriam looked shocked, her eyes widening and her lips pressing into a thin line. Finally, she managed to whisper, "Isadora?"

"It's been her all this time, Mum," Astrid said. "All these years, pretending to be Fetter, gathering information, making plans. Lying." Tears streaked down her face, and Thaddeus felt the sting of his own tears all over again at the enormity of Isadora's betrayal.

"By Flora," Miriam whispered. "Isadora. That sneaky witch." She seemed to come back to the moment and looked at each of them. "She didn't hurt you, did she?"

"No, she didn't hurt us," Teofil said. "But, Mum, she's off to find the dragon. She wants to use it."

Miriam looked at Thaddeus then, meeting and holding his gaze before pulling him into a tight, comforting hug. "Oh, Thaddeus. You must be so worried. Don't fret. Your father is alive. He's in a bad way, though, very bad. But he's strong willed."

Relief flooded Thaddeus, filling him, pushing out the exhaustion, the fear, everything else. His father was still alive; he wasn't too late after all. There was nothing left but relief now, and he wanted so badly to see his father, hold his hand, talk with him and explain everything that had happened to them on the journey so far.

"He's safe?" Thaddeus asked, his voice muffled against Miriam's shoulder.

She pushed him back to arm's length and smiled. "He's safe. Like I said, he's weak, but he's holding his own."

"I have something that will help him." Thaddeus placed a hand on the canteen. "Hopefully, it will cure him. We went on a detour. We found it, Mrs. Rhododendron. We found the Well of Tears."

Chapter SIXTEEN

"YOU FOUND the Well of Tears?" Miriam furrowed her brow as she stared at Thaddeus. "Is that what you said?"

Thaddeus nodded, unable to keep from grinning. "It is!"

"Well...." Miriam faltered, momentarily at a loss for words. "How did this come about?"

Thaddeus looked around her to the dark forest, searching for his father. "Can we talk as you take us to my dad?"

Miriam smiled and nodded. "Of course, my dear. I'm such a ninny. So sorry, Thaddeus my love, come along. He's not far."

Teofil explained Isadora's deception as they followed his mother through the forest. Thaddeus only half listened to the story, his thoughts occupied by concerns for his father. How would he look? Would he recognize Thaddeus? Would the water from the Well of Tears work for his injuries? If it had been able to counteract Isadora's spell that had been going for years and years, it would surely work on troll poison, wouldn't it? And would they have enough left to possibly change back his mother?

The others came to a stop at a cluster of tall trees whose trunks had twisted together as they had grown. Miriam turned to face Thaddeus, and when she took his hands and he saw her expression of love and concern, the fear inside him tripled in size and he felt as though he might choke on it. Something burned in the back of his throat, and his heart pounded.

"I have to warn you, Thaddeus, he hasn't been eating, though I've been nagging him to do so," Miriam said. "He's lost some weight, so he'll look very thin. I had to move him here to the shelter of these trees because the trolls came looking for their counterpart, and there were just too many for me to fight off. If it had been one or two, I could have handled them, but there were four, and I didn't want to be responsible for starting another war with the trolls."

Thaddeus nodded. "I understand. I just want to see him and have him drink the water."

"Very well, follow me." She looked at the rest of the group. "You three stay out here for now. The space inside is small. We won't have room for you all. Gather more firewood for tonight; that would be a help."

Thaddeus looked at Teofil and smiled nervously when he took his hand and squeezed it. Then he turned and followed Miriam, slipping between the tree trunks.

The trees had grown together a dozen feet or more above the ground, leaving a rough circle of space between the trunks that measured just over ten feet across. A small fire of moss and leaves had warmed the area and provided a little bit of light, enough for Thaddeus to be able to see his father lying at the other side of the space. It may have been a trick of the low light, or because of the poison in his system, but Nathan's face looked at first to Thaddeus as if it were just skin stretched tight over a skull. His cheekbones were very prominent, and the hollows of his eyes were ringed in either shadow or bruised skin.

Tears blurred Thaddeus's vision at the sight of his father in such a state. He had always been so healthy, so strong and vibrant. To see him like this left Thaddeus stunned and terrified.

"Oh my God," Thaddeus said with a gasp. "Oh, Dad."

Miriam took his hand and squeezed it, drawing closer as she gave him a sympathetic smile. "It's all right dear. I know it's a shock at first. But come sit beside him and let him know you've returned."

Thaddeus swallowed hard as he crossed to his father and knelt at his side.

"Nathan," Miriam said in a gentle voice. "Nathan, wake up and see who's come back."

Nathan moaned in response but kept his eyes shut tight.

"Come on, Nathan," Miriam continued. "Wake up and see who I found in the forest."

Thaddeus watched his father's dry, cracked lips slowly part and his eyelids flutter before opening. He stared up for a moment, still partly asleep, and then his gaze drifted over to Thaddeus. At the blank expression on his father's face, Thaddeus's nerves stretched even tighter, worried that while he had been gone the troll poison had removed all memory of him from Nathan's mind.

"Dad?" Thaddeus said in a quiet, tentative voice.

A few more seconds of Nathan's blank stare nearly made Thaddeus turn and flee the warm, claustrophobic confines of the shelter within the trees, but then recognition dawned on his father's face, and he whispered, "Thaddeus. You're back."

The choked laugh that bubbled up from Thaddeus's gut brought a relief that swarmed through his body. He took his father's hand and clung gently to it, frightened at Nathan's weak grip and how the bones felt so close beneath his skin.

"That's right, I'm back, Dad. And I've got something for you. It's going to make you feel a lot better."

"You found your mother," Nathan said with a smile that made him look like a grinning skull. "Is she here? Is she safe?"

Thaddeus hung his head a moment and took a breath, fighting back waves of guilt. When he was able to look at his father again, he smiled and shook his head. "No, not that. Not yet, anyway. I'm going to need you to help me with that journey."

Nathan managed to roll his eyes and let out a weak laugh. "Not in this condition, I'm not."

"Well, here," Thaddeus said as he pulled the canteen from his belt. "This will help you feel much better."

"What is it?" Nathan asked, wrinkling his forehead. He slid his gaze over toward Miriam. "Not more mooshberry juice? I can't handle any more of that stuff."

Thaddeus chuckled along with Miriam as he unscrewed the top of the canteen. The water sloshed about inside it, and his stomach seemed to follow suit. What if the water did nothing for his father? What if the metal of the canteen had somehow leached the magical properties from it? What if there was only enough left to prolong his father's decline into death?

No way to know but to let him drink it.

"Here, you'll need to sit up," Thaddeus said. "Mrs. Rhododendron, can you help me with him?"

"Of course, dear," Miriam said and leaned in over Nathan. "And I've told you to call me Miriam, Thaddeus. Mrs. Rhododendron makes me sound like an old fuddy-duddy of a woman."

"Well, you're definitely not that," Thaddeus assured her. Since he was kneeling on the ground, Thaddeus put the canteen between his thighs and gripped it tight with his legs so it wouldn't fall over, then worked with Miriam to get his father into a sitting position.

Nathan groaned and winced as they moved him, trying to help them sit him up but too weak to offer much in the way of assistance. They all heaved a sigh of relief when he was finally sitting upright against one of the tree trunks.

"Well, that was awful," Nathan muttered.

Thaddeus smiled and nodded. "It sure was. But this should help. Just take a few shallow sips for now, okay?"

Nathan regarded him. "It's not mooshberry juice?"

Thaddeus shook his head. "It's not. I promise. It's water, that's all. It might have a bit of a taste to it, but nothing like mooshberry juice."

He held the canteen up to his father's lips and slowly, carefully, tipped it. Nathan took a couple of swallows, but then a bit of the water ran out over his lips, and Thaddeus pulled the canteen away, saving as much as possible. By his estimates, the canteen was now three-quarters full, and he screwed the cap on tight.

"How do you feel?" Thaddeus asked.

Nathan ran his tongue over his lips and sat back against the tree with his eyes closed. "Good. Better, now that you're back."

"Besides that," Thaddeus said, feeling impatient with his father, the healing process of the water, their journey, all of it. "Does it feel like the water is helping you heal?"

A sigh slid out of his father's lips, and he had just parted them to reply when his eyes rolled back and he slumped over against Thaddeus. Convulsions rattled Nathan's thin body, jarring as he shook within Thaddeus's arms.

"Oh dear Flora," Miriam exclaimed. "Hold him tight so he doesn't hurt either of you!"

"I'm trying," Thaddeus said through gritted teeth, and lifted his chin to avoid his father's wildly thrashing head. "He's stronger than he looks."

The spasms stopped as suddenly as they had begun, and Nathan lay still against Thaddeus a moment, panting as he caught his breath. His father's thin frame felt hot in Thaddeus's arms, feverish, and once again he worried that he had been too late returning with the water.

"Oh...," Nathan said with a horrible smelling exhalation, and then he pushed away from Thaddeus and vomited up a long, thick runner of black sludge. It splattered on the ground, and Miriam and Thaddeus both scrambled back away from the stuff as Nathan brought up more of it, bracing himself on thin, shaking arms.

Once the vomiting had passed, Nathan wiped his mouth with the back of his hand and looked at Thaddeus. His gaze was much sharper than before he had drunk the water, and his eyes were now clear and bright. His skin, once tinted gray, shone with vibrant health.

Thaddeus smiled as tears blurred his vision. "It worked. Oh my God, it worked."

"What the hell is that stuff?" Nathan asked between breaths. "And how can we get more?"

"This is all that's left," Thaddeus said, holding up the canteen and shaking it so the contents sloshed around. "It's water from the Well of Tears."

Nathan's eyebrows went up, and he looked at Miriam, then back at Thaddeus. "The Well of Tears? It's real? You found it?"

Thaddeus smiled and nodded. "It is real, and we did find it. It was Fetter's—" He glanced at Miriam. Her expression tightened, and she looked away. Thaddeus battled back the sadness and anger that threatened to rise up within him and continued his explanation. "Well, we decided to go there first to get the water and come back and save you. And it worked! I knew it would, because it healed my leg and my hand. See?" He held his hand out for Nathan to inspect.

"But you were supposed to find your mother," Nathan said as he ran his thumb lightly over Thaddeus's palm. "Don't get me wrong, son, I'm grateful you came back with that water. But your mother is out there still, afraid and alone."

Thaddeus's happiness abated a bit, and he dropped his gaze to the thick black gunk that his father had coughed up. "I know. I'm sorry. But coming back to help you heal was all I could think of once we started talking about it."

"Everyone's back?" Nathan asked, tipping his head to look around Thaddeus. "All of you returned?"

Thaddeus glanced over at Miriam again, then met his father's gaze. "Not all of us. Come outside and we'll explain."

A short time later, after helping Nathan out of the shelter within the trees and his greeting them all, they settled into a circle around the fire Teofil had started. As the flames threw flickering orange light on them, Teofil and Astrid told the story of how Isadora had disguised herself as Fetter and lived within the Rhododendron family all these years. They explained how she had manipulated them into searching for the Well of Tears in order to help her change back into her true form, and how she had ridden off into the forest on the Bearagon, threatening to find Claire in her dragon form before Thaddeus could.

As the gnomes told their adventure, with some comments added by Dulindir and himself, Thaddeus sat beside his father. He studied Nathan's profile as he thought about Isadora's words before she had ridden the Bearagon off into the trees: *Shame he won't be able to share any more family secrets with you.* Had she said that just to be cruel, or was there some meaning behind it? Thaddeus had already uncovered some whoppers of family secrets recently; what else could be left? Did he really want to know, or were secrets best left to those who kept them? He needed to think on it before he asked his father about the meaning behind Isadora's words.

"That's quite a story," Nathan said once their tale had been told. He reached out to take Miriam's hand and gave it a squeeze before releasing it again. "I'm sorry, Miriam. I know this must be difficult for you."

Miriam nodded and wiped her eyes. "It is. But it helps explain so many things I noticed about Fetter over the years. His general attitude and struggle to conduct magic with any growing, living thing. Rudyard and I tried our best, but he just never caught on like the rest of the children." She pressed her lips together and gazed out into the darkness gathering around the trunks of the forest trees. "I just want to know what that witch did with my son."

"I think he might still be alive," Astrid said in a quiet voice. "Held prisoner somewhere, perhaps? It makes me sad to think of it, him wondering why we've not found him yet, or if we've even been looking for him all these years." She brushed aside a tear, and Teofil put an arm around her for a quick hug.

"Awful, awful woman," Miriam said, and then fell silent.

"We will need to continue our original quest," Nathan said, looking at Thaddeus. "Your mother needs to be our first priority. After that, we can search for Fetter." He looked back at Miriam. "We will find him, Miriam. I promise." She nodded and gave him a tight smile before dropping her gaze to the flickering fire.

Nathan looked at them each in turn, studying them as if trying to gauge their ability to go on. "We'll rest here, but just for one night. Tomorrow we'll strike out again for the mountains. I'm certain she would have flown to a high, rocky peak. And those mountains, especially the tallest one, are somewhere she's familiar with."

"They are?" Thaddeus asked. "How?"

"We visited them once," Nathan replied in a low, sad tone, "A long time ago."

"Oh," Thaddeus said. "Well, as we were flying back here in the gliders, I saw a section of the forest that had been burned. A long strip of it, as if maybe by dragon breath."

"Do you remember in which direction it lay?" Nathan asked.

"Pretty sure," Thaddeus said with a nod. "It was right before we turned to follow the line of the forest at the plains. It looked like it was pointed toward the mountains."

Nathan smiled and put a hand on the back of Thaddeus's neck. "You built a glider and flew in it over the Lost Forest. No wonder you always did well at science fairs. You're quite the brave man now, Thaddeus. I'm proud of you."

A warm glow of satisfaction surged within Thaddeus's chest, and he grinned as he pushed aside his questions. For now. "Thanks. We all did very brave things as we went."

"Teofil talked to flesh-eating vines," Astrid said.

"Astrid came up with the idea for the gliders," Teofil offered.

"Dulindir's hair glows with starlight at night!" Astrid exclaimed. "Show them!"

Dulindir smiled and closed his eyes. A moment later, the long length of his hair shimmered with warm white light, and Nathan and Miriam both drew in a breath.

"He helped us a lot," Astrid continued. "We've been told so many stories of how the Wood Elves behave, and he's done nothing like that."

Miriam smiled, but there was suspicion in her gaze as she looked at Dulindir. "All beings are unique in and of themselves, dear. Just as all gnomes or witches are not the same, this is sure to be true of Wood Elves. I'm glad you've found a new friend."

Nathan yawned, and it proved contagious; soon all of them were yawning as well.

"Let's get some rest," Miriam said. "Children, first the troll poison will need to be scooped out of the ground within the tree shelter. After that, there should be just enough space for all of you to lie down. Nathan and I will sleep out here and keep guard."

Thaddeus hugged first his father, then Miriam, and followed Teofil into the space between the trees. Together they used flat rocks to dig up the dark, slick mess Nathan had left and tossed it far out among the trees. The moss-and-leaf fire continued to smolder, the smoke escaping through the gaps in the trunks as it heated the shelter. Thaddeus stretched out on the ground and sighed when Teofil lay beside him, putting an arm around him and pulling him close.

"Sleep well," Teofil whispered before placing a gentle kiss on his earlobe.

"You too," Thaddeus replied, then sighed as he drifted off to sleep.

Chapter SEVENTEEN

THEY WERE losing the light and would need to make camp soon. Even so, Thaddeus didn't want to stop, not yet, but he had to keep the others in mind, especially his father. When they had first started out again, his father had asked Thaddeus to take the lead, and Thaddeus had agreed, enjoying the rush of pride he felt at his father's request.

Now, he stopped and turned to the rest of the group. All of them looked tired, and Nathan was panting for breath. Despite the water from the Well of Tears, the aftereffects of the troll poison seemed to be lingering. Yes, it was time to stop.

"I think we've gone far enough for today," Thaddeus said. "Let's set up camp."

"We can go farther," Nathan said. "Don't stop on my account."

"My feet hurt," Astrid muttered. "I'm glad we're stopping."

"Well, if Astrid says we should stop…," Nathan said, and everyone laughed.

Later, as they all sat around a small fire, Thaddeus looked at them each in turn and wondered how he had ever lived before knowing them. This entire world that had been hidden from him before now, a world of magic and mystical creatures, lay open and inviting to him. A world where anything was possible, anything at all. Even finding someone to love him.

As if brought on by Thaddeus's thoughts, Teofil took his hand and leaned in closer. "You've changed."

Thaddeus frowned. "What do you mean?"

"You're different from the boy who moved in next door at the beginning of the summer." Teofil smiled and squeezed his hand. "I like it."

Thaddeus blushed and dropped his gaze. "Well…."

"But I like that you still blush easily," Teofil said. "Don't ever change that part of you."

"I'll try," Thaddeus said. "But how have I changed?"

"You're much more confident. More in control and in charge. This summer, this journey we're on, has changed you, helped you grow."

"I hope so," Thaddeus said. "I needed to change. Something felt… wrong about who I was back then."

"You knew you were special," Teofil suggested. "You just needed to understand why."

"You helped, you know."

"Me? How?"

Thaddeus shrugged and looked away a moment, then back at him. "You love me. I never thought anyone would do that."

Teofil leaned in closer. "Well, I do love you. And I'll continue to do so, no matter what happens."

"Good."

"Thaddeus," Nathan said from across the fire, catching his attention. "How far do you think we've traveled?"

"Difficult to say for sure," Thaddeus replied. "I read somewhere that, on average, a man can walk twenty to twenty-five miles a day. But with the forest to deal with, probably less than that. Maybe fifteen miles?"

"No wonder my feet are sore," Astrid said with a moan.

"I haven't walked this much in almost twenty years," Miriam said, then smiled brightly. "It feels wonderful."

"For the record, Leopold and Vivienne said they would meet us at a point closer to the mountains," Nathan explained. "He mentioned something about a village at the foot of the tallest one. I'm pretty sure I know which village he meant."

"Will they have beds there?" Astrid wondered, turning left and right to stretch her back.

"And baths?" Teofil added.

"And warm food," Thaddeus threw in. "Maybe even pizza?"

"Pizza?" Teofil, Astrid, and Dulindir asked together.

"Oh my gosh, you guys have never had pizza?" Thaddeus looked at his father, who smiled and shrugged. "Well, you're in for a real treat, trust me."

"Let's not get too excited about it," Miriam cautioned. "We still have a long way to go to get out of the Lost Forest."

Thaddeus nodded in agreement, then looked off into the trees in the direction of the tall, rocky peaks they needed to reach. His mother would be there, still in dragon form; he felt it. And, most likely, Isadora, the power-hungry witch who had started all of this years ago, when

Thaddeus had only been a baby. He wondered what life had been like before Isadora's attack. Maybe, if he asked questions about the past and listened carefully, he could figure out what other family secrets lay in wait for him to discover. He considered his options and finally decided on a course of action, then turned to his father.

"What was our family like?" he asked. "Before Isadora attacked the village? Were you and Mom happy? Did you have a lot of friends? What was it like?"

Nathan and Miriam exchanged a quick glance, and Thaddeus thought he saw a startled and uncomfortable look pass between them. Could he have hit on the very family secret Isadora had alluded to? But when his father met his gaze, Thaddeus saw his smile and the gentle sadness in his gaze as he replied.

"Times were good before Isadora attacked," Nathan said. "They were very good. Your mother had wanted to have a baby for many years, but her pregnancies never seemed to take."

Thaddeus felt a chill. "Miscarriages?"

Nathan nodded. "Several. But when she became pregnant with you, she knew it was different. She said it felt right, that you felt good inside her. Still, she was careful not to exert herself while she was carrying you."

"What did she do to pass the time?" Thaddeus asked.

"She read a lot of books," Nathan replied.

"And she knitted," Miriam offered with a gentle laugh. "Oh, your mother knitted quite a lot of things. All of my children wore something while growing up that had been knitted by your mother." She looked at Teofil. "You wore hats and socks and a soft, alpaca wool jumper."

Thaddeus grinned at Teofil, imagining him in a small wool sweater. "You wore things my mother made. I love that."

"You did too, Thaddeus," Nathan said. "I managed to recover quite a few items she had made and brought them along with us when we... when we left."

"Really?" Thaddeus asked. "I never knew that. Did you keep them?"

"Of course," Nathan replied. "They're in a bin in the basement. I'll show them to you when we get home."

Thaddeus noted the optimism in his father's words and sent a wish up to the stars, to Flora, to God, or any all-knowing entity that might be listening, that they would, indeed, all make it home again.

A short time later, Astrid let out a yawn that started a chain reaction. They divided up times for someone to keep watch, Miriam volunteering to take the first post, and the others turned in. Thaddeus lay down alongside Teofil and smiled when he felt his arm slip around his waist.

The next morning, they were packed and ready to move by the time the sun was up. Thaddeus took the lead once again, checking his compass to make sure they were headed in the right direction. It couldn't be much farther to the end of the forest; he had to believe they would be coming out of the trees before too long.

Hours later, Thaddeus was glad when he did, indeed, set foot out from the dark of the Lost Forest and into the sunshine that seemed to flood another stretch of grassy plain. The mountain range was clearly visible now. The tall, rocky spire of the center mountain loomed closer than ever, and the others gathered around him to stare at it.

"I can't believe we're finally leaving the forest," Astrid said.

"I've only left the Lost Forest once in all my life," Dulindir said.

"Just once?" Astrid asked.

"Just once," Dulindir replied, his gaze fixed on the mountain off in the distance. "A long time ago."

"Sun's almost down," Nathan pointed out. "We should make camp here on the edge of the forest for the night, get a fresh start tomorrow across the plains. We'll be exposed to the sun tomorrow, so be sure we have enough water for the trip."

They all got busy getting things ready for the night ahead. Thaddeus set out to look for firewood and found his father a few yards away from the others. Nathan stood with his head down, supporting himself with a hand on a tree. He looked tired and pale, and the sight of him in this condition made Thaddeus's stomach clench.

"Dad?"

Nathan started and looked around. "Thaddeus. I didn't hear you come up."

"Are you all right?" Thaddeus asked, stepping up beside him.

"I'm fine," Nathan assured him. "Just tired."

"You look more than tired," Thaddeus said. "You look worn out."

Nathan shook his head. "I'm fine. Really. I just need a moment to catch my breath is all."

"Well, let's gather firewood together, okay?" Thaddeus suggested.

"I'd like that," Nathan said with a smile.

They worked in silence for a bit, Thaddeus's mind churning as he wondered if this moment might be the right time to ask about the family secrets. When he looked over at his father, however, and saw how pale and used up he appeared, he realized his curiosity could wait. It didn't seem fair to dig too deeply into the past when his father still felt so weak, especially about things that most likely had no bearing on their current situation. At least he hoped they didn't.

Instead of asking if there were more family secrets, Thaddeus said, "I performed magic while we were gone."

Nathan looked at him in surprise. "You did? What kind of spell?"

"We were being swept away by the Wretched River at night, so it was dark," Thaddeus explained. "I was being pulled under by water sprites, and I conjured a ball of light."

Nathan smiled and held the sticks he had gathered close to his chest. "You're coming into your own, Thaddeus. I'm very proud of you. Very proud." His smile turned a little sad, and he added, "Your mother would be very proud of you as well."

The faint moonlight that managed to make its way through the canopy of leaves sparkled in the tears in Nathan's eyes, and Thaddeus felt the sting of his own tears.

"I want to learn more," Thaddeus said. "Magic that is. There's so much I don't know."

"I will teach you," Nathan said. "As we make our way to the mountains, and in the days after that, we'll work on spells."

Thaddeus smiled. "I'd like that."

"Come on," Nathan said. "Let's get this wood back to the campsite. We're close, but we've still got a ways to go."

Thaddeus walked beside his father through the forest, back to where Teofil and the others waited for them. Just through the trees and beyond the grassy plain, the moon hung above the rocky peaks of the silhouettes of the mountains, and Thaddeus sent thoughts of love out to his mother.

"Soon, Mom," he whispered to the night gathered in the woods around them. "We'll come to rescue you soon. I promise."

R. G. THOMAS has been reading books from an early age. As a young gay man, however, he found very few characters with whom he could truly identify. Now that he's an adult—or at least older than he used to be—he likes to write stories that revolve around gay characters. The Town of Superstition is his YA fantasy gay romance series that includes wizards, witches, and other magical creatures.

When he's not writing, R. G. loves to read, go to movies, watch some TV, and putter around in the small suburban patch of ground he calls a yard. He visits his mother once a week, not just for the free cookies, and enjoys spending time with close friends drinking wine and making up ridiculous things that sometimes show up in his books. Although he hates the process of travel, he does enjoy experiencing new places. His dream trip is to one day visit the country of Greece, and he is currently saving his nickels and dimes to make that a reality.

Twenty years ago he met a man who understood and encouraged his strange, creative mind, and who made him laugh more often and more freely than anyone else. Today they are legally married and still laugh often as they live in a suburb just north of Detroit with their two cats who act as both muse and distraction to him while he writes.

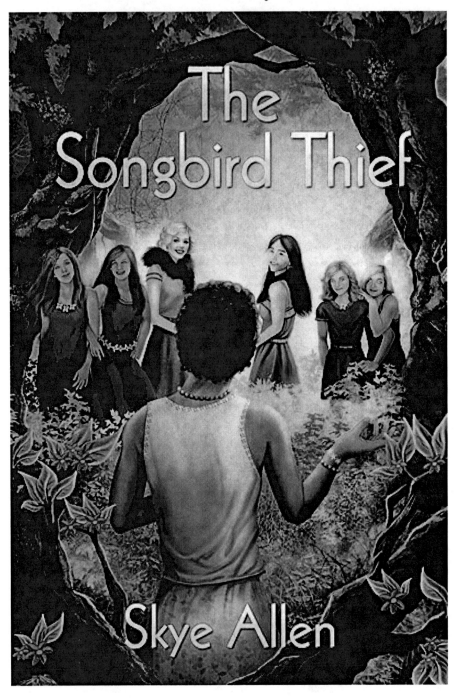

The Songbird Thief

Skye Allen

www.harmonyinkpress.com

CPSIA information can be obtained
at www.ICGtesting.com
Printed in the USA
FFOW02n0543190617
36837FF